PRAISE FOR
LOVE, ME

"A second-chance romance on steroids, I tore through
Love, Me in a single sitting. It had me breathless and unsure
until the last word—I loved it."

—**Annabel Monaghan, bestselling author of**
Same Time Next Summer

"In *Love, Me*, Jessica Saunders has created a highly relatable
protagonist, a charming cast of characters, and the most alluring
book boyfriend. A perfect escape from everyday life; the
warmhearted, accessible prose will draw you in from the
get-go and keep you reading late into the night."

—**Jacqueline Friedland, *USA Today* bestselling**
author of *He Gets That From Me*

"A sweet and honest look at first loves and second
chances with a dash of sexy celebrity mixed in.
Jessica Saunders is a new writer to watch!"

—**Allison Winn Scotch, *New York Times* bestselling author of *The Rewind***

"I loved Rachel Miller, the super-relatable star of this book whose
very normal life becomes extraordinary overnight and throws
everything off balance. More than just a romance, *Love, Me* is
a love letter to anyone who has ever been at a crossroads in
their life and had to dig deep to find their inner compass."

—**Jessa Maxwell, author of *The Golden Spoon***

"Full of '90s nostalgia and heartwarming tenderness,
Love, Me is a sincere look into the connection, depth,
and magnitude of first love."

—**Neely Tubati Alexander, author of *Love Buzz***

LOVE, ME

Dear Annabel,

LOVE, ME

You are the best! Thank you

A NOVEL

for everything

Jessica Saunders

JESSICA SAUNDERS

**UNION
SQUARE
& CO.**

NEW YORK

**UNION
SQUARE
& CO.**

NEW YORK

UNION SQUARE & CO. and the distinctive Union Square & Co. logo are
trademarks of Sterling Publishing Co., Inc.

Union Square & Co., LLC, is a subsidiary of Sterling Publishing Co., Inc.

ISBN 978-1-4549-5079-0
ISBN 978-1-4549-5080-6 (e-book)

Library of Congress Control Number: 2023011523

For information about custom editions, special sales, and premium purchases,
please contact specialsales@unionsquareandco.com.

Printed in Canada

2 4 6 8 10 9 7 5 3 1

unionsquareandco.com

Cover design by Sara Wood
Cover image © Lady:amesto/Shutterstock.com
Interior design by Rich Hazelton

For Suzanne

PROLOGUE

"Man of the Hour" by Liz Randolph, *Hollywood Reporter*

Jack Bellow is waiting for me in the lobby of the Chateau
Marmont. I can count on one hand the number of actors
who have beaten me to an interview, and it throws me off to
see him sitting there. My uneasiness is misplaced. Mr. Bellow
immediately greets me with a big hug, despite having spoken
only once before, over text, to schedule this meeting. He
offers to grab me coffee so I can get myself organized. He's
in no rush, he tells me, so I should take my time.

Mr. Bellow is quite literally the most disarming celebrity in
town. I immediately tell him so, and he laughs. "I figured out
pretty early on that being nice scored me more points."
Where better to start this interview than his childhood.

"We were as middle class as they came. I grew up on
Long Island, divorced parents and a younger sister. We
mostly lived with my mom and stepfather and they were
pretty relaxed. I generally did the whole play-outside-until-
Mom-called-me-in-for-dinner thing."

Mr. Bellow is notably still close friends with Alexandra
Hirschfeld, a screenwriter and up-and-coming filmmaker with
whom he went to high school. "What you see is definitely what
you get with Jack. He's an easy guy. I don't think he thinks of
himself as particularly interesting, or even all that good-looking,
so he never takes his success for granted."

To an outsider, Jack Bellow is anything but ordinary. He
graduated from the State University of New York, Albany, and
then attended Juilliard for its renowned MFA drama program.

Mr. Bellow referred to Albany as his lost years, spent mostly partying and showing up for classes when it suited him. He majored in English, and it was a lack of direction upon graduating that led him to pursue acting, something he had loved during his high school days. He was vaguely aware of Juilliard when he applied, but had no idea how exclusive a program it was. Mr. Bellow reflects on his Juilliard experience as life-changing. He knew nothing about the craft, and while he denies that he employs any kind of method acting in his work today ("Stanislavski who?" he joked), he credits his education as giving him a better command of his body and an appreciation for putting in the work.

Success came relatively quickly for him, when he landed a role on the legal drama *Sanctions*, soon after graduation. From there, he was cast as David Crump on the much-beloved sitcom *Plus Size*, which ran for several years in the 2010s, and he became a household name. Mr. Bellow as David, along with his co-star Jenny Pelch as Margaret, were the most "will they or won't they" couple since Ross and Rachel. I let him know that my friends and I were obsessed with *Plus Size*, and even went in costume as the four leads for Halloween in college. I quickly regretted my admission, but Mr. Bellow, as I am learning is typical for him, loved this and promptly asked to see a picture, which I dug up on my phone.

Being a child of divorce must have been difficult for him. He denies this, not surprisingly. His parents were better off apart, he says, and he and his sister had each other when shuttling between their houses. "I'm sympathetic to kids that go through it, I know it can be traumatic. In my new movie, I play a divorced dad, so I was able to channel those emotions and put myself back there. But for us, it ended the tension that we had been living with on a daily basis. Sometimes I do think it makes things better for the children, not worse."

Seamless, which will be released this Spring, is the story of two divorced couples who essentially swap spouses. The script resonated with Mr. Bellow because he had yet to play a father and he wanted to step into those shoes for a bit. "It was exciting to see how relationships can shift over time, and that even though the characters behaved badly, their decisions were guided by love," he said, almost wistfully.

Ever since his divorce several years ago from actress Fiona Drake, Mr. Bellow is notorious for refusing to speak about his love life. Nevertheless, his current relationship with Cassandra Willis, the former supermodel turned actress, is well documented. One gets the sense that perhaps this gorgeous star is finally looking to settle down again. Mr. Bellow is between films right now and has the freedom, he says, to select projects that mean something to him. He said he made a few mistakes early on (though I can't think of any), taking on nearly any role offered to him. For now, he has a stack of scripts on his desk he's working his way through.

I ask him a question I've wondered about many successful actors: Is being a celebrity all it's cracked up to be? He lives a life most of us only dream of—does he ever think about what life might have been like if he'd become, say, a teacher?

"And married my high school sweetheart?" he responds with a laugh. "Honestly, all the time."

In true Jack Bellow fashion, that's all I can get him to say.

1

Present Day

RACHEL MILLER WAS AWOKEN AT 3:00 A.M. BY THE SOUND OF her seven-year-old whispering in her ear that she needed to go to the bathroom. Rachel tried to stifle her annoyance as she untangled herself from the sheets, careful not to disturb her sleeping husband.

"Come on, kiddo," she whispered, reaching for Emma's hand and leading her back down the hall to the bathroom directly adjacent to her daughter's bedroom. Rachel tucked her in shortly after, and returned to her own bed, only now she was, frustratingly, wide awake.

Four hours later, an exhausted Rachel stood naked in her closet debating between two nearly identical black Theory pantsuits. She grabbed one down, and then reached for a cream-colored blouse, debating whether the tone washed out her pale skin. She put it back and selected an emerald green silk tank. She knew it brought out her eyes, and green was a lucky color, wasn't it?

"Brush your teeth! Are you brushing yet? Twenty minutes, guys," Rachel called out to the ether, as she clasped her bra around her waist.

Emma, fresh as a daisy, came bounding in, her reddish-blond curls shooting out all over her head. "Mommy, I see your boobies!"

"Emma, sweetie, did you do your teeth?" Her daughter breathed out her proof. "Okay, go downstairs and eat."

Rachel's ten-year-old son, Max, shouted from down the hall that he couldn't find his Chromebook.

"Dan, help him, please. I can't do this this morning," Rachel shouted in response, as she walked into her bathroom to continue getting ready.

"It's down here," Dan called from the kitchen, otherwise paying no mind to his family bustling around him.

Rachel stared into the mirror and began to diligently apply her makeup. She had gotten away with little more than blush and mascara when she was younger. The circles under her hazel eyes now required serious concealer and she had swapped out her sheer lip gloss for actual lipstick. She pulled back her shoulder-length auburn hair into a sleek bun, thankful as always for the advent of keratin treatments. Aside from the extra ten pounds that she hadn't been able to shake post Emma, Rachel was mostly satisfied with her appearance. She grabbed her favorite heels, giving her petite stature three extra inches for confidence, then walked downstairs and into the kitchen.

"I didn't hear you come to bed," Rachel said to her husband, as she poured herself coffee. "Did you stay up late?"

"Nope," Dan said, looking up from his phone. "You probably passed out five minutes after you went upstairs, like you always do."

Rachel ignored his comment and sat for a minute next to him at the counter, silently running through the argument she had to deliver in court that day. "Damn, I forgot to make lunch."

Dan looked up again, briefly considering her, perhaps wondering if this involved him, then returned to scrolling on Instagram.

Rachel jumped up and quickly assembled two turkey sandwiches, and threw them into her children's lunch bags with a clementine and a pack of mini Oreos each. That would have to do.

"Finish up, sweetie," she said, looking at her daughter slowly eating her Cheerios. "We need to get a move on."

"Max, we're leaving now," Rachel yelled up the stairs. A few minutes later, Max made his way out of his messy bedroom and ran down the stairs. Rachel handed him a muffin to eat in the car and pointed at his backpack to remind him to take it.

"Bye, Dan," she called out to her husband as they left, shutting the door behind them.

Rachel pulled her car out of their garage, hurt that Dan hadn't offered to manage drop-off that day or help in any capacity. He didn't even wish her luck. He knew how important this motion was, didn't he?

Seven minutes later she arrived at Sutton Elementary, in their picturesque Westchester, New York, town of Ridgevale, and lined up behind the other SUVs.

"Max, honey, don't forget you have Hebrew school today. Becca's doing carpool. And, Em, Justine is bringing you and Olive home to our house for a playdate. Sound good?"

Her kids shook their heads yes and jumped out of the car.

Rachel rolled down the window. "Okay, bye, guys, be good today. I love you."

"Bye, Mommy! I love you," Emma called out behind her for all the world to hear. Her fifth grader gave a wave and walked off toward his friends.

Rachel had a half hour to be in court. She turned on the radio and zoned out. Was her son acting more distant? she wondered. He used to be so attached to her. Maybe she should plan a trip to Legoland for the two of them or something. Do ten-year-old boys still like Legoland? Rachel sighed, and tried to focus on the motion she had to argue.

She found a parking spot and checked her phone before walking inside the courthouse. There were a few unimportant e-mails and one from Jerry Rich, her boss, which she looked at quickly. "Good luck today.—J. R." Rachel knew this was not Jerry offering his support. Her client, Carraway, had the potential to give them much more business and Jerry was already salivating. She hoped that landing more work from them would propel her into equity partnership and maybe, finally, get Jerry to treat her as a peer. Rachel shook off her nerves and walked into the White Plains Courthouse, greeting Marcelo, the same security guard that had been assigned to the attorney check-in point for as long as Rachel had been practicing.

"Ms. Miller, how's it going?" Marcelo asked.

"Doing well, Marcelo. And how many times have I told you to call me Rachel?"

She handed him her cell phone before walking through the X-ray machine, though it pained her to relinquish it. She reminded herself, as she did before every court appearance, that the school would call Dan if they couldn't contact her, and then her mom if they couldn't find him. If something came up, which it *wouldn't*, she silently reprimanded herself, it would be dealt with, even if she didn't know about it when it was happening.

Rachel entered the lobby of the sprawling courthouse and crammed into the rickety old elevator, momentarily holding her breath as it shuddered on each floor. She got off on three and headed over to the list outside the courtroom to sign in. There it was. *Randall Preston v. Carraway, Inc., et al.* Mr. Preston's attorney, Lou Vasquez, had already signed in for the plaintiff and was standing in the hallway flanked by a colleague and his client. Seeing Lou, one of the preeminent plaintiff's lawyers in New York, was intimidating, but she knew her case was solid. He spotted her across the hall and gave her a salute.

Rachel sat down on the bench outside the courtroom and flipped through her notes, until she saw her old law school friend, Gabe Lancaster, coming out of the elevator. Gabe was an in-house litigator at Carraway, and when the company was served with a personal injury lawsuit in New York, he asked Rachel to handle it.

Gabe gave her a quick hug and asked her if she was ready. She could sense his nerves. There was a lot riding on this motion for both of them, but Gabe seemed far more anxious about it than she was.

"It'll be fine," Rachel said reassuringly. "The arguments are solid, and the expert Vasquez hired is shit. We know this."

"Thanks," he said, the admiration for her coming through. "Why can't all my outside counsel have your confidence? Okay, distract me. What's been going on in your life?"

"My life." Rachel smiled. "We're so boring. The kids are great, gymnastics, soccer, you know how it goes."

"And the husband?" he asked.

Rachel laughed. They had all gone to law school together and Gabe had never forgiven Dan for stealing Rachel out of his study group third year.

"He's fine. He's Dan."

"Still the life of the party, then?"

She laughed. "You know him, still doing keg stands." And generally ignoring his wife, she thought to herself.

Rachel saw her opposing counsel walk into the courtroom, so they followed suit and grabbed seats toward the front. She took in her surroundings, which was more like a school auditorium than a courtroom, with its wooden pews and high-hat lighting, and flipped through her legal pad one more time. The Honorable Edith Bronheim entered, and Rachel and her fellow attorneys rose in tandem. Once papers were shuffled and the judge was comfortably seated, the court secretary called Rachel's case first for oral argument.

Rachel took a deep breath and approached the podium. "Good morning, Your Honor. My name is Rachel Miller for the defendant, Carraway, Incorporated, and may it please the court." She went on to argue that the Carraway pain-blocking device implanted in the plaintiff's back was not defective, challenging the plaintiff's lack of evidence and lackluster expert. "This is a case that should have been thrown out months ago, Your Honor, but for the requirement that we undergo needless discovery before getting to this point. Carraway was forced to undergo significant legal expenses and as such, we are seeking an immediate dismissal, as well as costs. Thank you, Your Honor."

Rachel stood silently, waiting for the judge to ask her questions. Instead, Judge Bronheim nodded to her and called the plaintiff to argue his case. Rachel sat down at the defense table, satisfied, and listened to Lou Vasquez blather on about the defect in the warnings and that the device implanted in his client's spine caused him further injury. He was clearly searching for any possible fact to hang on to that might necessitate trial.

The judge interrupted him about five minutes in. "Okay, Mr. Vasquez. Thank you. I'll take this under advisement and will issue a written opinion. What's my next case?"

Rachel knew this was a good sign. Lou looked at his colleague, who grimaced, confirming Rachel's assessment. She gathered up her things and led Gabe out of the courtroom.

Once outside, Lou walked up to them. "Nice performance in there, Ms. Miller. Should we sit down and talk about settlement?"

"Well, I don't see why not, Lou."

Less than a half hour later, Carraway agreed to pay the plaintiff $130,000 for his troubles. Lou Vasquez walking away with a third of that was a significant loss for him and a great day for Rachel.

"I think this means you're in," Gabe said, as he and Rachel walked downstairs together. Carraway, like most companies, had several lawsuits around the country, and Rachel's firm, Silver and Frank, was vying for lead counsel.

Rachel smiled gratefully at Gabe as they approached the front desk to retrieve their phones and exit the courthouse. "I really appreciate you trusting me with this, Gabe."

"Of course, Rach. You did great."

"Ms. Miller, I mean Rachel, sorry," Marcelo interjected, a bit bashfully, "here's your phone. It's been buzzing like crazy."

Rachel took her phone from him and glanced at it quickly. She had seventy-six missed text messages on her Ridgevale mom text chain and three missed calls from her best friend, Becca. She frowned. At least it wasn't the school calling.

She gave Gabe a peck on the cheek. "I gotta go. I'll check dates and we'll set up a meeting."

Rachel walked toward the parking lot and looked at her phone again. She couldn't figure out where the mom text conversation started and scrolling up from the bottom wasn't making sense. Screw it, she thought, as she turned on her car and plugged in her phone. Becca could fill her in. Rebecca Darner, Rachel's best friend since freshman year of college, and a fellow Ridgevale mom, was way more in tune to the goings-on of the other mothers anyway, and frequently distilled the gossip for Rachel.

"Oh my god, Rachel. Finally!" Becca said when she answered her call on the first ring.

"Why do I have eight million text messages on my phone?" Rachel asked as she pulled out of the court parking lot and headed to her office.

Becca took an audible breath. "I was at drop-off this morning and Michelle asked me if it's true you dated Jack Bellow in high school."

"Okay . . ."

"And then Amy walked over and showed me her phone."

"Wait, all these texts are about me?" Rachel's stomach had started to drop.

"So you haven't looked at your phone at all?"

"I was in court and didn't have it with me. What's going on?"

"Please don't freak out," Becca said. Then she dropped the bomb. "It's about you and Jack."

2

Fall 1997

RACHEL STONE SAT IN THE BACK OF THE AUDITORIUM WAITING
for the auditions to start. Her heart was racing. This was definitely a mistake. Her parents had been all over her about building
up her resume now that she was a junior. She'd already joined the
school paper in September, but according to the college counselor
they had dragged her to, one extracurricular wasn't enough to get
into a top school.

"You have a beautiful voice," her mom said pointedly. "Try out
for the musical. Isn't it *Grease* this year?"

"You'd be terrific, honey!" Her dad was always in support of
her mother's ideas. They launched into a duet of "Summer Nights"
and Rachel rolled her eyes but couldn't help but join in.

She mostly agreed to audition because her best friend, Alex,
was in the drama club. It wasn't a crazy idea; she used to love taking musical theater classes and voice lessons. She had even starred
as Dorothy in the middle school production of *Wizard of Oz*, but
then Michael Shultz started a rumor that Rachel had a crush on
the Tin Man and that ended her theatrical career.

Where is Alex? she wondered. She felt like she needed to pee
for the third time since she entered the auditorium. She stood up
to leave, smoothing down the mane of reddish-brown hair she
had spent hours blow-drying straight that morning, grateful for
the cooperative October weather.

"Rach!" Finally. Rachel turned toward the voice of her oldest
and best friend, Alexandra Hirschfeld. Alex lived three houses

away from Rachel, and there was rarely a day the two of them weren't together. Alex was standing next to a tall, good-looking boy with crystal blue eyes who was wearing a faded gray T-shirt and carrying a guitar case, his JanSport casually slung over his shoulder. He was perfection. Rachel was suddenly self-conscious of her tight baby-doll shirt, which showed off her newly arrived size C-cup chest. (Her mom had said she had "finally blossomed" just that morning.)

"H-h-hi," Rachel managed to stutter.

"Hey, you." Alex smirked. "Have you guys met?"

The boy smiled at her then, his eyes glittering, and shook his head no.

"Rachel Stone, meet Jack Bellow. Jack, meet Rachel. Rachel has been my best friend since practically birth." Alex pulled on Rachel's arm to move her away from her seat and up to the front with the other kids.

Rachel knew exactly who Jack was, and Alex of course knew that. They'd been calling him HDG, for "hot drama guy," since Rachel spotted him passing by her locker on the first day of freshman year. She had seen him with his friends in town, too, but she'd never said hello. Alex had become friendly with him in drama club the year before and had promised to finally introduce them if Rachel auditioned for the show. A little extra incentive.

"Glad you decided to try out," Jack said, as they walked down the rows of auditorium chairs.

"I hope I'm not terrible," Rachel said nervously. Talking to her crush was heightening her anxiety.

She sat down next to Alex, behind a heavyset girl with her hair piled on top of her head doing scales, loudly. Rachel looked around and noticed that the drama club was a bit of a motley crew, as her dad would say. Other than Jack, there were only a few guys that might be considered good-looking. She saw two girls from her pre-calculus class, who always dressed like witches, as if they were starring in the movie *The Craft*. They were talking to a skinny blond girl wearing a Tori Amos T-shirt who Rachel didn't recognize. Next to them was a senior Rachel knew from her neighborhood who was on the football team. She gave him a quick nod, surprised to see him there.

Jack leaned over Alex and said to Rachel that he was surprised they hadn't met before. "Sorry if this sounds super weird, but could I have maybe seen you at the diner with your parents?"

Oh my god, she thought. He thinks I'm such a loser. "If it was a Saturday morning, probably." She tried to play it cool, particularly since she wasn't ready to give up her weekly pancake ritual with her family.

"I thought so. It's nice that you all spend time together."

"They're not too bad. You're a junior too, right? Which elementary school did you go to?"

"Parker. You went to North with Alex?"

"Yup. It's funny going to such a big school. I have camp friends who've known every single person in their grade since, like, kindergarten," Rachel said.

"That's why you need to hang out with us drama freaks. Meet more people."

Rachel was momentarily embarrassed. The wealthier North Avenue kids in their Long Island town had a reputation for sticking to their own.

"Ha, we're not freaks." Alex hit Jack's arm. "Well, maybe just you. Anyhoo, I told Rachel she has nothing to worry about. She has a sick voice."

Rachel smiled at her weakly, feeling the butterflies again.

"You're fine, Rach. It's so easy. You sing, like, one verse of a song, everyone does a choreographed dance that you'll obviously be fine with, and then pairs of people get called up to read scenes. Plus, you're gorgeous. You'll get in."

"Then why don't you audition, Al?" Rachel joked, deflecting the compliment.

Alex laughed. "Oh yes, maybe I can be Sandy." Alex was a self-professed nonactor. She had always dreamed of being in the movie business. Their playdates as children usually involved her directing Rachel in a play or using her dad's camcorder to make movies with their dolls. She joined drama to get experience backstage and was thrilled when she was asked to assistant stage manage the production.

"Okay, I guess I better go find Brenda and get this thing started." Alex grabbed her backpack and mouthed good luck to Rachel as she went in search of their drama teacher.

Rachel and Jack sat there quietly for a second. "So, you play guitar?" Rachel asked dumbly, pointing to the guitar sitting next to him.

"Sort of. I've been teaching myself."

"That's so cool. I've always wanted to learn."

"Once you figure out the chords it isn't that hard. I can show you," Jack said.

He was cut off as Brenda Danziger, the drama teacher, walked onto the stage. She greeted them loudly with a voice that projected all the way to the back of the auditorium. Although she was a teacher in the school, she insisted on everyone calling her by her first name.

"Hello, friends! Welcome to the auditions for *Grease*! Most of you know the drill. I call your name, you go to the stage and perform a few bars until I tell you to stop. We clap for everyone, and remember," she said in a singsong voice, "we do not talk when others are singing. Let's get started. Noah Rittenhouse, you're up," Brenda said, pointing at a short, stocky freshman with visible acne.

Noah was followed by a succession of sophomore girls and then Ben Danforth, who Rachel knew from her advanced placement English class. Jack gave him a thumbs-up as he walked onstage. Rachel immediately pegged Ben as an obvious Danny Zuko.

"Ben's my boy," Jack whispered. Ben had a ton of confidence and Rachel sensed that most of the girls were probably very into him. As he left the stage, Rachel heard her own name, and her stomach went ice cold.

Jack leaned over to her. "You'll be great! Seriously. Pretend we're all naked."

Rachel stumbled over her bag getting out of her seat and Jack put his hand on her back to steady her. She smiled at him, then walked up the stairs to center stage. The spotlight shone bright and Rachel stood in the circle it created. It was hard to see the people in the audience, which helped.

Brenda called out, "Say your name, what song you're performing, and go."

Rachel took a deep breath. "Okay, Rachel Stone, singing 'On My Own' from Les Mis." She heard a chuckle in the audience, but someone shushed them. It was a little ridiculous—she was maybe the seventh girl that day singing the song—but it was the only one she'd prepared. She took another breath and began to sing.

She commanded the stage, her voice powerful and clear. All her nerves dissipated the moment she opened her mouth to sing. Why did she ever stop performing? As she started the second verse, Brenda cut in. "Okay, nice job. Cindy Cullen, you're next."

Rachel got a smattering of applause as she left the stage. Alex gave her an exaggerated thumbs-up, and Rachel stuck her tongue out in return. As she went back to her seat, she saw that Jack had moved up a row to talk to Ben and she was disappointed.

When it was Jack's turn, he sang "More Than Words." He had a nice, mellow voice and played his guitar. His light brown hair draped over his eyes as he leaned forward, and Rachel couldn't stop staring. She hoped no one noticed. He got a lot of applause, and a few people even cheered. After he sang, he came back to the seat next to her. Rachel's heart rate immediately sped up again.

"How bad was I?" he whispered, although she sensed from his smile walking off the stage that he was pleased with his performance.

"You're kidding! You were so good. Maybe you'll get Danny Zuko." Rachel laughed nervously, slightly embarrassed by her effusiveness.

"Wow, thanks. That's totally Ben's role, but maybe I'll be one of the guys he hangs out with," Jack said. "You were awesome, by the way. Alex was right."

They were starting to get looks so they stopped talking as the rest of the auditions continued. Jack's arm was an inch away from hers on the armrest between their seats. Rachel felt a magnetic pull that moved her own arm directly next to his as Jack moved even closer, so their pinkies touched. Rachel felt a straight shot to her belly. They didn't make eye contact, just looked straight ahead as their arms were glued together.

When the singing finished, everyone, including Jack, jumped up to go onstage for the dance portion. "You coming?" Jack asked Rachel. Rachel was flustered from being in such close contact with him and waved him on as she grabbed a sip from her water bottle.

"Hey!" Her old friend from elementary school, Nicole Mensky, was standing in the aisle, apparently waiting for her. "I forgot you could sing!"

Rachel complimented her on her own audition.

"Come stand with me onstage. I need someone to help me with choreography." Nicole was probably remembering the ballet and tap classes they had taken together as little girls.

"I'm sure I'll be the one following you," Rachel said modestly.

"I saw you sitting with Jack," Nicole said curiously as they walked up to the stage. "I didn't know you were friends."

"Oh, we aren't. I mean, I don't really know him. Alex just introduced us." Rachel felt her cheeks turning red. "He seems nice."

"The nicest! He used to go out with Jen, but they broke up a few weeks ago, right before school started," she said, nodding at the girl in the Tori Amos shirt.

Jack didn't have a girlfriend. She wondered if Alex knew. Before she could ask for more details, the choreographer came onstage to get them started.

Nicole was still a terrible dancer, but Rachel had no trouble keeping up and was more than happy to give her old friend a few pointers. When it was time to read scenes, Rachel was paired with the pimply freshman, Noah.

After auditions, she went to gather her things and spotted Jack and Nicole talking and looking at her. She awkwardly waved goodbye to them and headed out of the school, where her mother was waiting out front as promised.

That night, Rachel was on the phone with Alex as they watched *Dawson's Creek* together, their Tuesday-night ritual. They were both in love with Pacey, and a little bit with Joey, too. At the first commercial break, Rachel asked Alex about Jack.

"I knew it! I mean, I wasn't going to bring it up because I literally wanted to see how long it took you."

"Alex! Was I so obvious? Could he tell?" Rachel was mortified and grateful that Alex couldn't see her face.

Alex laughed her off. "No, I'm totally kidding."

"It's just that he's so freaking cute. I know I've been saying this for, like, a year, but he's even better up close."

"You've actually been saying this for two years," Alex teased. "But yes, he's definitely hot. And the good news is, you're like Cindy Crawford compared to most of the girls in drama."

Rachel laughed. "Like a foot shorter, and missing the mole, but we're practically doppelgangers."

"You know what I mean. I'm sorry it took me so long to introduce you. Thankfully, he and Jen finally broke up."

"I saw you eyeing her, Alex," Rachel said with a smile in her voice, giving it right back to her friend. Rachel was the only person Alex had told that she liked girls. In true fashion, Rachel had taken to pointing out pretty girls to her friend and mulling over their dating potential.

"Shut up. Let's talk about your boyfriend."

During commercial breaks, Alex gave her friend the lowdown on Jack and Jen, and the politics of the drama club. The girls squealed together when Dawson ran after Jen Lindley and Rachel thought to herself, for the first time, that high school might be getting interesting.

3

Present Day

"Okay, so Amy shows me a picture of you—well, you can't totally tell it's you, but you're definitely with Jack—and you're not wearing a shirt, and his hands are covering your boobs. I think it was taken in, like, a school bathroom?" Becca's voice was animated as she described the photo.

Rachel could see it in her mind perfectly. They were posing like that Janet Jackson album cover. Alex had taken the picture of them in the girls' dressing room. She and Jack were both always on Rachel to let go a little.

"That's weird. How does Amy have that picture on her phone?" Rachel asked, trying to stay calm.

"Oh, Rach." Becca paused, her voice sympathetic. "I hate to tell you this. It was posted on the *Daily Mail*. They put up a bunch of pictures of you and Jack."

Rachel felt her heart stop. "Wait, what?"

"There are some letters, too," Becca said quietly.

"I don't understand." Rachel's voice sounded strained, even to her own ears. The blood was rushing to her head.

"I guess because he's so famous now, people find anything about him interesting, even stuff from over twenty years ago? I don't know, it's not like he's Meghan Markle."

"What are people saying?" she whispered, still looking to her best friend to boil it down to the most salient points.

"Nothing bad, I promise. Everyone is flipping out that you used to go out with *the* Jack Bellow, obviously. I mean, a few questions about how this stuff got out there and if you knew beforehand. Things like that."

Rachel was having trouble catching her breath. "How did this happen?" she asked, her voice getting stuck in her throat.

Becca was silent.

"I can't go to my office. Oh my god. What am I going to say to Dan?"

"This will blow over, Rach. You know how celebrity gossip is."

"Yeah, and I also know how much our friends enjoy a scandal." Her mind flashed to the endless discussion following their friend Sarah when her husband had an affair.

Rachel ended the call, her stomach churning, as she drove home instead of to her office in the city. She immediately tried Dan, but he didn't pick up and she didn't bother leaving a message. What would she say, anyway? Becca had texted her the link, and Rachel almost pulled to the side of the road to look at it, but she needed a few more minutes of semi-normalcy. A bunch more texts from her friends had come in as she drove, and she willfully ignored them. She finally pulled up in front of her house.

Rachel rushed inside, her heart beating rapidly. She grabbed her laptop out of her bag and sat down on the floor in her foyer, not able to wait another minute. She typed in the website address and there it was, right on the home page. Her head was spinning as her eyes bounced around the page.

Exclusive: The Unseen Photos of Jack Bellow.
Always a heartthrob, see our favorite Hollywood nice guy cavorting with his high school gal pal and the love letters he sent her. Is she the reason Jack isn't ready to settle down? What will Cassandra Willis have to say?

Rachel landed on the photo of her and Jack with his hands partially covering her breasts and gagged. She had to force herself to keep going. She quickly scrolled through the slideshow of other pictures and saw one of Jack kissing her, and another of them at the prom. She flipped past a group photo of all of them at the diner, with Jack and Alex and a few of the other drama kids. There was a picture of Rachel and Jack in her and Becca's old dorm room, naked under that stupid flowered Laura Ashley comforter. Jesus. And the letters!

Dear Rachel,

I can't believe you're going away all summer. I have a pit in my stomach as I write this. I know it's partially because I'll miss you, but also I guess I'm wondering what will happen to us. I've never felt like this about anyone before. These last eight months have been crazy and amazing.

What are you going to tell your friends about me? Are you going to write me? Are you going to forget me? What if another guy asks you out? I'm embarrassing myself, right?

Here is what I love about you. And yes, I used the word *love*. I love how your hair smells like coconut. I love your toes. They are so cute. I love how you're so much smaller than me. I love your boobs. I can't help it! I love them. I mostly love the way you are so easy to be around, you always know exactly what to say to make me feel better about things. How do you do that?

Promise to write me, okay? I'll be at my dad's for the first two weeks and then back home the rest of the time. I know you know this. I already made plans to see your

parents while you're gone. Your dad wants to take me fish-
ing, apparently. I wish we were going to be together.

I love you,

Jack (Jackie, Jack Jack, Doody, Sweet Cheeks)

*   *   *

Dear Rach,

I'm sitting in math. You're leaving for Florida tonight with your
parents. I don't know why I'm so sad that you're leaving.
Maybe because I want to be with you for New Year's. Everyone
is going to Ben's house. I think Nicole and maybe a few other
girls are going to stay over. Ben said Jen is probably coming. I
promise I won't talk to her. I mean, I'll talk to her a little because
I know you would yell at me if I was being an asshole.

I guess you and your camp friends are going to parties
down there. You've told me so many stories about them and I
can't help but worry you're going to hook up with one of Cori's
friends. Okay, I know you're laughing at me right now, but I'm
at least a little serious. Just don't do anything I wouldn't do.

I already miss you. I love you so much.

Jack

*   *   *

To my favorite person in the world:

I don't know why I'm writing you this right now, since I literally
just saw you, but I feel like I need to capture what you mean to
me. Friday night was perfect. I know I had wanted to do it for
a long time, but you were right to want to wait until we were
(almost) seniors. I didn't know I could feel even closer to you
than I already did, but I do. I am listening to Beastie Boys right

now, which isn't romantic at all but it makes me happy, and I'm so happy. I hope we get to see each other tomorrow so we can "bond" again as you so cleverly call it. Forever isn't stretching it. I honestly can't bear to imagine us not together.

I'm looking at that picture of us on my desk, the one from the *Grease* cast party. You look so beautiful. I wish you were here. I miss you right now. Writing this down is good for me because it gets my thoughts of you out of my mind. I guess every guy thinks about their first time, but they (or maybe just me?) imagine some faceless big-boobed blond babe bouncing up and down. Look at all that alliteration! Mrs. Katz would be proud. But what we had was so much better. I hope I measured up to Dawson. Or the other guy. I forget which one you like.

I think I'm rambling. I guess all I want to say is that I think you are incredible. Not just because you are insanely pretty, but you are just the sweetest, kindest person I ever met. So much of who I am is because of you. Do you realize that? I want to be with you forever and ever.

Love, Me

Rachel stopped reading. She had loved Jack's letters. She and Alex started calling him "The Poet" when "Hot Drama Guy" felt like an inappropriate code name for her actual boyfriend. She couldn't begin to imagine how the *Daily Mail* had this. She hadn't seen these letters in years, not since her parents sold their house on Long Island to move closer to her and Dan in Westchester, and dumped a bunch of boxes on her in the process. The website didn't use her last name, but there was no chance anyone that knew her wouldn't recognize her. And look, there in the comments was her full name. Posted by Anonymous. Of course. It was probably Brett Harrison, he hated her. She was elected editor of the school paper senior year and got into Cornell when he was waitlisted. Brett was always posting about Jack's accomplishments to their high school Facebook page, as if they were friends.

Rachel had done a lot of work on herself not to think about her first boyfriend. It wasn't easy, not with him constantly on her television screen and the cover of magazines, but she had mostly moved past it. Plus, she knew it drove Dan nuts. She purposefully hadn't mentioned dating Jack Bellow to any of her Ridgevale friends, happy to finally have it behind her. Becca thought she should be bragging about it. How many people can say they lost their virginity to a movie star?

Rachel thought back to when Jack was cast on *Sanctions*, his breakout role. She was already a full-fledged attorney by then, and found it ironic that her high school boyfriend was finding success playing a lawyer on television. She, Alex, and Becca watched that first episode and they all shrieked the first time he came on-screen. He looked far more muscular than he had in high school, but otherwise it was the same Jack. He had significant chemistry with the female lead, and Rachel was not at all surprised to later read that they were dating in real life. It was strange to see him kissing another woman, even though it had been years since they were together.

She ended up sending Jack an e-mail to congratulate him after his first episode aired. As much as he had hurt her, it was so long ago, and she was really proud of him for doing what he set out to do. They spoke a few times after that. They mostly caught up on their old friends and jobs. Jack was still close with their friend Ben, who was apparently outearning all of them as an investment banker in the city and dating several different women at a time. Neither Jack nor Rachel brought up how things had ended between them, which was probably for the best. They even talked about getting together when he was in the city next, but it never happened. It was another four or five years before they actually saw each other again.

Rachel groaned out loud as she realized Jack would think that she was responsible for this. But at least he was used to the attention; Dan was going to be horrified. Her husband had this weird, very much one-sided competition with Jack Bellow. *Sanctions* had been airing for about a year, and Jack had just started getting all this attention for it. Rachel casually mentioned one night when a commercial for the show came on that Jack Bellow was her high school boyfriend, and Dan flipped out. He wanted to know every detail about him and when they last spent time together, not understanding how she had never mentioned that she'd dated a famous celebrity. He even insinuated that she must still be interested in him. Rachel was surprised that he was jealous, he was ordinarily so laid-back, and it wasn't like he was ever particularly possessive over her.

She finally managed to convince Dan that she had moved on from Jack, and her history with him faded into the background as they got more serious. Sure, over the years, Dan would comment jealously that "her boyfriend" was on-screen, or wonder out loud how Jack managed to land so many of the hottest actresses. Occasionally, he'd even ask her if she wished she'd ended up with Jack, instead of him. But Rachel had moved on. She couldn't totally avoid Jack, obviously; his picture was constantly popping up around her. She thought about him sometimes, but who didn't occasionally wonder about their first love?

She had to get in touch with Dan before someone else told him about this. And her parents. Oh, fuck.

4

1997–1998

JACK MET RACHEL EVERY MORNING BY HER LOCKER SO THEY COULD see each other before first period. She could not believe that they were one of those hallway make-out couples. It happened so fast, once they were both cast in *Grease*. Rachel was surprised to get a good part playing one of the Pink Ladies, Frenchy, and Jack was cast as Doody, which made Rachel laugh every single time she had to say it. She wondered how much influence Alex had over the casting, since Rachel and Jack were playing boyfriend and girlfriend in the show.

The cast list had gone up the Wednesday after auditions and Alex met Rachel at her locker after school to give her the good news. When they saw Jack, he said that he was stoked to be playing her boyfriend. Rachel felt her pale skin turning pink. She had been thinking about nothing but Jack since the audition day, but she had been too embarrassed to talk to him again. Other than seeing him in the hall and saying hello a few times, she sort of avoided the drama kids altogether.

"A group of us are going to the diner today after the read-through. You guys should come," Jack said.

Rachel looked over at Alex. "Sure, we'd love to," Alex said, answering for both of them. She was clearly not going to let her friend hide behind homework and miss a chance to finally hang out with her crush.

"I can ask my mom to give you guys a ride, if you want," Rachel finally uttered. Jack Bellow was asking her to hang out.

"Jack just got his license! Can you drive us?" Alex said.

Jack laughed, keeping his eyes on Rachel as he spoke. "Chill, Alex. It's just a junior license until I'm seventeen. But yeah, I can take you guys. You'll need to get a ride home since I have to go to work later."

They walked into the auditorium and there was a huge circle of folding chairs on the stage. The name of each role was taped to the chairs and Rachel found her seat. She was sitting next to Jack's ex-girlfriend, Jen, who was playing Rizzo, and the other Pink Ladies. She had briefly worried that people would be annoyed, since it was her first time in a high school play and she had one of the lead roles, but no one seemed to mind. The read-through itself was surprisingly fun. She loved listening to everyone test out their characters.

After rehearsal, a crew of them left for the diner, and it seemed like anyone in the cast could join, if they wanted. Rachel somehow ended up riding shotgun in Jack's car, and Alex sat on Nicole's lap in the back seat next to Ben and two other boys. They all crammed into a booth and Jack steered Rachel into the seat beside him. When the waitress came to take their order, Jack asked Rachel to share cheese fries with him. Rachel caught Alex's eye across the table in that moment and she seemed as shocked as Rachel that things were going this well.

When the food arrived, the group launched into a discussion about whether George Clooney was a terrible Batman or if it was just a bad movie. Rachel hadn't seen it and turned to Jack.

"Where do you work?"

"The pharmacy in town. Not particularly exciting," he responded with a laugh. "But I like making my own money."

"That's awesome."

"Well, my dad's not the best about paying child support or whatever, so me working sort of takes the pressure off my mom, I guess."

Rachel was immediately embarrassed. Her parents wouldn't dream of her paying for anything. "That must be really hard," she said sympathetically.

"Don't get me wrong, making my own money is great. I can basically do what I want. That's why I bought my car. I mean, it's my uncle's old station car, but at least I don't need to ask my parents to take me anywhere. They'd probably just fight over whose turn it was or something."

Rachel smiled, but inwardly cringed at how good she had it. Her parents rarely fought and money was something she never thought about. Her mom was a psychologist, but worked part-time and always volunteered at the school when Rachel was younger, and her dad was an accountant. Her parents were willing to pay for dance and piano lessons, and even sent her to a several thousand dollars a year sleepaway camp each summer in upstate New York.

Jack must have sensed her discomfort and waved her off.

"Honestly, it's fine. My mom is remarried now, and her husband, Stan, is pretty laid-back. And my dad is great. I'm just happy I don't have to listen to them yelling at each other anymore." Rachel loved how honest Jack was being with her. She took so much for granted.

"My parents are still, like, madly in love. It's sort of gross."

Jack laughed. "You're lucky, trust me."

"No, I know. My parents are pretty great. It's just me, so they're kind of devoted. Do you have siblings?"

"Yeah, a sister, Megan. She's a freshman. She sang the same song as you at auditions."

"Meg is your sister? She's so sweet! She came up to me after to tell me that I did a good job."

Jack smiled. "She annoys the hell out of me, but she's a pretty good kid."

"Well, now I'm jealous of you. I just stopped begging for a younger sibling, like, last year."

"She's up for grabs," Jack joked.

Rachel was disappointed when Jack said he had to get going for work a few minutes later. He reached over and hugged her goodbye, which was exciting, but then she watched him hug the other girls, too. Oh well, she thought.

Alex told her on the phone that night that she definitely thought Jack was into her. "He legit only talked to you, Rach. This is happening."

"I don't know, maybe he was just being nice because I'm new to the drama club?"

Alex laughed her off. "Or maybe he realizes what an awesome human you are?" Rachel had plenty of friends, and she always made a point to be nice to everyone, but she didn't see herself quite the same way Alex did.

At rehearsal the following week, Brenda asked if anyone could help reorganize the prop room. Rachel wasn't needed for any of the scenes they were rehearsing and volunteered. She had serious organizational skills. Her mom liked to joke that all you needed to do was tell Rachel to do her math homework, and she would spend the next two hours cleaning to avoid it. Rachel would argue that she focused better when things around her were in order.

The prop room was located backstage in the auditorium and was really just a small storage room with a few tables and cubbies. Rachel quickly assessed that it had no logical system and set to work. She started by moving all the tableware together to one shelf, and was amazed by the number of plates, cake stands, and silverware the theater company had accumulated. She heard a quick knock on the door and turned around, and there was Jack.

"I thought you could probably use some help," he said.

"Yes! I guess I'm a total sucker for volunteering for this!"

"Kind of, yeah," Jack said, teasing her. She pointed him to the opposite corner of the small room and Jack began gathering canes, walking sticks, and an errant mannequin, placing them neatly against the wall. Rachel tried reaching up to the top shelf to move a fake plant.

"Hey, let me help you," Jack said, moving toward her. Rachel realized her tank top had ridden up as she was stretching, and her stomach was showing. She pulled the tank down and awkwardly straightened her flannel shirt that was hanging off her shoulders. Jack easily reached above her head, plucking down the plant and handing it to her.

"Here you go," he said, standing right in front of her.

"Thanks." Rachel was nervous to have Jack in such close proximity but hoped he would stay close. He didn't move away.

"Should I get the other plants down?" he asked her, reaching over her head. "You're so tiny, you don't even have to duck."

She stood there, almost frozen, as this boy that she had been thinking of nonstop stepped closer to her. He reached above her head, and she could smell his Old Spice boy smell, with a hint of something stronger, like cologne. He brought down the fake cactus and set it next to him on the lower shelf.

They looked at each other for a moment as Rachel held her breath. He moved a piece of her hair away from her face.

"Hi," he said.

"Hi," she said back.

Jack leaned down and Rachel turned her face up toward his, waiting. He gently pressed his lips to hers. Rachel felt her heart beating faster than it ever had. He wrapped his arms around her, pulling her even closer. The kiss deepened and Rachel felt her whole body tingle. They stopped kissing after what felt like ten minutes, and she looked up at him shyly. She had kissed a couple of boys at camp that summer, but none that made her feel this way.

"Wow," he said. "I've been wanting to do that for weeks."

"You have?" Rachel asked him.

"Are you kidding? I thought you were the cutest girl I ever saw at auditions. Well, to be honest, I've thought that since I first saw you hanging out with Alex last year," Jack admitted. "But now I also know you're smart and easy to talk to."

Rachel was in disbelief that this gorgeous guy, her crush of two years, liked her back. She still thought of herself as the scrawny, undeveloped middle schooler with frizzy hair. Despite coming home from camp that summer with boobs and a waist.

"Alex definitely told you that I liked you, didn't she?"

"She may have given me an enthusiastic yes when I said I was going to ask you out."

"You're asking me out?" Rachel asked him, still somewhat shocked by Jack's interest. She had never had a real boyfriend before; at camp they mostly just swapped around with the boys in their division, but it never meant anything. Jack Bellow actually liked her.

"Isn't that obvious? Do you want to be my girlfriend?"

Holy crap. She couldn't wait to tell Alex. "Um, yeah?"

From that day forward, the two were inseparable. They spent most afternoons before rehearsal making out in the prop room or Jack's car. When he wasn't working after rehearsal, they spent hours on the phone. Jack would occasionally say how he wished he could take her on a real date, instead of to the diner or for pizza, but Rachel was happy to be with him anywhere. She didn't want him to spend his hard-earned money on her. Plus, her dad always handed her a twenty before she went out; it was more than enough for both of them.

A few times early on Rachel went over to Jack's house. She adored his little sister, Megan, who would hang in his room and listen to music with them for as long as Jack could tolerate. His mom mostly stayed out of their way. Rachel was in their kitchen with them one day, making instant noodles; when Nancy, Jack's mom, walked in.

"Oh," she said, looking at them. "Hi, Rachel, it's nice to see you again. Jack, can I speak with you for a moment?"

Rachel stood there uncomfortably, as she heard Jack and his mom whispering in the hallway. She thought she heard him saying "A&P."

"Hey, sorry," Jack said, coming back into the kitchen a few moments later.

"Is everything okay?" Rachel asked.

"All good. I guess I forgot to go food shopping, so she was kind of annoyed."

Rachel couldn't imagine her mother ever expecting her to grocery shop. Maybe she should offer. "Is it okay for me to be here?"

"She just gets in a mood, sometimes," Megan said, embarrassed. "Ever since our dad left. Which makes zero sense since she has a perfectly good husband now."

Rachel gave Megan a hug. "Hey, don't worry about it."

Jack apologized to her again later when they were alone in his room. "Sometimes I just want a normal mom who, like, makes my friends freaking cookies and cares when I get home at night."

"I get it," Rachel said reassuringly. "Maybe we can hang at my house more."

Rachel's parents immediately took to Jack. Since Rachel had no siblings, there was plenty of room for Jack in their home. He soon became a permanent fixture at their dinner table. He was polite and thoughtful, often bringing her mom, Elaine, chocolates from the pharmacy, and offering to help her dad, Mitch, with tasks around the house. It also didn't hurt that her mom often saw patients in the late afternoon, giving them a chance to fool around without the risk of getting caught.

Rachel came home one Saturday morning after sleeping at Alex's and found Jack in her kitchen, with her mom. His eyes looked red, and her mom looked sad, too.

"What's wrong?" Rachel asked nervously.

"Nothing," her mom said quickly. "Jack just came over to wait for you to get home. Isn't that sweet!"

"Saturday pancakes?" Rachel asked Jack, throwing an arm around him, and boldly kissing him in front of her mom.

"Mitch," Elaine called out. "Time to go for breakfast, honey, Rach is home."

When they were talking that night before bed, Rachel's mom wouldn't tell her what she and Jack had been discussing, just that things weren't so easy for his family, and Jack was lucky to have Rachel as his girlfriend. Fortunately, Rachel, and her parents, were committed to giving him the love they felt he was lacking.

5

Present Day

RACHEL TRIED TO BAT DOWN HER ANXIETY AND CALLED HER BOSS. She had nearly forgotten the huge achievement of that morning. She filled Jerry in, and let him know what Gabe said about getting more business from Carraway.

"Excellent news! Let's have them to the office next week, strike while the iron is hot. I'll have Joan set it up." Jerry made no inquiries as to whether this worked for Rachel. "Oh, and put together a PowerPoint for the meeting. You can work off that pitch we did for Merrymount."

After Jerry clicked off, Rachel stared at her phone. How was she going to do any work today? It was just after noon and she felt like it had been a full week since she had driven her kids to school that morning. She needed to get in control of this situation. But first she had to call her mother.

"Mom, hi," Rachel said when Elaine Stone answered the phone on the first ring.

"Hi, my sweet baby. I was just thinking about you! How did the hearing go?"

As much as Rachel was sometimes irritated by her mother, she still craved the endless love her mom had for her. "Great, we settled the case."

"That's fantastic, honey, I'm so proud of you!"

"Thanks. I'm calling about something else, actually." Rachel kept staring at her computer screen, looking at her eighteen-year-old self. "So this is kind of crazy, but, um, there are some revealing pictures of me posted online. I don't know why or how. I'm with Jack."

"Rachel! What do you mean? Wait, when did you see Jack?" Elaine fired questions at her daughter.

"It's old high school pictures. I have no idea how they got out there, or why they were even published. I'm sick about this, Mom. I can't believe it's happening."

"How bad could it be, sweetie? Can you show it to me?"

Rachel texted the link to her mom and waited as she looked.

"Wow," said Elaine, then seemed to remember herself. "Okay, sweetie. Let's not go crazy. These are very old pictures, and maybe no one knows it's you? He's dating that pretty model, isn't he? What's her name? Carol or Kerry or something? Trust me, no one cares about Rachel Miller," Elaine said, both reassuring and critical, as was her trademark.

"Cassandra Willis, Mom. And she's ridiculously famous."

"That's it! She's stunning."

"This is so helpful, Mom."

"Oh, sweetie, I'm sure it'll blow over. What did Dan say?"

"I haven't spoken with him yet. I know he's going to freak out. He was always so weird about me and Jack dating."

"Well, he'll just have to deal with it." Elaine paused. "God, I forgot how sweet you and Jack were together. Look how young you are!"

"Mom!"

"Rach, what's done is done. Okay? Let's just breathe. Remember, in for four, out for four," her mother said, demonstrating loudly into the phone.

"Okay," Rachel said, trying to steady her breath like her mom had been showing her since childhood. "Can you tell Dad? He probably shouldn't go online today."

"I wonder if my friends have seen this," Elaine mused.

"Mom!"

"Sorry, sweetie. Why don't you go splash some water on your face. We'll figure this out. Want me to come over?"

Rachel thought about it. She wanted to fall into her mother's arms and unload all her problems on her. But, since becoming a mother herself, she finally understood that adage about only being as happy as your least happy child. She was an adult, she needed to manage her own life, and she knew it wasn't fair to put her issues on her seventy-two-year-old mother.

"No, Mom. I'm fine. I'll be good."

She hung up and texted Dan to call her. She wondered what he was going to say about all of this. If you had asked her a few months ago, she would have said he would be livid at whoever published the photos and mortified that his friends were seeing his half-naked wife. Now, who knows, they were so out of sync lately.

Rachel thought back to the night before, when she tried to get him to come up to bed with her. She wasn't looking to have sex—they were far too tired on weekdays—but she thought it might be nice to actually get into bed together at the same time, like they used to. Maybe put on an old episode of *Seinfeld* and snuggle. He said he'd be up right behind her, and she tried to stay up and wait; she even put on a cute pajama set instead of her usual T-shirt and underwear. He definitely didn't come up a few minutes after her like he implied he had that morning. She'd read for at least twenty minutes before closing her eyes.

Rachel looked to see if anything else had been published. Nothing yet, as far as she could tell. She googled her own name and saw her LinkedIn profile. Litigation partner at Silver and Frank, where she had worked since her second year of law school as a summer associate. Cornell undergraduate and Fordham Law School.

She saw and reread her *New York Times* wedding announcement. They both looked so young. Dan had a full head of blond hair, which he wore spiked up in front. He was still a few years shy of his now-receding hairline, and she was far from needing the Botox she was having injected in her forehead every four months. And they were madly in love.

She typed in Jack's name. There were about a million hits. Pictures of him with his girlfriend, Cassandra. Pictures with their friend Alex, who was a screenwriter and was directing her first movie in London. Endless interviews. Links to profiles of him in *Rolling Stone*, *InStyle*, an interview of him in the *Hollywood Reporter* from earlier that year (with what Becca insisted had a passing reference to Rachel). Of course, she had read them all.

Rachel's phone rang, breaking her out of her reverie. Finally, Dan. No, not Dan. A 212 number.

"This is Rachel," she answered.

"Is this Rachel Stone Miller?" asked the man's voice on the phone.

"Yes, speaking, who is this?"

"Hi, Rachel, this is Kurt Parker, from *TMZ*. Do you have a few minutes?"

This was not going to disappear, as she had hoped. It was really happening.

"Can I ask what this is in reference to?" she uttered, knowing full well why *TMZ* was calling.

"I'm not sure if you're aware, but there were several photographs published of Jack Bellow today, with a woman from his past. There are a few comments identifying you. Can you confirm that you used to date Mr. Bellow?"

Was she supposed to deny? What else do they have on her? She switched into deposition mode. Better to ask questions of him rather than give anything away.

"I'm sorry, where were these pictures published?"

"They were published on a different site. We'll be reporting on the story and I was hoping to get a comment from the woman in the photos. Presumably, that's you?" he asked.

"Can I call you back?" Rachel said. "Or is there something you can send me to look at?"

"Listen, Ms. Miller. Several sources have already confirmed this is you. I'm just looking for a comment."

She stalled. She had no clue what to say. "I guess, no comment?"

"If you change your mind, here's my number." She didn't bother taking it down. "My deadline is 5:00 p.m."

What is happening? Rachel thought as she hung up with the reporter. She sent an e-mail to Kaitlyn Howell, a friend and colleague who used to work in public relations and now oversaw her law firm's communications. Within thirty seconds her cell phone rang.

"Holy shit, Rachel. Did you actually go out with Jack Bellow?" Kaitlyn asked excitedly.

"I am seriously freaking out over here. Can you help me?" Rachel said, panicked. She quickly filled Kaitlyn in on the little she knew so far.

"Hey, you're okay," Kaitlyn said gently, hearing her friend in distress. "I'll look into it. Send me the name of the reporter who called you and I'll find out what they're running."

"Yes. Do that. Maybe I should talk to someone about making them take it down? Isn't there some right to privacy argument I can make?"

"I don't know, you're the lawyer."

"I'm serious, Kaitlyn. Jerry still treats me like a junior associate half the time. This will undo any minuscule positive opinion he has of me. And what will my clients say?"

"Sorry. I get it. Let me make some calls. And I can reach out to Angie Kim in the IP department for you, maybe she can draft a cease and desist."

"Yes, do that," Rachel said, happy to form any kind of plan. "Thank you."

"Try not to freak out. This is definitely not major news yet. I hadn't heard about it until you e-mailed, and you know I'm a celebrity gossip fiend. We won't discuss how pissed I am that you never told me Jack Bellow was your high school boyfriend!"

"I can't even joke right now." Rachel's voice went up an octave.

"It's not like you should be embarrassed about dating a gorgeous movie star!" Kaitlyn hung up, promising to investigate and report back.

Rachel needed to distract herself. She shot off a text to Gabe, suggesting a follow-up meeting with the Carraway team about bringing legal work to her firm. Then she turned back to her laptop and opened up the PowerPoint she had done last year for the Merrymount pitch. Jerry was right, it was a good start. Of course this presentation was far more important, and if they landed the business, she would be the originating partner. She tried to make some edits, but she couldn't concentrate. Her phone continued to vibrate. She hoped it would be Dan, but it was more texts from random friends asking about her and Jack. She was going to have to deal with them, too.

6

Rachel gave up on work and tried Dan's cell again. "Where are you? It's urgent. Call me."

She called Becca. "I think I'm losing my mind," Rachel said, not bothering to say hello. "I can't get ahold of Dan. Did Matt hear from him?" Their husbands had been best friends since high school.

"Nope. He said he called him, but nothing. Could this be a publicity stunt on Jack's end? I was talking to Amy and she mentioned that he has a movie coming out."

"Yeah, about the divorced couples," Rachel responded, not bothering to pretend she wasn't deeply aware of Jack's career. "But, Becca, why are you talking to Amy about this?"

"Rach, come on. People are asking me a million questions. I haven't said anything that isn't on the website. And everyone keeps commenting on how hot you were. God, I was always so jealous of your tits."

"Becca! My kids could see this."

"Sorry, you're right. I just hate seeing you so wound up."

"It's fine. If this was Jack's doing, don't you think he would give me a heads-up? I haven't spoken to him in years, plus he's dating Cassandra Willis. I kind of feel like having her as your girlfriend is far more interesting than sending love notes to someone like me twenty years ago."

"Did you try Alex? Maybe she has info."

"It's hard to imagine she would know anything. She's in London filming her movie. . . . Oh, wait. Cassandra is the lead, so maybe she will know something. Let me try her."

Rachel called Alex, but her phone was off so she left a message. "Hey, Al. I need you to call me. Not sure if you saw yet, but there were some pictures of me and Jack published, and old letters, too—remember those love letters he wrote me? I'm freaking out. Please call me. Love you. Call me!"

Just as she hung up on Alex's voice mail, her phone rang. Kaitlyn again.

"Okay, I called an acquaintance who works at the *Daily Mail*. All she knew was that they bought a bunch of old information on Jack for a significant amount of money, and they published most of the usable stuff. They haven't gotten any response from Jack's team yet."

"So what does that mean for me?" Rachel asked her friend, happy to confirm at least that Jack wasn't behind this.

"Honestly, I don't know. The good news is that there doesn't seem to be much more coming out, at least not by the *Daily Mail*. So maybe this blows over in a few days."

"I seriously hope so. Everyone in my freaking town already seems to know."

"I'm going to keep digging," Kaitlyn said compassionately. "Hopefully this is nothing. In the meantime, don't talk to the press or answer any questions."

Like she would ever talk to the press.

"Oh, before I forget, you might want to call your assistant. Someone just linked to your firm bio in the article comments. It's possible you're going to get some calls."

"You're kidding me," Rachel yelped, stomach acid sloshing in the back of her throat. "I'll call her now."

She looked at the photos again, still open on her screen, unsure why she was torturing herself but unable to stop. She zoomed in on the picture from their dorm room. That was the last visit, wasn't it? Before everything fell apart. Jack's arms still looked like string beans, not the oversized muscles of a movie star. Becca was right, she did look pretty amazing back then.

Rachel finally dialed her assistant, Beth. There was nothing she could do to stop this from blowing up at work. She had spent all this time building her professional image, but what happens to your career if your co-workers see you half-naked?

"Hi, Beth, um, I'm not coming back in today," she said uneasily when her assistant answered. "Yup, hearing went well. So, this is weird, but we may get some calls from reporters. I dated someone in high school who is famous now, and old pictures of me were published online. It's sort of ridiculous. Just don't say anything, okay?" Beth agreed immediately, and just as quickly, Rachel realized she already knew about it.

She had better call their nanny, Justine, too, to fill her in. Justine also played dumb, but clearly had heard the news about her employer. "Just call me if the kids say anything, okay, and please don't comment on this to anyone!" Had anyone in her life not heard about this? And why wasn't Dan calling her?

She finally forced herself to scroll through the fifth-grade mom text group. It seemed they'd forgotten she was on there. Lots of questions about who knew Rachel dated Jack and how the letters and photographs got out. Rachel silenced the group. She couldn't bear to read further.

There were a few individual texts from the women with whom she was closer.

> KATIE: Hey there, just thinking about you, here if you need.

Katie was a good friend who worked fifty hours a week at a hedge fund. They joked that she was even less in tune to Ridgevale's gossip than Rachel. She hearted Katie's message.

> PAM: Rachel! How did you never tell me this? I'm
> dying! Love you!

Pam was always sweet, she wouldn't judge her. Rachel quickly texted back.

> RACHEL: xx

And then Amy Booth, president of the Sutton Elementary School PTA. The closest thing Rachel had to a frenemy. Rachel met Amy when she first moved to town and their boys were in nursery school together. Their families had immediately hit it off, but as Max got a little older, he started gravitating toward other boys. Rachel was adamant that he never leave anyone out, but she also encouraged him to spend time with kids that made him feel good. Unfortunately, Amy felt that her son was being excluded, and that Max was the one to blame. Soon after, the invites to backyard barbecues and birthday dinners slowed down. Rachel always pretended that she was too busy with her job and her kids to care, but she had privately admitted to Becca that it stung.

> AMY: I can't believe you never told me you went
> out with Jack Bellow!

Like Rachel owed her that information.

Amy was the least of her concerns. She started thinking about Jack. Maybe she needed to call him.

7

THE DAY PASSED SLOWLY WITH RACHEL CONTINUING TO FEND off texts and calls from friends. It seemed like her entire orbit had seen the *Daily Mail* piece, and a Google alert she had secretly put on Jack's name a few years back alerted her that other news sites had picked up the "story." Rachel never felt so exposed. She spoke with her intellectual property colleague, who explained the concept of fair use and told her that since Jack was a public person, it would be a losing battle to get his old photographs taken down. She was just the injured bystander.

"How could they publish the letters, though?" She was horrified that her privacy could be invaded like that. "Couldn't the *Daily Mail* get sued? It's not like I authorized any of this."

"Well, since Jack is the author of the letters, it's really his battle to fight. I suspect that the website felt it was a pretty low risk. Truthfully, whoever sold these is at risk of a claim, too. But I doubt someone as famous as Jack Bellow would pursue a lawsuit. Kind of comes with the territory."

So there was nothing she could do. Fortunately, neither of her kids seemed to have heard anything about it at school that day, and certainly, neither noticed that their mother was in the midst of an emotional breakdown as she hustled them to the bathroom for showers after dinner.

While Rachel spent the day in a state of heightened alert, Dan remained radio silent. She had already put Emma to bed and sent

Max to read in his room by the time she heard the garage door opening at 7:45 that evening.

She pounced on him the second he walked inside. "What the actual fuck, Dan? I've been trying you all day! For all I knew you were dead." She knew he wasn't dead because she had been tracking his movements on the iPhone Find My app for the past two hours.

"Whoa, Rachel. What's going on?" he asked, putting his hands in the air. "Can I come inside the house?" He threw down his bag and jacket on the mudroom bench, ignoring the hooks that Rachel had their handyman install above it.

Rachel leaned against the wall, steadying herself. Was he serious right now? she wondered.

"I know you don't call me, but there is zero chance you didn't look at your phone in the last six hours." She opened up the website for what felt like the hundredth time that day and handed him her phone. Dan stared at it for a solid minute.

"Rach." He paused. His voice had a nervous edge.

"Why didn't you call me?" Her voice cracked. She hadn't cried yet, but something about seeing Dan finally made her eyes fill. "Everyone has seen this. I already got a few calls from reporters and I have been freaking out all day."

"Rach, come." Dan took her arm and led her toward the family room. "Let's sit down. You need to breathe."

"I'm breathing, Dan," she snapped. "Jesus. You and my mother with the fucking breathing." She allowed herself to be led to the couch and sat down. Dan grabbed her a glass of wine and handed it to her.

"I don't understand how this is happening," she said, the desperation creeping into her voice.

"Drink."

Rachel felt the wine warm her, and despite her anger at his absence all day, the comfort of being in her husband's presence soothed her.

"You feel a little better?"

Rachel nodded.

"Okay, first. This is not the end of the world. It doesn't even say your full name."

"Dan, we're past all that. Everyone knows it's me. Reporters have been calling all day. Our friends, too."

She saw him take that in.

"And you! There is no way you didn't see this!"

Dan collapsed next to her on the couch. He looked down at his hands as he twisted his wedding ring. He wouldn't look at her and she could see his pulse beating in his neck.

"Now you're freaking me out," she said.

He reached over and grabbed her hand. "I walked around the city all afternoon because I didn't know what to do."

"So you did know? And you didn't even text me?"

"Rach." His voice came out strained.

"Oh my god. Did you have something to do with this?"

"Babe, they told me this wasn't coming out yet. I was supposed to have time to prepare you."

"I don't understand. What did you do?" Rachel put down her wine and stared at her husband. It somehow hadn't occurred to her that he could be the one responsible.

"I sold some of your high school stuff."

"What are you talking about? Why would you do that?"

Dan looked at her and shrugged. The truth had come out and there was no longer a reason to pretend. "We needed the money."

Rachel looked at him in shock. Both of them did well at their law firms. Rachel had gotten a pretty sizable pay bump when she made junior partner several years before and her salary had continued to increase in the years since. Dan didn't earn as much, but he certainly did fine.

"Remember when I went to Vegas last year with Matt and Greg and I won a few thousand dollars playing poker?" he asked, avoiding eye contact with his wife. "I kind of kept it up."

"Last I checked you haven't been back to Vegas."

"Yeah, obviously not. You can do it online. It's basically gambling as if you were at the casino from home."

"I'm familiar with online gambling, Dan," she seethed.

"Yeah, well, these sites totally suck you in. So many of my friends' play poker online, it's not a huge deal."

Rachel stared at her husband as he rambled.

"What are you talking about? What does this have to do with these pictures of me and Jack?" Her voice rose in volume.

"I've been so bored at work. And you're always too tired to hang out with me at night. It kind of just passed the time."

She looked at him in disbelief.

"I took a few losses. I tried to win the money back, but it just kind of spiraled."

"How much did you lose, Dan?"

He looked at his wife and exhaled. "About a hundred thousand. A little more. I know it sounds crazy. What was I supposed to do, Rach?"

Rachel covered her mouth with her hand in shock and stood up from the couch, beginning to pace. "Maybe for starters, you tell your wife?"

"I wanted to figure this out. It's not going to break us. I thought maybe if I got the money back it wouldn't matter."

"How is this even possible?" She admittedly didn't keep up with their finances as closely as she should, but she knew they didn't keep that much cash in their joint checking account.

"We had that savings account, like the rainy day fund?" He was questioning her, as if she might have viewed online poker as an acceptable use for that account.

"So if I'm understanding this," Rachel said, the anger rising in her voice, "you gambled away the entirety of our savings, and instead of telling me about it, and trying to come up with a solution together, you stole my personal letters and photographs and sold them to make that money back?"

"I didn't touch our investments," he said, defensively. "That cash was just sitting there."

"Sitting there for a new roof or to pay the mortgage if we lost our jobs!" She was furious.

"I know what it looks like. I didn't think it would be such a huge deal. Of course, I planned to tell you first."

She glared at him, her head spinning as she processed what he was telling her.

"I don't know why they published everything today, they said it would be next week," Dan justified. "I got in over my head, obviously."

Rachel tried to steady herself. Her body felt ice cold. Somehow, she had spent the whole day convincing herself either that Dan totally had his head up his ass and wasn't paying attention to her calls, or that he was mad at her. She certainly wouldn't allow herself to believe that her husband could betray her like this.

"I'm sorry, I know I completely messed up. I didn't think it through. I just knew if I told you about the poker you would make such a thing of it."

Rachel looked at Dan, unable to speak, listening to him attempt to rationalize the situation. She wasn't sure if she was more shocked by him selling her out like this or by him having a secret gambling habit.

"You had this whole box of souvenirs of you and Jack from high school. Clearly there was no other reason for keeping it."

What? Who was this person?

"I'm so sorry, babe," Dan finished, and started to cry (cry!). He seemed to finally comprehend the gravity of what he had done to his wife.

Rachel stared at her whimpering husband, finally finding her voice. "So you were scared I'd find out about your gambling? But then you used me to fix the problem?"

"I didn't know what to do. I only knew I needed to get the money back. And if I told you, you'd be so angry and want to go to your parents. I just, I don't know, I guess I lost control."

"Lost control?" He had completely gone off the rails and flipped over several times. "I don't know who I'm talking to right now."

"I know you haven't been happy with me lately," he said, sadly.

"When did I ever say that?"

"It's the way you look at me. And whenever I say I don't like my job, you're so dismissive."

"I'm sorry I didn't love the idea of you quitting your job to invest in a restaurant with your brother, which you'd never before expressed interest in doing. And that's irrelevant, Dan. Unless that's why you did this to me? Because I didn't jump at the idea of my lawyer husband suddenly becoming a restauranteur?"

"Rachel."

She didn't respond.

"Fine." He wiped at his eyes and composed himself. "I've obviously been stressed about the money. Then a few weeks ago I finished work early and went to that dive bar I used to meet Matt at after work, you know?"

She shook her head, annoyed, wanting him to continue.

"Jack came on the TV, in that ridiculous Ford commercial that's always on. Then this other guy sitting at the bar points at the screen and says to me, out of nowhere, that he can't figure out what's so great about Jack Bellow, but that his wife is obsessed. Of course, I laughed because I've been saying that for years. Then we got to talking and I told him about how you used to go out with Jack, and kept all this old stuff from when you were together. The guy said he bet I could get a lot of money for it, and he had a reporter friend I could e-mail. It was like a sign or something."

Rachel looked at her husband, wondering how they were having this conversation.

Dan continued. "Anyway, I reached out, and the numbers were huge for a celebrity like Jack. I couldn't pass it up."

Rachel's head was spinning. "You've spent the last, like, twenty years horrified that I once dated Jack. So now you're so cool with it you felt like plastering it all over the internet?"

Dan looked at her guiltily.

"You understand we could get sued for this."

He stared at her dumbly. "They were your pictures and letters. And he's a public figure. This is totally fine."

"Did you even go to law school?" Her voice was scathing. "It's the content in the letters, Jack still owns that. And how did you even explain to that website that you had the right to sell this?"

He stared down at the floor, avoiding eye contact. He wanted to hide from her anger, like he was one of their children scared to get in trouble.

"You pretended to be me, didn't you?" she whispered. She didn't wait for his answer.

Rachel considered the man she had loved for so many years and felt, in that instant, her whole being reject him. "You know what, I can't look at you anymore. I'm leaving."

8

Rachel grabbed her bag and walked out of the house. The reality was she had nowhere to go, but she hadn't eaten yet, and the idea of making dinner and then sitting down with her husband was absurd. For a moment she thought about what Dan was going to do about food, but she quickly shook off the thought. He's a big boy, she told herself, he can figure out how to make a sandwich for himself. And let him deal with Emma when she comes out of her bed looking for water or Tylenol or a late-night cheese stick. She got in the car, and aimlessly headed toward Greenwich.

She drove the twenty minutes north, the conversation with Dan running on a loop in her mind. How was she ever going to forgive him for this? The gambling alone was mortifying, that he would lose their money like that. But to do this to her, to sell her out like this, it made her ill. That he would pretend to *be* her? Who the hell had she married?

Rachel ended up parking by a crowded upscale steakhouse she and Dan had been to a few times with friends. She straightened herself up and walked into the restaurant, asking the hostess for a seat at the bar. As she settled in, the bartender walked over and handed her a menu.

"What can I get you?" he asked.

Rachel ordered a glass of Pinot Noir. After the bartender set it down in front of her, she ordered a Caesar salad and a ribeye, medium rare. May as well treat myself, she thought. She sat there drinking her wine and looking around. She happened to love this restaurant, but she also knew it was a hangout for divorcées. Rachel woke up this morning not overly happy, but generally content, and that she was now contemplating what being single might look like was bewildering.

When the couple next to her got up, a good-looking older man sat down. He was probably in his late fifties and didn't have a wedding ring. He looked at Rachel and smiled.

"Looks like we're both dining alone tonight."

Rachel smiled in response, not wanting to encourage a conversation.

"What's a good-looking girl like yourself doing eating alone?" Her technique of not responding was clearly unsuccessful. "I'm Tim. I don't think I've seen you here before."

"Nice to meet you. I'm not usually eating at the bar," she said, politely.

"Newly separated?" he asked.

"No." She couldn't help chuckling, he was so eager to connect. "Just needed a little alone time." You know, just need a little time to myself to figure out if my husband is a sociopath, she thought to herself.

"Oh, I've been there. Well, enjoy your meal. I'll leave you to it," Tim said, realizing he was not going to score with her. Fortunately for them both, a couple of large-breasted women in their early fifties, pumped full of Restylane, wandered over to order cocktails and started chatting with him.

Rachel went back to trying to make sense of everything.

She looked around the restaurant. The last time they were here was with their friends Pam and Mike a few months ago. Things were already off with them at the time. Dan had been acting distant, but she knew he wasn't happy with work, and

Rachel was too exhausted to make a big thing of it. She mostly chalked it up to being married with young kids. Her mom always said they were in the thick of it. Parenting, working—this was all normal. Rachel now realized Dan was also probably consumed with his gambling. But that night they were both drunk, and he was flirty with her at dinner, touching her thigh a couple of times under the table and even kissing her before getting up to use the bathroom.

When they got home, as soon as the babysitter left, Rachel grabbed Dan and started to kiss him. "Come upstairs with me. Or maybe we should stay down here?" she'd said to him with a giggle, making a move to undo his belt.

He chased her up the stairs and threw her onto their bed. Rachel was completely uninhibited that night. She couldn't remember the last time she and Dan had connected that way. He touched her everywhere she liked and didn't stop until she'd finished.

She remembered how she lay there when they were done, practically twitching.

"Think I knocked you up?" he had teased, knowing her IUD was firmly in place.

"Bite your tongue!" She was so happy to be with him like that again.

It was short-lived. They had a fight the next day. That was when he floated the restaurant idea by her, suggesting that maybe he talk to her dad about giving him a loan. She wouldn't hear of it. She knew he wasn't happy at his law firm, but he refused to interview for other positions and instead was putting in zero effort at work.

"Are you trying to get fired?" she had asked him, the last trace of romance from the night before evaporating.

"I'm not you, Rachel. Being a lawyer isn't everything. I couldn't cut it at Silver and Frank, and I guess I can't cut it at Parker Daly Schmidt, either."

"That's ridiculous." She felt like she was talking to one of their children. "This is about not trying, Dan. You barely make an effort. I send you all those links to conferences, which you ignore, and we have plenty of friends you could ask to send you business. How else are you going to make partner?"

"I network plenty!" he insisted.

"Getting drunk with existing clients doesn't count," she retorted.

"Don't you understand this isn't what I want? And why does it even matter to you? I know you love being the successful one."

"Or maybe you can't stand that I'm on the cusp of making equity partner and you can barely manage your own deals."

"There you go. You clearly don't think I'm good enough for you." He threw her words back at her.

"Find another job if you're so unhappy. And grow the hell up."

They barely spoke the rest of the day, and if Rachel was honest with herself, they'd barely spoken in any meaningful way since.

She took another sip of her wine, debating whether she could order a second glass and still drive home. Rachel didn't know how she was going to get over this, but she heard her mother's voice in her head telling her not to do anything rash.

She picked up her phone and texted Alex.

RACHEL: Did you see the pictures from high school?
We need to discuss. Please call me!!

She was probably asleep, Rachel figured. She googled Jack's name again and this time there were several more recent articles posted. There were also more pictures from their high school yearbook, showing them as "Cutest Couple." She hated to consider what Jack was thinking. He would clearly hear about this, and he was going to rightfully assume it had come from her. No one else had those letters. She finished up her dinner and headed home. This was all so overwhelming.

When she walked into her house, Dan was sitting in the kitchen, waiting for her.

"We need to talk about this," he said.

Rachel scoffed. "I'm not going to rehash this with you. I'm going up to bed."

"Rach, please.

"No. Not tonight. Being around you is not good for me right now."

Rachel went upstairs, grabbed her pajamas and toothbrush from her bedroom, and walked down the hall to the guest room. She knew she'd never sleep if Dan was next to her in bed. Still, she lay there for a while, trying to quiet her racing mind. Was this her fault for putting too much pressure on him? Should she be worried about the gambling? How could Dan do this to her? She was losing it. Eventually she took an Ambien. She needed to turn off her brain.

9

Fall 2003

THE FIRST TIME THEY MET WAS IN THE LAW SCHOOL LIBRARY AT Fordham. Rachel had a textbook open next to her from which she was painstakingly transferring notes onto a legal pad. They were three weeks into their first year of law school, and she had already been called on in their Civil Procedure class. Dan wasn't particularly suited to the Socratic method. The fear of embarrassing himself in front of the hot girls in his section was the impetus for him to do the assigned reading, which was what brought him to the library that day.

"Hey, you're in Section B, right?" Dan asked her quietly, walking over to her cubicle. Rachel looked up at him and nodded. "Can you tell me the pages we need to read for Contracts?"

Rachel looked in her backpack and pulled out her Contracts notebook. "Pages 72 through 108."

"Thanks. I'm Dan Miller, by the way," Dan said, putting his backpack on the cubicle across from hers.

"Hey. Rachel Stone." She smiled at him and then went back to her textbook.

"Mind if I sit here?" Dan asked.

"Go ahead." Rachel put down her pen and looked at Dan for a moment, taking him in. He was just over six feet and had a stocky build. His short blond hair was slightly spiked up in the front, showcasing his warm brown eyes. He was wearing khaki cargo shorts and Stan Smiths, with a blue T-shirt untucked. In his easy smile, Rachel could sense that he was the kind of person that people wanted to be around.

They sat there quietly working for a while, until Dan stood up and asked if she wanted to take a coffee break. Rachel agreed and got up, straightening her books and putting her notebooks in her bag. She pushed in her chair and turned around, noting that Dan's cubicle was in disarray with three open textbooks and his backpack wide open on his chair. She fought every urge to fix up his space.

She and Dan walked out of the library. Rachel was petite and often gravitated toward taller men, but Dan dwarfed her in both stature and girth. They headed to the campus coffee shop.

"Where'd you go to college?" Rachel asked him.

"Michigan. But I took a couple of years off to figure out what I wanted to do. You?"

"Cornell. I just graduated." Dan asked her if she knew his friends who went there. She did, and though she didn't admit it to Dan, she had hooked up with one of the guys he mentioned, Greg Sherman, a few times.

Dan opened the door to the coffee shop for Rachel and they walked up to the counter. They both ordered coffee, and he convinced her to get a donut with him, too. Rachel went for her wallet, but Dan insisted on buying. They grabbed a table outside, enjoying the slight breeze as summer transitioned to fall.

"Why'd you go to law school?" Dan asked her.

"It's a little lame. I kind of had no other real plans, and my parents suggested it, so I guess I figured, why not?" she responded, embarrassed by her admission.

"I get that. My reason isn't much better. I got this idea in my head that being a lawyer was an easy guarantee to be rich—well, unless you become a prosecutor or something. So here I am. I don't know why I'm telling you that," he said with a laugh.

Rachel smiled. "That's kind of funny, because I was thinking I might want to be a prosecutor."

"Guess we can't get married then," he joked. "I can't even imagine going to court."

Rachel laughed. "I hear you. I used to act in high school, so being in court and arguing in front of a judge kind of appeals to me."

"No pun intended."

Rachel laughed again at his silly lawyer dad joke.

"Hey, my roommates and I are having a party tomorrow night, do you want to come?" Dan asked.

"Yeah, I'd love to. I missed that mixer thing because I had a friend's birthday party. Did you go?"

Dan said he did, and that Section B was a bit lackluster in the fun department. "But everyone seemed nice. Just very into studying."

"And you're not?"

"No, it's not that. I just can do both, you know?" he said, backpedaling.

"I'm kidding! This place is filled with dorks. It just doesn't bother me because Cornell was the same way."

Dan breathed an exaggerated sigh of relief. "You scared me for a second. Should we head back to the library, nerd?"

As soon as they returned to the library, Rachel dove right back into her Civil Procedure textbook. Dan continued with Contracts. She noticed that he kept glancing up at her as he worked. After another hour he said he was too restless to sit there.

"I'm going to head back to my place. Give me your info and I'll send you my address."

"What do you mean?" Rachel asked, still immersed in her reading.

"For the party tomorrow. Bring friends if you want."

"Oh, sorry. Yes, for sure. My roommate will definitely come, and maybe I'll ask another friend too if that's cool."

Dan told her to bring whoever she wanted. He took her number, saving it in his phone as "Rachel Law School." After he left, Rachel kept thinking about Dan. There was something about him. She eventually lost interest in studying and packed up her stuff, calling Alex on her way home to see what she wanted to order for dinner that night.

Rachel and Alex had moved into the city together after graduating college. Alex was working as a production assistant and the only reason either could afford to share their one-bedroom converted apartment in Murray Hill was that their parents were helping to pay for it.

The next night, Rachel, Alex, and Becca, who was always up for a party, headed out to Dan's apartment. Alex had been perfecting a boho vibe at the time and wore a western-style coin belt over a tunic and jeans. Although the late September air had a chill, Rachel and Becca were dressed similarly in True Religion jeans, tight tank tops, and open-toed shoes. Dan's place, fortunately, was only three blocks away from theirs.

At just past ten, they walked down the beige hallway of a building much like their own and headed toward the loud lyrics of "Cry Me a River." The apartment was already full of people drinking out of red Solo cups and singing along to the music. Rachel saw Dan outside on the deck manning the keg. It was the largest New York City balcony she'd ever seen. She walked outside toward him, pulling her friends with her to say hello.

"Rachel," he said loudly, obviously drunk. "You came!"

Rachel laughed. "Hey, Dan, these are my friends Alex and Becca." Both girls said hello and he offered them beers.

Becca grabbed Rachel's arm. "Oh my god, Rach," she shouted over the music. "Matt and Greg are here."

"You know my boys?" Dan asked. "Oh, right. Cornell. Yo, Sherman, Darner, get over here."

The guys walked over, and Rachel and Becca were both highly embarrassed. They got over it quickly as both Matt and Greg gave them big hugs.

"Hey, ladies. I guess you finally graduated. Welcome to our party," Greg said. It turned out that Dan and Matt were best friends from childhood, and that the three of them had lived together since they all graduated from college two years earlier.

"It's kind of crazy to see you here. How've you been?" Matt asked Becca, stepping closer to her.

Becca and Matt were borderline boyfriend and girlfriend through most of Becca's sophomore year. They hadn't spoken since Matt's last Slope Day, a Cornell tradition that involves drinking from dawn until you can no longer stand. It was a day neither of them remembered particularly well, but ended with Matt in someone else's bed and Becca crying in Rachel's. Dan handed each of them a beer and, within moments, Matt and Becca wandered off to catch up somewhere quieter.

Greg saw some friends he knew, and Rachel and Alex went inside to check out the apartment and see if they knew anyone else there. As more people arrived, Dan continued handing out beers and greeting guests. Rachel watched him throw his arms around nearly every person who walked out onto the balcony.

The two girls stood in the kitchen looking around, quickly dumping their beers and switching over to tequila. As they were chatting, Alex got a call from a girl she had hooked up with the weekend before. She and Rachel debated whether she should go meet her and eventually agreed that Alex was unlikely to find a better option at Dan's apartment. When she left, Rachel went off in search of Becca. Instead, she found Greg, who asked her if she wanted to smoke a bowl with him, so Rachel followed him into his bedroom.

Greg's adult bedroom mirrored the one in his college apartment. He had a Phish tapestry over his desk and although she had only slept in his bed on a few occasions, she recognized his tan plaid comforter. He had a giant glass bong sitting on his nightstand but reached into a drawer and pulled out a small glass multicolored bowl.

"Come sit," he said, patting his bed.

Rachel laughed a little nervously and sat down next to him. He handed her the pot and she took a hit, feeling it immediately.

"It's so random that I'm seeing you here," Rachel said. "I literally just met Dan yesterday in the library."

"You're hot library girl?" he asked her, surprised. "Oh well."

"What does that mean?" Rachel said.

Greg shook his head at her. "Nothing. Dan mentioned he had invited a cute girl from law school to the party. So how have the last two years of your life been?"

Rachel filled him in on some of their mutual friends from Cornell. Greg was a commercial real estate broker, and apparently spent a lot of his time taking his clients out drinking, which suited him. After a little while, Rachel asked him if he knew where Becca and Matt were and Greg said he saw them go into Matt's room.

"I'm glad you're here," Greg said, as he got up and shut his bedroom door. He sat back down on the bed, leaving barely an inch between him and Rachel. "You know, Matt and I were just talking about you and Becca the other day. Our favorite roommates. I think this must be fate."

He leaned in and kissed her. Rachel wasn't sure if she wanted to be kissed in that moment, but she couldn't think of why not and let it happen. Greg's kisses got more enthusiastic, and he began pawing at her under her tank top. She wasn't feeling it and eventually told him to stop.

"You know, I think I'm going to find Becca," she said to him, standing up.

"What do you mean? I thought you were into me."

"I'm gonna head out. I'm sorry." Rachel wanted to get out of his room.

"We're just having fun. Why did you come in here if you didn't want to hook up?" Greg asked.

Rachel thought about all the fraternity house and college town bedrooms she had stumbled into at Cornell after a night out. She often questioned whether she should be there, or even if she liked being with the guy she was with at the time, but that was what she and her friends all did. Being a law student made her more discerning.

"I don't know, Greg. I didn't realize smoking someone's pot at a party required that I have sex with them." She quickly walked out of his room, leaving Greg sitting on his bed, and bumped right into Dan.

He looked at her quizzically. "You okay?"

"Yeah. Your friend is kind of a douchebag, though. Have you seen Becca?" Dan pointed her toward the balcony.

She headed off in search of Becca and could feel Dan looking at her. Becca was standing with Matt, and she looked happy.

"Hi, Bec, I think I'm going to head out," Rachel said. "But you stay if you want."

Becca asked if something happened, and Rachel could sense Matt listening, so she shook her head. "I'm fine, I just want to go to bed. Call me later?"

They hugged goodbye and Rachel left. She saw Dan out of the corner of her eye on her way out but didn't bother saying good night. As she was standing at the elevator, she heard her name.

It was Dan. "Hey, are you okay?" he asked her, kindly. "Greg is pretty messed up. I'm sorry if he made you feel uncomfortable."

Rachel looked up at this sweet guy. "Hey. I'm totally fine. I guess I gave him the wrong impression. You go back to your party. Thanks for having me."

Dan said okay and that he'd see her around at school, but after that night, Rachel mostly avoided him. It wasn't easy, once Becca and Matt started officially dating again, but she didn't see the point of socializing with Greg's roommate if she didn't have to.

10

Present Day

RACHEL WOKE UP THE MORNING AFTER HER WORLD TURNED upside down, still tired from the Ambien and planning to crawl back into bed after getting her children to school. There was no way she could work that day. She had spent years barely taking a vacation, and even then she always had her laptop with her. It was time to cash in on all that goodwill.

The children were up already and in front of the television. Beds unmade and hair askew, but half-eaten bowls of cereal in front of them took one responsibility off her plate.

"Guys, twenty minutes until we leave. Go brush your teeth and get ready," Rachel said as she walked into the kitchen to get coffee. Dan was nowhere to be seen. He must have left for the city already, which was just as well because Rachel couldn't bear the thought of seeing his face that morning.

Emma listened without issue, immediately bounding upstairs. Max was slow to rise, as usual. "Where did Dad go?"

"I guess he had an early meeting, sweetie, he already left. Now go on up." How puffy did her eyes look? she wondered. Might her ten-year-old actually notice, given his general inattention to anything other than PlayStation and food?

Her son walked around the kitchen island, passing his mother, to place his bowl in the sink. Rachel couldn't help but pull him in for a kiss. Though he was nearing her height, he briefly melted into her. Her baby boy. She hoped no one said anything to him at school. She wasn't ready to tell him about the photos yet. She was really hoping to avoid mentioning it altogether.

Rachel finally ushered her children out of the house and into the car, without brushing her teeth or changing out of her pajamas.

"Why aren't you dressed yet, Mommy?" Emma asked.

"Oh, I'll change after, baby." Emma accepted this answer and chattered away the rest of the ride about a boy in her class who liked to wear pajamas to school, even though it wasn't Pajama Day. Rachel was too zoned out to respond, and fortunately, Emma seemed content simply to have an audience.

When Rachel got home, she checked her phone and saw she finally had a text from Alex.

> ALEX: Hi! Sorry!!! This will be okay. I promise. I'll try you later if I can. Things are crazy here with the movie. Love you.

Super helpful. Rachel sent an e-mail to her assistant that she was taking the day off again, not bothering to explain why, then headed to the guest room and immediately fell back to sleep. She got up a couple of hours later, feeling more refreshed. As she stood under the shower, she thought back to the day before when she was busy preparing for her motion and annoyed with Dan for trivial stuff, and now her entire life was in dissaray.

She poured herself a cup of coffee and checked in with her mother.

"I've been so worried about you, sweetie. How are you feeling?"

She told her mother what Dan had confessed. "So, basically, on top of the fact that I'm mortified that these pictures and letters are out there, I have no idea if I want to be married to my husband anymore. Who does this, Mom?"

Elaine had been listening to her daughter quietly and seemed to be weighing her response. Her parents adored Dan. Unlike Rachel, who hated having her mother constantly psychoanalyzing her, Dan never took anything personally. He was happy to play the role of dutiful son, as his own parents had moved to Florida and he and Rachel rarely saw them.

"I'm just trying to make some sense of this, honey," Elaine said finally. "Gambling can be very addictive, you know. You make a bad bet, and then you feel compulsive about making back the money. It's a terrible cycle, I saw it in my practice from time to time."

"How do you go from occasionally playing poker with friends to wiping out an entire savings account?"

Elaine mulled this over. "Maybe he saw gambling as an outlet. Or a way to get some control, even though the opposite happened."

"What does that mean?" And why was her mother defending Dan?

"I know this isn't politically correct of me, but it's sometimes hard for men when women are more successful than they are."

"Mom, that's so ridiculous. Plenty of women make more money than their husbands these days."

"I know it's a different time. I'm just sharing what I've observed. And you told me he's been distant for months. Maybe it's time to call your old therapist?"

Rachel sometimes regretted how open she was with her mother, but she tended to pull things out of her. "Sounds like I'll learn that this is all my fault."

"No one's going to say that, sweetie. But something bigger must be happening here. Didn't you tell me that Dan hates people knowing about you and Jack?"

"That's what's so confusing to me. Like even if we really needed money, why wouldn't he just come to you and Dad? It almost seems spiteful. Not to mention that this could impact our children. Max will be so embarrassed if he hears."

"Hmm." Elaine was apparently stumped. "Well, you aren't going to figure this out in a day, and I'm sure it will blow over. Barely any of my friends have mentioned it to me!"

"Well, that's reassuring," Rachel said sarcastically.

"I'm sorry, I'm just trying to help. I understand you're hurt. All I know is that you can't make any decisions about your marriage yet. Let the dust settle a little."

Rachel got off the phone, feeling no better than she did before. Her mom was right about one thing, though, she thought. She couldn't figure this out in a day.

She logged into her computer after she made herself a second cup of coffee. Her phone pinged with a text from Dan.

DAN: How's everything going? Just checking in.

Guess all it takes is a marital crisis for him to reach out during the day, she thought. She ignored it and silenced her phone. There were several e-mails awaiting her, which she ran through quickly to determine which needed immediate responses. She sent a couple of e-mails from reporters over to Kaitlyn, but otherwise ignored them. Her junior associate had sent her a draft motion for summary judgment that morning to review. Editing a brief seemed like a relatively straightforward task.

Forty-five minutes later, or eight tenths of an hour in six-minute billing increments, Rachel stopped typing. The brief was in relatively good condition and Rachel was happy to see her associate had done his research and put together a solid draft.

Just as she finished, Kaitlyn called. "Okay, so I spoke with a friend of a friend at *Entertainment Tonight* and she told me they are all over this Jack story. It seems to be a slow news week. They would love to interview you, but I told them no. Right?" Kaitlyn asked.

"Are you kidding? Obviously no!"

"Okay, just wanted to confirm."

"Do people seem to know at work? Have you heard anything?"

"Well, I think probably people do know. Not like management or anything. I've just heard a little buzz."

"This is all so ridiculous. I haven't seen Jack in ages. I really need this to go away."

"I know. I completely get it. But this is Jack Bellow we're talking about; this isn't going away overnight. Hopefully we can hold people off and if he doesn't comment, people will definitely lose interest after a bit. The news cycle moves fast. Let me know if you hear from other reporters." Rachel thanked her and hung up the phone, turning back to her e-mails.

At around 2:00 p.m., she stopped working and got back into bed. She was flipping through Netflix trying to find something to watch when she received a text.

UNKNOWN NUMBER: Hey, stranger

She waited for a second text to come through. It was probably another reporter.

Her phone buzzed again.

UNKNOWN NUMBER: It's Doody.

She breathed in quickly.

RACHEL: Jack

UNKNOWN NUMBER [JACK]: Hey, you.

RACHEL: Do you hate me?

JACK: All press is good press, isn't that what they say?

RACHEL: Ugh. Not to me. I'm so sorry. This is a shit show.

JACK: Nah, it'll blow over.

He kept typing as she stared at her phone, waiting.

JACK: I'll be in the city next week for work. Free for dinner Thursday night?

The idea of seeing Jack was simultaneously enthralling and horrifying. How was she going to explain why his old letters to her were published? It's not as if the source being her husband absolved her of blame.

She started typing, then stopped. She texted Becca instead.

RACHEL: Jack texted me!!! He asked me to dinner!! WTF!!

BECCA: Ummmm. Do it!

RACHEL: Dan?

BECCA: It's fine. One night. You kind of owe this guy a dinner.

If Becca thought it was fine, she probably could do it. It was just dinner with an old friend. One that half the world was obsessed with, but it didn't mean anything.

RACHEL: I think that works.

JACK: Okay great. Let's say Carbone at 7:00. Looking forward.

Rachel put her phone facedown on her bed and felt her heart racing. She was seeing Jack again.

11

Summer 1998

RACHEL WORKED AT HER SLEEPAWAY CAMP THE SUMMER AFTER eleventh grade. She hated leaving Jack, but she didn't want to miss out on being a junior counselor. For someone like Rachel, who was so serious about school, camp felt like the only time she really got to be a kid.

Rachel's bunkmates were sick of hearing about Jack, but also incredibly jealous that she had a boy so madly in love with her. They crowded around her bed every time she got a letter from him. *"Dear Rach, I know it's only been a week, but I miss you every second. I'm counting down the days until you come home..."*

Jack was working at the pharmacy that summer and spending weekends making movies with Alex and some of their other friends. The boys got the moviemaking bug after their health teacher assigned them a group project to make a film about the the dangers of doing drugs their sophomore year. Since then, they would create ridiculous how-to videos and projects mirrored after their favorite shows, *Mr. Show* and *The State*. Alex was never more in her element and anointed herself the group's director.

The first weekend Rachel was back from camp, the friends all went to East Hampton to stay at Ben's summer house. That had required some convincing of Rachel's parents, who were assured by the Danforths that the kids would be heavily supervised and that there would be several other adults present. Mitch and Elaine Stone had not contemplated that the adults would be significantly drunker than the children for most of the weekend.

Jack had been many times before, but this was the first time the girls were also invited. Since the musical, they had become a solid group. Rachel and Jack, of course, but also Alex, Andy, Ben, Nicole, Kelly, Danny, and unfortunately for Rachel, Jack's ex-girlfriend, Jen. Danny and Nicole were off and on together since ninth grade. Kelly and Ben were both into each other and everyone figured this would be the weekend where they finally hooked up.

The plan was for them all to sleep in the basement, some on the couch and the rest in sleeping bags on the floor. But Ben had told Jack that he and Rachel were welcome to take the small guest room down there. He knew they had a lot of time to make up for. Ben was planning to make the weekend count with Kelly, but he wasn't as much of a stickler for privacy.

They arrived Friday morning and after throwing down their things, they headed down to the beach. Ben had packed a cooler full of Natty Light and wine coolers, and Nicole had picked up bagels for sustenance the morning before they left. Jack and Rachel spent the day jumping waves in the Atlantic and endlessly kissing in the water. Jack couldn't keep his hands off Rachel, who was wearing a very skimpy black bikini that she wasn't allowed to bring to camp, which had a strict one-piece rule.

That night, Ben manned the barbecue while the adults went into Southampton for dinner. They made a small bonfire on the beach and the friends talked long into the evening, plotting out their senior year. Jack broke out his guitar and everyone sang along with him. It was all perfect, and Rachel could not remember ever feeling that happy.

The group started pairing off until just Alex, Andy, and Jen were left by the beach. Jack and Rachel headed back to the house. When they got there, Rachel was surprised when Jack led her into a small guest room off the basement. It was sparse, meant more for a live-in housekeeper than a guest, but it had a full-size bed.

"How did you get Ben to give us this room?" Rachel asked Jack as she surveyed the space.

Jack laughed, a little nervously. "I guess he thought we would want to be alone."

They could hear their friends laughing outside the room, and Rachel wondered if they would be able to hear them, too. She whispered to Jack that they should be quiet.

He sat on the edge of the bed and pulled her next to him. She leaned her head on his shoulder and picked up his hand to kiss it. Sometimes Rachel wondered why he had chosen her, of all the other girls.

"Are you having a good time?" he asked her.

"Are you kidding? The best. I'm so happy that I finally get to be with you again."

Jack turned to Rachel and kissed her on the nose. She laughed and kissed his back. "I missed you so much, babe," Jack said. "Can we never be apart again?"

Rachel responded by kissing him and climbing onto his lap. They sat like that for a while, kissing and holding each other to make up for the eight long weeks apart. Then, still kissing her, Jack pulled her down with him onto the bed. He put his hand under her shirt, letting his fingers drift up and down her back. Rachel felt him harden beneath her, which still thrilled her, having that power over him. She sat up and pulled her tank top over her head. With some effort, Jack unhooked her pink bra and pulled it down her arms, and then he took off his own shirt.

Jack pushed her back down on the bed and leaned over her, kissing her eagerly. She felt him poking against her and she rubbed against him in response. Jack kissed her breasts and stomach and moved farther down, as he slowly peeled off her underwear. Rachel grabbed ahold of his hair, moving her hips slightly as the pleasure mounted. With his mouth on her, she had so little control over her body. He kept going until he could hear her breathing accelerate and Rachel felt herself almost vibrate under him.

Rachel's body eventually settled, and she pulled Jack toward her.

"I'm ready, Jack," Rachel whispered.

"Are you sure?" he responded.

Rachel nodded. They lay there, together, for a moment. He looked down at her, taking in her beauty, and ran his palm over her soft belly. Then he reached around her head under the pillow and produced a gold-foil-wrapped Trojan. She laughed louder than she intended.

"I had high hopes for this weekend," he said, smiling, but shyly.

She helped him pull down his boxers and looked at all of him. Jack sat up to open the condom. "Do you want me to help you put it on?" she asked.

He handed her the open condom as she placed it on him and attempted to roll it downward. It smelled rubbery and felt greasy. She didn't know it would be lubricated and wiped her hand on her thigh. Jack reached down to help, and slowly unrolled the condom, careful so as not to rip it, and then pinched the tip as the directions instructed.

They looked at each other when it was on. "Should I lie on my back?" she asked.

Jack nodded and Rachel lay back again. They kept their eyes glued to each other as Jack moved on top of her and slowly, slowly eased himself inside.

"Are you okay?" he whispered. Their eyes stayed locked, and Jack watched her face, eager but not wanting to hurt her.

Rachel shook her head that she was fine, and Jack pushed farther until his entire length was inside her. It hurt initially, but not like she had expected. She breathed through it and tried not to tighten up around him. Jack's eyes were closed as he moved back and forth inside her, and Rachel, not knowing what else to do, wrapped her legs tightly around his back. Moments later, as she was just starting to feel something, Jack stopped moving.

"What's wrong?" Rachel whispered.

"I finished," Jack said self-consciously.

Rachel hugged him and then helped him ease out of her, together making sure the condom stayed on him. "That wasn't what I expected."

"I guess it was fast, I'm sorry." Jack was embarrassed.

"No, no, I just mean, like, it didn't really hurt and was starting to feel good. I kind of want to do it again." Rachel laughed, entirely comfortable with him.

Jack jumped out of bed and peeled off the condom, discarding it in a tissue that he put on the dresser. "Don't let me forget that," he said. He walked over to his backpack, fished around for a moment, and pulled out a fistful of condoms.

"Jack! I don't mean right this second. Come snuggle with me," Rachel said, pulling the sheets around her, reaching her arms out to her boyfriend. Jack tossed a condom at her and she grabbed it and waved it at him. He jumped back into bed and pushed her down, putting his whole body on top of hers.

"I love you so much," he said, the smile on his face coming through in his voice. "Can we be together like this forever?"

"Yes! What are we going to name our babies?" Rachel asked him. "I'm very into Victoria for a girl, and what do you think about the name Ethan for a boy? Maybe we'll have twins!" Jack told her they should get through high school first before they started thinking about babies, but they could name their kids whatever she wanted.

They continued talking about the future. Jack told her he had been thinking that summer about pursuing acting one day, and Rachel thought she might like to be a journalist. They joked about being a famous couple. Jack promised that whatever he did, he would make a ton of money and give her everything she wanted. After a while, he fell asleep. Rachel stayed up a bit longer, looking at him beside her. She meant it when she said she wanted to be with him forever. Only Jack made her feel this good.

The rest of the weekend was perfect, and when Rachel finally got Alex alone to tell her the news, Alex shrieked. She knew it would happen. She also had news of her own. She and Jen had kissed the night before. Andy had dared them to do it, but still. A night of firsts.

The group spent the rest of the weekend drinking and swimming and planning for senior year. They were debating what show Brenda would pick for their senior musical. *Grease* had been a huge hit, but they all agreed it was sort of a clichéd choice. "Oh my god, the way our parents started dancing and singing along to 'We Go Together,' I died!" Kelly said. Ben jumped up and performed an over-exaggerated shimmy.

It was the late nights, the tech rehearsals, and the set building that bonded them. Rachel thought back to the night, about a week before the show opened, when they were on a dinner break. They were eating pizza in a giant circle, right in the middle of the hallway outside the theater. Alex suggested playing Never Have I Ever, a game that most of them had never heard of. Alex explained that players took turns stating something they'd never done, like skip school or make out in a car, and if you had done that thing, you had to take a drink.

"Like of alcohol?" his sister, Megan, piped in, surprised. Jack had finally let her sit with them at Rachel's urging.

"How about instead of drinking, you have to kiss someone in the circle!" Ben suggested lasciviously, raising his eyebrows at the group.

"Meg, go back to your friends," Jack had said, shaking his head. Rachel gave her an apologetic shrug, so Megan stuck her tongue out at her brother and got up and walked down the hall to the other freshmen.

They started out sort of lame. When it was Rachel's turn, she said she'd never tweezed her eyebrows. The guys looked confused, like was that a thing? But it got a lot of the girls kissing people. Finally, Ben went, and he decided to spice it up by saying in a nasally robotic voice, "Never have I ever had sexual intercourse." Then he immediately turned and kissed Kelly, showing the group that he had, in fact, had sex. It was otherwise a troop full of virgins, and everyone was eyeing Rachel and Jack, but they didn't make a move. Thinking back on it, Rachel realized that the next time they played, her answer would be different.

Rachel was so grateful to Alex for bringing her into the group. She didn't understand why the drama kids had a dorky reputation; she hadn't met anyone more fun than her friends.

12

Present Day

AFTER A WEEK, THE INITIAL SHOCK OF DAN'S BETRAYAL HAD settled in a little, and despite a few additional articles coming out, the news around her and Jack seemed to be dying down. Rachel, nevertheless, continued to sleep in the guest room each night, eating dinner early with the kids, then heading there right after they'd gone to sleep. Anything to avoid being alone with her husband. She still wasn't sure whether she would be able to forgive him, and she knew if she got back into bed with him her mind would race for hours, making sleep impossible. For now, it was best to avoid any real conversation. After a few nights of trying to apologize, Dan kept his distance. Instead, he attempted to make things up to her by doing more around the house, like taking out the garbage without being asked.

On Wednesday, Rachel finally approached him. "I'm meeting up with Jack tomorrow. For dinner in the city," she said, trying to make it sound like an everyday statement. She had practiced with Becca, who repeatedly assured her it wasn't a terrible idea.

"You've got to be kidding me," Dan said.

"I owe him that much after all the crap we've—you've—put him through. So you need to come home early and relieve Justine, okay?"

"Okay, whatever," Dan said, with a look of true sadness on his face.

Rachel almost felt guilty, but she pushed the feeling to the side.

Somehow, Max hadn't heard that his mom was the talk of the town yet. The mothers of all his and Emma's friends knew, though. They had been texting her for details all week. They were being nice about it to her face, but by ignoring most of their questions, Rachel assumed that most people thought she was the one who'd sold Jack out. She preferred not to admit the current disaster state of her marriage, so she let it go. Becca had downplayed the extent with which their friends were discussing the situation, but Rachel had been at enough girls' dinners to know that this was a huge topic of discussion.

Rachel was trying to compartmentalize at work as best she could, and after a meeting earlier that week that secured them the Carraway national counsel work, she had little choice. She was knee-deep in boxes, reading corporate documents and old e-mails to which she had not previously had access. The work was a good distraction, and Rachel knew there was a lot riding on how her firm, and especially how she, performed.

Jerry stuck his head into her office mid-morning. "Doing okay?" he asked. He was so fickle, but bringing in a client that had the potential to earn the firm millions clearly elevated Rachel in his ranks.

"Yup. Just getting up to speed."

"I heard you made a little news. I'm sure it will blow over. Just don't let it distract you," he said, walking out of the office.

"Oh," Rachel replied. She buried herself in boxes, wishing she could crawl inside of them and hide. She spent the rest of the day camped out in her office, ordering lunch to her desk and ignoring everyone but her assistant.

Rachel woke up Thursday morning after another restless night and groggily got in the shower. For the first time in a week, instead of ruminating about her marriage, she was kept up by thoughts of seeing her ex-boyfriend again after all these years. She was a little unsure what to wear, not wanting to try too hard, but wanting to look attractive. And young. She had already booked a blowout for herself during lunch.

Dan came into the bathroom as she was sitting in her robe, putting on makeup. He stared at her for a minute. She rarely spent this much time getting herself ready.

"You look really pretty," he finally said to her, almost shyly.

Rachel couldn't help herself and smiled. "Thanks."

"Are you going to come downstairs for breakfast?"

"What do you mean?" she asked him.

"I just—did you want me to feed the kids?"

The moment between them passed. "I didn't think you needed that instruction. Please give your children breakfast. Oh, and make them lunch and take them to school."

Dan wasn't used to her being so flippant. He started out of their bathroom, then turned back to look at her. "Are you really going out with him tonight, Rachel? Don't you think we should be focusing on us?"

"Dan, seeing Jack has nothing to do with you. I know you don't understand, but I feel terrible about what happened."

He looked at her. "You say you don't want the attention but you're basically asking for it if you're seen with him, Rachel."

"I really need to get ready for work. Can you get the kids moving, please?" She resumed curling her eyelashes.

Dan gave her a resigned look and walked out of the bathroom to get their children ready for school. Rachel shrugged it off. Let him think what he wants. She couldn't remember ever feeling this betrayed, not by anyone, much less her own husband. She had wondered herself if meeting Jack in public was a mistake. But was it better to meet him in a hotel room? And so what if people saw them? It was just two old friends having dinner, she rationalized.

When she finished her makeup, she went to pick out her outfit. She loved her closet. It was what sold her on the house. It was an oversize walk-in with a large double-sided dresser in the middle. Her drawers were perfectly organized, and her hanging clothes were color-coordinated by season. Alex always teased her for being a smidge OCD, but she wouldn't have it any other way. Rachel finally settled on a floral Veronica Beard dress that Becca had made her buy earlier that year, claiming it accentuated her boobs and still-narrow waistline. Sexy, but modest enough for work with a blazer. She threw some blush and mascara in her bag so she could freshen up before dinner. Emma ran up to kiss her goodbye before school, and she was seemingly enchanted by her mother's appearance. Rachel made a mental note to take better care of herself.

Concentrating at work was impossible, but she tried to get through some more of the old boxes Carraway had sent over. She perused a few gossip websites, happy to see that neither her nor Jack's name was mentioned. She kept looking at the clock, willing the hours to pass so she could go see him.

That afternoon her mother called to check in, as she had been doing daily. When Rachel told her that she was going to have dinner with Jack that night, Elaine was not happy. "I don't think that's a good idea, Rachel. What do you need to see him for?"

"You don't think I owe him an explanation, Mom?"

"Not particularly, no. Jack is doing just fine. This is par for the course for him. You don't need to get involved with that," she declared.

"It's just dinner. It's been so long."

"Honey, I think it's a mistake. I know how you felt about Jack. He had this hold over you. I'm concerned that this will add to your confusion, not make you feel better." Her mom was likely remembering the many nights Rachel called her crying in college after Jack had broken her heart.

"I'm a big girl. I know what I'm doing," she replied, eager to get off the phone.

Her mom told her to be smart and call her the next day. "I just don't want you to lose sight of how much you love Dan. The two of you have a lot to work out."

"Okay, Mom. Talk tomorrow." Rachel hated how her mother could get in her head.

She picked up her phone to text Alex.

> RACHEL: Meeting Jack for dinner tonight. Is that crazy? Dan and Elaine are both giving me shit about it. Miss you. Call me when you get a break!!

Her phone buzzed back a minute later.

> ALEX: Ah! Fun! Enjoy, babe.

Not exactly the endorsement she wanted, but Alex would tell her if she was making a huge mistake, wouldn't she?

13

Summer 2005

DAN MUST HAVE DONE WELL IN SCHOOL, BETTER THAN RACHEL had expected from their minimal interaction. Both were hired by the same white-shoe law firm as summer associates after their second year of law school. Being a summer associate, as Rachel understood it, generally meant that you were wined and dined and paid well to do very little work. The goal was to get the students to sign on with the law firm after graduation the following year, and that's when they sucked the life out of you.

The new class of summers and their junior associate mentors were invited to a Yankees game at the start of the program. Rachel immediately spotted Dan at the private bar the firm had arranged for them. Despite going out of her way not to talk to him over the last two years, Rachel knew no one else at the event and made a beeline for him.

"Hey!" Rachel said, tapping Dan on the shoulder to get his attention. "Becca told me I was going to see you tonight!"

"Hey, Rachel," he said, bending down to kiss her on the cheek. "I was stoked when Matt mentioned we both ended up at Silver and Frank."

He gestured to the two guys next to him and introduced her. "This is Rachel Stone, she's at Fordham with me. Kevin is at St. John's, and Joe goes to BU."

Rachel smiled and they moved over so she could get a drink. "Of course, you've already met our entire class of summers."

"What can I say?" He laughed. "Do you know Jaime Friedland? She's also from Fordham. And there are a couple of people here that I went to college with. I can introduce you around."

Rachel collected her vodka soda and they said goodbye to the guys Dan had been sitting with as they walked off to meet the other summers. Dan easily broke into the other conversations, introducing both himself and Rachel if he didn't know someone already. Rachel bumped into an acquaintance from Cornell and started chatting with her. It seemed like this was going to be a fun summer.

When the game started, Rachel saw Dan had saved her a seat with him and his new friends.

She smiled at him gratefully as she sat down.

"I'm sure it's very uncool of me to admit this, but I was sort of bummed that you and I never hung out," Dan said earnestly. "I mentioned it a couple of times to Becca, but it seemed like you weren't interested."

"It wasn't you. Greg was sort of a creeper and I just felt like I needed to avoid the whole situation. I know you guys are friends, so I probably shouldn't say that."

"I get it. You're not the first girl to say that about Greg," Dan said, shrugging. "If it's any consolation, I'm saving up to get my own apartment the second we graduate."

"It is. And I already know, considering Becca is planning on moving into your apartment the second you move out." She laughed. They had both been keeping tabs on the other. "I shouldn't have blown you off like that."

"All good." He smiled, and she knew she was forgiven.

"So tell me how you're a different sort of frat boy from your frat boy roommate," she joked.

"Cute. I guess I'm not really a player? I'm a frat boy that calls the next day."

Rachel smiled, letting him off the hook. She figured that even if Dan hung out with an asshole, he wasn't necessarily one himself. They watched the game together, chatting throughout about Fordham and their law school friends. At the end of the game, they all migrated down to a bar in Midtown, and as people started leaving, it seemed logical for Dan and Rachel to share a cab home to Murray Hill. Rachel gave her address and then turned to Dan.

"It's fine," he said. "One stop, sir." He turned to Rachel. "I can drop you off and then walk, it's like three blocks."

They got to Rachel's apartment and Dan paid, refusing to accept money from her. "But you didn't even get dropped at your own place!" she objected.

"It's not a big deal," he told her, getting out of the cab. They stood there for a moment until Rachel said she better go in.

"Hey," Dan said. "I know it's about two years after the fact, but I invited you to my party because I wanted to ask you out."

"I sort of knew that. Greg told me you called me the hot library girl," she said, laughing and a little surprised by her own boldness.

"I was so pissed at him for ruining my shot!"

Rachel took a step closer to Dan. He was nearly a foot taller than her and made her feel tiny. "Do you still think I'm cute?" she asked, looking up at him flirtatiously.

Dan took his cue and leaned down to kiss her. They both felt an immediate spark and neither wanted the kiss to end. Rachel finally pulled back. "Whoa."

"Yeah," he replied. "So, maybe we can, um, hang out again? Want to have dinner on Saturday?"

Rachel agreed, then stood on her toes to kiss him again, briefly. "Do you still have my number?"

Dan opened his phone and brought up "Rachel Law School," showing her. She showed him her phone then, which said "Dan Library."

"I guess I'll see you Saturday. And maybe tomorrow at work? Is that weird?"

"No," Dan laughed. "I'm sure 50 percent of our summer class ends up hooking up." She gave him a squinty look. "Not that that's what this is. I'm just saying."

Rachel laughed again. Dan was easy to be around. "I'm kidding."

"Okay, okay. I'm leaving. See you Saturday." He turned and walked down the street, and she watched him go.

That weekend, Dan took Rachel for sushi in the village. Becca said he'd accosted her in the apartment he shared with Matt, asking for restaurant suggestions. She also told Rachel that in the nearly two years she'd been with Matt, she'd never seen Dan this excited about a girl. She was holding out hope for the two of them.

Rachel wasn't as sure. She thought Dan was adorable, though she'd never really gone for the football player look. There was just something about him. He had the cutest dimples, and his eyes sparkled when he smiled. He made her laugh, too. But a side of Rachel questioned if maybe he wasn't serious enough for her. He must have done well in school, she rationalized, to have landed at a law firm like Silver and Frank.

Becca, as usual, told her she was overthinking. "It's dinner, Rach. He isn't asking you to marry him. Although, that would be kind of amazing." Becca was already envisioning her own wedding to Dan's best friend.

Rachel met him at the restaurant, and he was already there waiting at the table. He stood to kiss her hello, and she was wrapped in his giant hug.

"You look really nice," he said sweetly.

She smiled shyly. "You look nice, too."

The conversation flowed between them. Dan seemed interested in what she had to say, and they learned they had very similar upbringings, he in New Jersey and her on Long Island. He had an older brother who also lived in the city, and he seemed to have a wide network of friends.

"Have you worked with Jerry Rich yet?" she asked him once the conversation turned to their summer jobs.

"No, but actually, he's friends with my dad. That's kind of how I got this gig."

"That's awesome." Dan working at Silver and Frank that summer suddenly made a lot more sense to Rachel. "Well, I heard if Jerry likes you, you're in for life. I'm hoping I get to do work for him." Rachel was gunning for a spot on the litigation team.

Dan shrugged. "I'm not planning to work that hard this summer. This is how they get you. It's supposed to be fun!"

Before she knew it, he had her doing sake bombs, and any reservations she had about him were gone. She'd never laughed so hard. Maybe this, his exuberance, is what she needed in her life.

They spent several hours talking and eventually wandered over to a nearby bar, neither wanting the evening to end. After ordering a couple of beers, Rachel leaned into him. He grabbed her hand and she started laughing.

"What?" he asked her.

"Look at our hands together. You're like a bear."

Dan put his palm up to Rachel's. "Or you're just really, really small."

They laced their hands together then and Rachel smiled shyly at him. Finally, Dan leaned in to kiss her. It was as electric as it had been the other night.

Dan pulled back. "I know I'm being completely uncool, but I really like you."

Rachel had butterflies dancing in her lower belly and was too overwhelmed to say anything, but she felt it, too. She leaned in to kiss him again, and murmured, "I can't believe I'm making out in a bar. Is this allowed after college?"

"True. We're gross. Maybe we should go back to my apartment?"

Rachel laughed, knowing he was only half serious and having zero intention of rushing things with him. "What's a little PDA in NYC?"

14

Present Day

THE DAY WAS NEVER-ENDING. RACHEL FELT A NERVOUS ENERGY, but also a level of excitement at seeing Jack that she hadn't expected. Before finally heading out to meet him, she ran to the bathroom and touched up her makeup. She combed her fingers through her hair, which thankfully looked amazing post-blowout, and gave herself a once-over. She scooped up each boob in her bra for a little lift. Not terrible. She walked out the door of her building, flagging a taxi to take her to the Village.

Rachel walked into the restaurant and spotted Jack immediately, even though he was sitting in the back in a secluded area facing away from the entrance. She took in the swirl of his hair, so much shorter than it was when they were young, and his long, tanned neck. Her stomach was a jumble of nerves and she contemplated passing by the bar for a glass of wine before heading to the table. The hostess approached her and asked if she had a reservation.

"Oh no, I'm here to meet someone. I see him over there," she said, and began to walk toward him, the opportunity for liquid courage quashed.

She took a breath and walked to his table. "Hi, Jack."

He looked up at her and gave her his now-trademark smile, his blue eyes gleaming. Other than the scruff of a beard and the crinkles around his eyes, his face looked the same. He rose out of the booth and gave her a hug. Gone was the scrawny teen; his chest and arms were lean and muscled. She let herself be enveloped by him, and was momentarily catapulted back to high school.

"Rachel," he breathed. "Come sit."

Rachel sat and Jack flagged over the waiter to take her drink order. He had a whiskey in front of him and she ordered a glass of Sauvignon Blanc.

"So, what's it been, five years?" He sounded almost nervous, and Rachel wondered why he could possibly be. She watched him take a long sip of his drink. Being back in his presence was oddly calming for her. Her mom was wrong, he no longer had any power over her. It was just nice to be near him again.

"Yeah, just about." She recalled an unpleasant visit to his apartment with Max one Thanksgiving several years ago and brushed away the memory.

Jack cleared his throat. "So, um, get me up to speed, Rach." Jack's life was public knowledge, whereas she assumed he knew very little about her, beyond seeing her once a decade and getting bits and pieces of information from Alex over the years.

Rachel was happy to ignore the elephant in the room and settled into filling him in on her life. She told him about Max and Emma, her job, the long hours. She said she loved her suburban community but was grateful to be a working mom since the women in town could be a little overwhelming for her. "Thankfully I have my college roommate, Becca. Remember her? We moved to the burbs together."

Jack laughed. "You think I would forget the girl who put a scrunchie on your door when I visited you and made us sleep in the common room? After we hadn't seen each other in a month?" He laughed at the memory. "How is Becca these days?"

"Oh my god, I forgot she did that! You wanted to kill her. Well, she's the same exact person, but now she's busy planning kids' parties instead of dragging me around to fraternity houses.

Our husbands are actually best friends, too, from high school. Following them out of the city was the only way we were going to move to Westchester."

"Ah," Jack said, seizing his opening. "And how is the husband?"

Rachel ignored the question and took a sip of her wine. "Are we going to order? I'm famished."

Jack took her cue. "Are you still a pasta girl? I am obsessed with the spicy rigatoni vodka here."

"Sure, and chicken parm?" she suggested.

"Yes! I haven't been out with a woman willing to eat real food with me in ages. I'm going to have to work out for two hours tomorrow."

They ordered and Rachel asked Jack to tell her about his upcoming movie. It was a story about two divorced couples, and he said he loved playing a father. "I got so close with the kids on set. I guess there is a reason people have children," he joked. "I've been doing action movies lately and I'd never been given a kid."

Their food came and Rachel split the chicken and pasta between them. Jack ordered another drink and Rachel asked for a second glass of wine. They were quiet for a moment.

"Wow, this is good. I can't believe we haven't been here before. Dan loves all the hot celebrity restaurants," Rachel commented without thinking.

"And how is Dan doing these days?" Jack asked again, taking the opening.

Rachel felt her cheeks grow warm and was grateful for the dim lighting of the restaurant. She had decided that unless Jack asked her directly, she wasn't going to admit to him that her husband was the culprit. He needed to see her happy, successful, loved. Yet, as she sat in front of him, the armor she'd intended to keep around her came down. She couldn't be anything but honest with Jack.

"He was the one who sold everything. I'm so sorry." Her eyes filled up, but she quickly blinked the tears away.

"Hey," he said, seeing her embarrassment. "I never thought it was you."

She shook her head. "I feel just as badly that it was him, trust me."

"Why did he do it?" he asked quietly.

The words poured out of her as she filled him in. "And then, instead of telling me, he decided to sell a bunch of my personal shit to get the money back."

"I doubt this is what you want to hear right now, but gambling can be an addiction. I have a couple of friends who went into treatment for it."

"So I'm supposed to send him to rehab and discount that he blew up our entire existence?" Rachel asked him, surprised he was rationalizing Dan's behavior and realizing yet again just how angry she was at her husband.

"No, I mean, that's up to you, obviously. I'm more saying that maybe he didn't have as much control over it as you think. And clearly he thought he had to get the money back somehow. Money does crazy things to people."

"Honestly, I don't even think he has a problem, I think he was just being reckless, or I don't know, bored." Would it be easier for her if he did have an addiction? A disease that could explain this deception away?

"Do you think you can work it out?" he asked gently. When they were kids she could say anything to Jack without judgment. They would analyze each other's emotions and understand each other in a way she'd never before experienced, not even with Alex. This was real life, though. Rachel barely knew how she felt about Dan anymore, and Jack was the last person who should help her figure that out.

"I've been thinking about how you're taking it," she said, redirecting the conversation. "I can't imagine you feeling great having those old letters out there."

Jack briefly squeezed her hand to reassure her. "I've heard that my obsession with my first girlfriend was being compared to Mark Wahlberg in the movie *Fear*." They both laughed.

"You always did want to reenact that roller-coaster scene," she said flirtatiously, unable to resist. She was wrong to think he no longer had a grip over her—she felt like a teenager just sitting across the table from him.

"This has definitely opened up a window into my psyche that I was not expecting," Jack said, taking a long swallow of his drink. "But it's not like people actually know me because they read some letters I wrote more than twenty years ago."

That stung. In some ways, Rachel felt like the real her was exactly who Jack had been writing to, not the present-day mom who managed a house and a job and the inner lives of her children, and barely had time to get through a novel.

"Honestly, everyone thinks people like me have these amazing lives," he continued. "I know that I can't complain, but things aren't always easy."

"So your life isn't perfect? Have you told *Us Weekly*?" Rachel asked, semi-joking, and relieved to turn the focus back to him.

Jack glanced around their booth, never sure who might be listening. Rachel took that as a sign that he didn't want to share with her, either. "Hey, I'm kidding, we don't have to talk about it," she said to him.

"It's not that. I've just been burned one too many times. Sometimes I think I would have been happier in a totally different life."

He looked at her meaningfully, and Rachel had to glance away. Was she the different life?

Rachel pointed out that she was surprised no one was bothering them. "I thought celebrities can't eat in public without being hounded."

Jack made a face she couldn't decipher, then explained that some places have a deal where no one is allowed to take photographs of famous people. "Carbone is actually one of the few restaurants I feel comfortable going. And New York is way better than LA."

Jack steered the conversation back to high school. They eased back into their old rapport, reminiscing about their friends. The conversation naturally led to their breakup.

"I wouldn't call it a breakup, Jack, it's my non-breakup breakup. I pretty much thought you were dead until you showed up on my television screen."

Jack looked at her with his penetrating gaze. "It's no excuse, but I was in a really difficult place at the time. I'm so sorry for hurting you, Rachel, I really am."

"It's okay." She realized she meant it.

"I actually always imagined we would end up together."

"What are you talking about? You're so full of shit." Rachel had spent years wondering what might have happened between them, but it was always her impression that Jack never gave her a thought after dumping her so unceremoniously.

"Are you kidding, I was so gutted when Alex told me you were getting married. She didn't tell you? I had this whole crisis, I could barely leave my trailer."

"She definitely did not tell me. I didn't even think you guys were in touch back then."

"She had to talk me off a serious ledge. It didn't help that I was going through my own breakup. But I knew you were happy, and I didn't want to mess anything up for you." Rachel thought back to that time. She was sort of crushed when she heard he was dating his *Sanctions* co-star, Amanda Coyne, and read obsessively about their relationship at the time. Of course she never admitted that to anyone. She didn't even understand why she cared so much, since she was already serious with Dan by then.

"And then when I saw you at Alex's party a few years later, I don't know, it felt like maybe there was something still there." Jack trailed off. "Anyway, look at us now. Present media crisis aside, we're fine."

Rachel remembered that night, the closest she'd ever come to betraying her husband. "If I'm not mistaken, you got married to someone else a few months after that party." She had been all the more embarrassed by her behavior back then, realizing how much she had misread his attention.

He laughed. "See where that got me!"

Rachel thought about how disastrously that marriage had ended, with the photos of his ex, Fiona Drake, and her co-star kissing in Paris, and immediately regretted bringing it up. Nothing in Jack's life was private. Just the taste of publicity she'd had over the last couple of weeks made her all the more sympathetic now. She felt terrible for him at the time, but he had seemed to move on quickly. At least according to the tabloids.

Jack let it go. The waiter put carrot cake down on the table, on the house, which was Rachel's favorite. She dug in as Jack watched her eat.

"Is it awful that I'm happy this happened?" Jack asked her. "I just never thought I'd get to be sitting across the table from you again."

Rachel nudged the cake and the extra fork toward him. "Take a bite, superstar." Jack patted his stomach and shook his head.

"So, what do we do now?" she asked him.

"You come back to my apartment?" he said, reaching for the fork in her hand and using it to take a bite of the cake.

"Very cute. Last I heard you have a gorgeous girlfriend."

The check arrived and the waiter took a moment to thank Jack for coming and letting him know how much he enjoyed his work. Jack handed off his credit card and told the waiter how wonderful everything was. Rachel bet he left a ridiculous tip, but she tried not to peek. She didn't even bother to offer to contribute to the cost of the meal. Instead, she thanked him for dinner.

"As much as I appreciated your dad giving us twenty bucks to go to the diner, I like finally being able to take you out," he said.

Outside the restaurant, Jack hesitated briefly, then asked Rachel if she wanted to go for a walk. She wasn't quite ready to end the night and agreed.

They started walking down Thompson Street, not talking.

"Tonight was nice," Jack said, almost shyly. "No one talks to me like a person anymore, everyone is so performative and complimentary. I miss being around someone who knows me from before and isn't impressed with all this bullshit."

"Who said I'm not impressed?" Rachel said, teasing him. "Well, honestly, you're still just Jack to me. I watched *Plus Size* obviously, but for a while I couldn't go see your movies. It was too weird watching you half-naked and kissing other women. But then Becca made me see that movie you were in with Mandy Moore. I forget the name, my brain no longer hangs on to details like that. Anyway, I loved it so much I ended up watching everything you've ever done. You're really good, Jack! I'm proud of you."

"Thanks. It sounds like you're kind of a big deal, too. I bet you're incredible in court."

Rachel laughed him off. It seemed insane to talk about her legal career in the same context as Jack's movies.

"Do you remember when your stepfather walked in on me naked and told you to have sex in the car, like a normal teenager?" Rachel couldn't stop laughing at the memory.

He turned toward her and stopped walking. "When you surprised me with the *Varsity Blues* bikini? My mom was livid! And Stan couldn't look at me for a week."

"Glad you didn't take a picture of me in that outfit, there's only so much embarrassment I can take."

"I still think about the whipped cream," he said.

Rachel looked up at him, feeling the charge between them. She was seventeen again. Jack leaned in, as if to kiss her. Rachel was pulled toward him but stopped herself as their lips almost met and hugged him instead.

"I should go. I've loved this, but I'm in a totally different world from you. Clearly."

"Can we see each other again?"

She gave him another hug around his waist, resting her head on his chest like she used to. She wanted to, she knew she did. But she had too much to figure out right now, and her lingering feelings for Jack were a layer she couldn't add.

"I can't, Jack. I'm so sorry about all of this. I think I better head home."

Jack stepped back and gave her a small smile in response, disappointed but not surprised.

"I'll get you a car." He shot someone a text and a black car immediately pulled up next to them.

"Do you have cars just waiting for you on every street in the city?"

Jack laughed. "You'd be amazed what I can do." Rachel could only imagine.

As he opened the door for her, she reached for his hand and squeezed it. "Be good, Jack."

He waved goodbye as the car pulled away. Rachel settled into the back seat and closed her eyes, picturing what it would be like to kiss him again. She remembered the softness of his lips on hers, and could almost taste him. She pretended for a moment that he was sitting there in the car next to her, and let herself feel his arms around her, telling her how he always loved her. She stayed with the fantasy the entire ride home and was disappointed when they pulled up in front of her house.

When she got inside, she felt too hyped up to go to sleep and headed down to the basement to look at her old high school stuff. Not surprisingly, Dan had put everything back haphazardly. She pulled out her yearbooks and some old albums, and then saw it. Her Jack box. He had given it to her for their first anniversary, decorated with memories of their dates and a picture of the two of them in a frame on top. She slowly opened it up, not wanting anything that was glued on to fall off, and was immediately taken back to high school. It was a time capsule. She lifted out her dried corsage from the prom. There was a small sample of Cool Water cologne, Jack's signature scent from the late 1990s. She remembered getting it at the mall before leaving for camp so she could smell it when she missed him. She sniffed it now, and despite the years it had been sitting there, the faint remnant brought her right back. There were so many photos of them. Oh, how she had loved looking at Jack's face.

She opened a note he had written her. He used to fold them in a tight square, she had forgotten about that.

> Hi, I finished my homework, it's late and I'm writing my love a note. Today was nice. We need to decide if we want to do open mic night. I was thinking I could play guitar and you could sing. Maybe "Stay"? You tell me. I'm getting excited about Valentine's Day. I kind of think you'll love the gift I got. Like *Seventeen* magazine caliber. I have a big smile on my face right now thinking about you. You are the best thing that ever happened to me. I love you forever and ever and ever.

Rachel wondered what the gift was; she couldn't remember. But she knew she'd loved it. She loved anything Jack gave her. She refolded the note and put it back in the box. Then she put everything else away and brought the box upstairs with her.

She peeked in on her sleeping children and gave them each a kiss. Emma was sweaty, so she pulled down her comforter. She breathed in her sweet scent and left the door open a crack just as she'd found it. She went directly to the guest room. She had no reason to talk to Dan.

As she got under the crisp white sheets, she grabbed her phone to turn it off. There were two texts waiting for her. One was from Dan saying he was sorry for that morning and that he hoped tonight was okay. The other was from Jack.

JACK: Who wore it best? Xx.

He'd attached a link to James Corden wearing the *Varsity Blues* bikini. Rachel chuckled and turned off the light, again thinking about Jack and what it might have been like to kiss him that night for real.

15

1998-1999

Rachel and Jack both arranged to have off last period senior year, and with her mom's schedule seeing patients, they were able to hang out nearly every afternoon with total privacy. Jack and Ben had found his stepdad's old *Playboy* magazines that summer, and Jack had a new wealth of knowledge about pleasing his girlfriend. Rachel, having grown up in what Alex referred to as a "naked house," was uninhibited with him and eager to try anything Jack suggested. It helped that everything they did together was new to him, too. She sensed Jack was giving Ben more details than she wanted, but she mostly let it go.

Alex sometimes cut last period to hang out with them. Rachel knew that she had been hoping something would develop between her and Jen, but after the night in the Hamptons, Jen had pretended their kiss never happened. Rachel kept encouraging her to try to meet other girls. She felt like Alex was missing out, and didn't have to. As close as the two of them were, and as grateful as Alex was for Rachel's support, Alex seemed to recognize that she could never truly understand.

"It's fine, I'm happy being with you guys," Alex told her on more than one occasion, knowing that Rachel was worried about her and wanting her to let it go. "I know my real life will start in college." Just as Rachel had her heart set on Cornell, Alex had long dreamed of attending NYU, planning to apply to the Tisch School of the Arts. She was convinced that if majoring in film and television didn't give her access to the school's gay population, living in the most liberal, exciting city in the world certainly would.

That winter, Jack finally got a starring role in the senior musical, playing Joe Hardy in *Damn Yankees*. Rachel, now a die-hard drama student, was cast as the reporter, Gloria, and got to sing a song with all the boys in the cast. Unfortunately, Jen was cast opposite Jack as Lola.

It was so obvious that Jen wanted to get back together with him. She kept suggesting extra rehearsals for the two of them and would zealously kiss him during their romantic scenes. Rachel worried that Jack would fall for Jen again; she was so pretty and skinny and cool. But Jack never faltered; he was completely committed to Rachel. Kind, adorable, smart Rachel is all he'd ever want, he'd say to reassure her.

There were only a couple of months left of senior year when Alex asked Rachel what was going to happen to her and Jack when they left for college. It wasn't the first time someone brought that up, but Rachel had been avoiding the subject. The couple had discussed applying to school together, but both knew that Rachel's grade point average and SAT scores put her in a different league from Jack. Rachel didn't intend to give up her dream of attending Cornell, where her father went. And Jack would never hold her back. He had always said he wanted to go to UCLA, attracted to the California weather, but with his grades hovering around a B+ and his financial needs, it was an unlikely scenario. Instead, he applied to SUNY schools as an English major and ultimately landed on Albany, which offered him the most money.

"I mean, what's the game plan for you guys?" Alex asked her as she sat on Rachel's bed.

"What do you mean?" Rachel said, holding up a sweater to get her friend's opinion. Alex made a face, so Rachel tossed it into the donation pile.

"I guess I'm just curious if you're really planning to travel back and forth between each other's schools."

"Well, Jack will have his car, and Albany's pretty close to Ithaca, so it's not such a big deal."

"Yeah, I know you guys say that, but is it realistic? Like, don't you worry that being with Jack is going to prevent you from meeting people?"

"Oh. Well, not really. My roommate seems totally awesome, and she already knows a few other girls going that she said she'd introduce me to."

"Rach. No offense, but you're being a little dense here. Don't you want to have other experiences? Like, meet other guys?"

Rachel looked at Alex, confused, and felt a lump forming in her throat. "Wait, did Jack tell you to talk to me? I thought he wanted us to stay together."

Alex laughed. "What are you talking about? Jack adores you. I'm just saying you're my best friend, and all I keep thinking about is the fun I'm planning to have at NYU, and all the new people I'm going to meet. I'm just worried about you. That's all."

Rachel breathed a sigh of relief and told Alex she didn't think hooking up with random boys in college was going to make or break her experience. She and Jack knew it would be hard, but they were committed.

Later that night, a bunch of them went to the movies and Rachel told Jack about her conversation with Alex when he dropped her home afterward.

"I think it could be tough, Rach, but I don't want to lose you," Jack said, trying to reassure her, but in fact doing the opposite.

"Does that mean if I said we could see other people and still be together on breaks and stuff, you'd want that?" She was near tears.

"Why are you hearing that? All I am saying is that going back and forth between our schools could be difficult. I love you. I don't want to be with other people. You know this."

Rachel started crying in earnest. "I'm scared to be without you."

Jack leaned over to her and took her face in his hands. "You will never be without me, babe. I love you so much."

And so, two and a half months later, after a year of only spending Rachel's family vacations apart, Rachel stood in Jack's driveway next to his sister and mother, as he and his stepfather packed the trunk of his old Civic. His father had come earlier to say goodbye and was already gone. Rachel saw him slip Jack some money as they briefly hugged. When Jack moved the money into his wallet, Rachel observed that it was just some fives and singles with a twenty-dollar bill wrapped around it.

Jack insisted on driving up to Albany alone, even though it meant getting to college and unpacking himself when his new classmates were surrounded by their families. Rachel didn't entirely understand why Jack wouldn't want his mom there, and she thought Nancy would appreciate the experience of bringing her son to college, but she didn't comment.

Jack forcefully closed the trunk and stepped back. He had just a foot of space between his life's possessions and the top of his car to see out his rearview mirror. He looked at his stepfather and extended a hand for a shake. Stan responded in kind and patted his stepson on the back, pulling him in for a half hug.

"Well, I'll leave you to it. Have a safe trip and call your mother when you get there," Stan said, putting his arm around his wife.

Nancy wiggled away from Stan and plowed over to her son.

"Are you sure you don't want me to come?" she pleaded. "It just seems like such a long drive. And what will your roommate's parents think, you unpacking your room by yourself?"

"I'm sure, Mom," he said, pulling her in for a hug. "I'll be fine. I got this. It's like a three-hour drive. I've driven farther camping with Dad."

Nancy grabbed him by the face and kissed both cheeks, breathing him in for the last time until Thanksgiving break. "Okay, you better call me. Not just when you get there, at least once a week."

"Got it. I promise."

Megan stepped up to her brother next. "Call me, too?" Jack wrapped his little sister in a giant hug that stretched out longer than his goodbye to either parent. Rachel knew Megan would miss having her brother home and had expressed that she was worried about the pressure of being alone with their mom. Jack would check in on her. They both would.

Megan turned to Rachel. "I guess I'm not going to see you, either?"

Rachel opened her arms to Megan, who had become like a little sister to her. "You have to come visit me at Cornell, Meg. And call me whenever you want!"

"Okay," Jack said, interrupting their goodbye. "I'm going to take Rachel home and head out. I love you guys. Thanks for the help, Stan," he said, nodding to him and hoping Stan would lead his family inside.

"So," Jack said, when he and Rachel were alone. "I guess I'll drop you at your house."

"I guess so," Rachel said glumly, getting into the passenger side of the car that had chauffeured her around for nearly two years. "I can't believe I'm saying goodbye to you."

"Not goodbye, babe. I promise to call you all the time, and we'll see each other in a month when I visit. And you can e-mail me whenever you want. We'll be like pen pals," he said, attempting to raise her spirits.

She leaned in to kiss him, and they kissed, like they had so many times before. With a sweetness and gentleness that slowly progressed into something deeper. He pulled away, with a smile, and pushed her hair behind her ear. He leaned in again to kiss her neck and smell her fresh shampoo scent. Rachel held his right hand, occasionally kissing it, as they traveled the seven short minutes across their Long Island town to her house.

Waiting outside for them, as expected by both teenagers, were Rachel's parents, Mitch and Elaine Stone.

"You ready, bud?" Mitch asked Jack.

"I'm set. Thanks for everything, guys, I mean, all you have done for me, seriously," Jack said, maybe referencing how Rachel's dad had gotten a colleague to write him a letter of recommendation that helped him land his work-study job, or maybe acknowledging how the family had essentially adopted him over the last two years. It didn't matter; her parents understood.

"We have a little something for you, hon." Elaine ran into the house and came out with a giant wrapped box. Jack looked at them mystified and opened it. It was a laptop. Jack had planned to get a loaner at school and was clearly overwhelmed.

"You're going to do great, Jack. Remember what we talked about," Elaine said to him. They exchanged a knowing look that Rachel didn't entirely understand. Both of her parents gave him a long hug, and Rachel noticed Jack tearing up when he hugged her mom. As Mitch and Elaine went back inside the house to give them privacy, Rachel realized that he was more emotional

saying goodbye to her parents than he had been his own. He'd
become a part of her family.

"This is really it, I guess. I love you, Jackie, so so much," Rachel
said, starting to cry. She wiped her nose on the red plaid flannel
shirt he had tied around his waist. "Something to remember me by,"
she said, laughing through tears at her snot on his sleeve.

"Hey," Jack said to her, looking into her eyes. "You know you
make me so happy, right? Like even when I can't figure out my
homework, or my parents are fighting, or any other shitty thing?
You just make me feel better than anyone ever has, Rach. I love you
so much."

Rachel was silent, the tears streaming down her face. There was
nothing else she could say to him to express how deeply she felt.
After another minute, he detached himself from their embrace. "I
better get going," he said sadly.

Rachel stood on her tippy-toes and kissed him again, one last
long kiss. He pulled back and headed to his car, getting inside and
giving her a final quick wave. She stayed outside for a long time,
sitting on the stoop by her sidewalk with her head in her hands, as
her love drove off. A part of her hoped he'd turn back and ask her to
drive up with him to Albany. As she cried to her mother that night,
Rachel felt a depth of grief so strong she could crack in two.

16

Present Day

WHEN RACHEL WALKED INTO THE KITCHEN THE MORNING AFTER meeting Jack, Dan was already sitting there drinking his coffee.

"So, how was it?" he asked her, somewhat coldly. She felt momentarily guilty, but she'd stopped herself from crossing a line. It was better not to engage.

"It was fine. Kids do okay?"

"Max had trouble with his math homework again."

Rachel walked over to the coffee machine and poured herself a cup. "I'll reach out to his teacher to see what she thinks about getting him a tutor. We probably should anyway."

"Okay," he said, still sounding curt. "Did you check your phone yet today?"

"No, why?" she asked.

"Why don't you look at *Page Six*?" he said with a sneer.

Rachel grabbed her phone out of her robe pocket and turned it on. She had several text messages waiting for her, which she ignored. She opened the home page of the *New York Post* website.

She saw a picture of herself and Jack outside the restaurant, hugging goodbye. There was a blurb underneath:

We all cringed a little reading the mushy love letters a very young Jack Bellow wrote to his high school sweetheart, attorney Rachel Miller. Now, the rumor mill is in overdrive as the two former lovebirds were spotted embracing outside Carbone last night.

Rachel was grateful she had resisted the urge to kiss him. She looked at her husband. "Obviously nothing happened, Dan." It was strange how she had already numbed herself to the embarassment of being in a tabloid.

"I told you not to go see him, Rachel. You said you wanted to put this behind you, but you realize you basically lit the whole thing on fire," Dan said coldly.

He got up and put his mug in the sink, then walked out of the kitchen.

She followed him. "Where are you going?"

"I'm sick of you giving me the silent treatment. I'm having dinner with my brother after work." Rachel watched him leave and slam the door to the garage behind him. Let him be jealous, she thought. She had done nothing wrong.

"Kids, get dressed," Rachel shouted up the stairs for what felt like the millionth time.

As she pulled up at the school, and the kids jumped out, she saw the women. They stood in a large clump at the foot of the school steps. A gaggle of eight Lululemon-clad mothers, all but two of them thin, not a gray hair in sight. Rachel parked her SUV in the school lot. She sat there for a moment, watching them, correctly assuming that the topic of conversation was her and Jack.

She and Becca walked together most Friday mornings, the day Rachel worked from home. She slowly got out of her car, adjusting her own leggings and matching pullover. She felt their eyes on her, but refused to listen to her inner voice telling her to run in the other direction. She could handle this. These were her friends. Well, mostly.

As she approached the women, they simultaneously moved closer to her, the buzz emanating from them like a swarm of bees. In the background, Rachel could hear the start of morning announcements and the muffled Pledge of Allegiance.

"Rachel!" Amy exclaimed. "What was it like seeing Jack again?" she asked, sweetening her voice, but Rachel felt the venom. She noticed her exchange a glance with her best friend and biggest follower, Heather Portnoy.

"Guess you guys have been watching *TMZ*," Rachel said, with a weak smile.

One of her better friends, Wendy, spoke up. "You have to tell us about Jack! I always had such a huge thing for him. He's on my list! Adam was dying when he heard about you guys because he knew I'd be so insanely jealous."

Rachel laughed, pushing down the discomfort from all the attention, as the women moved closer to her, eager for details. Jack was the total opposite of Adam Weinstein, a shorter-than-average, balding dentist.

"He's a good guy. Honestly, we hadn't been in touch for years."

"You must have been freaking out when the pictures were published. Do you know how it happened?" Dani, another woman whose daughter was in Max's grade, asked.

Rachel knew she could be honest with a few of these women individually, some of whom she'd been friends with for close to a decade. But she was never going to admit the stress she was under to the broader group.

"I'm not really sure." She tried to laugh it off. "I don't totally get why people care, it's not like the things Jack did or said in high school mean anything anymore." She thought back to what he said to her the night before, that it wasn't as if people knew him now because of some letters he'd written at seventeen. As much as that pained her to hear.

"It must be so hard on Dan," Amy said, clearly pushing for a reaction. "Seeing you and your ex so in love. And then these new pictures of the two of you together. Was that last night? Must be a lot." The judgment oozed from this woman.

"Oh, Dan's met Jack, it's really not a big deal," Becca chimed in, saving her. "Should we get going, Rach?"

Rachel smiled at her friend gratefully. "Yes! I need to be back for a 10:30 call."

Wendy jokingly booed, and said she wanted more details when Rachel had time. Rachel promised to call her soon, and a few of the other women as well who immediately requested more details.

"We'll set up a Zoom," Becca quipped, as she led Rachel away from the school.

"Remind me why I moved to Ridgevale?" Rachel whispered.

Becca laughed. "They're just excited to have something to talk about."

Now that they were alone, Rachel's eyes filled with tears. Between the gossip, and seeing Jack again, and now having Dan mad at her, it was all too much.

"Hey," Becca said sympathetically. "I know how shitty this all is. But it's going to go away. And it's not important what anyone else thinks."

"I feel like no one would believe me if I told them, 'Actually, it was my husband you all think is so great who completely sold me out.'" Dan was a beloved member of their community; it was his general frat guy "I love everyone" attitude that attracted people to him. Rachel loved that about him, too, so it never bothered her. But in this moment she was annoyed by his popularity.

Becca stopped walking and grabbed her in for a hug. Then she pulled back and put her hands on her friend's shoulders. "Rach, they all love you, too, you know. You're the first person to drop off soup or take someone's kid when they're sick. You make sure not a single kid or adult is ever left out of anything. Look how you take care of me, listening to me obsess over nonsense all the time and always giving me the best advice."

Rachel smiled weakly. "Amy is so mean."

"I know. Let me deal with her, you focus on you. Okay?"

She nodded, somewhat relieved. She knew her friends cared about her, and Becca would always have her back.

"No more energy on these women. Tell me about seeing Jack!"

"We're putting you in an untenable position," Rachel said, sadly. The closeness of the couples had every benefit until one of them was in the middle of a marital crisis. Rachel trusted Becca without reservation, she knew she would always support her. It seemed, however, that it was too much to ask that Becca keep what Rachel said from her husband.

"What do you mean?"

"Matt has to be there for Dan, and I need you. But you're married to each other."

Becca thought about this. "Do you remember what we said in the sorority house?"

Rachel shook her head.

"Sisters before misters." She got Rachel to laugh at that. "Rach, you've been my best friend for more than twenty years. I'm not going to let you keep shit from me because you're worried it may create some awkwardness between me and Matt. Let's be honest, if someone held a gun to my head I'd run off with you over him."

"I love you, Bec." The women hugged again.

"Now spill," Becca demanded, resuming their walk.

"I think we almost kissed."

"Shut the fuck up!"

Rachel gave her a rundown of the night before.

"Did he say anything about Cassandra?"

"Actually, no, he was a little cagey about everything. I don't want to read into it too much, but he doesn't seem all that happy."

"Any word from Alex yet?"

"Barely. Other than texting me that it'll blow over soon and not to stress. It's so strange for her to brush me off like this. I guess she really is busy?"

Becca looked pensive. "She's clearly stressed about the movie. She's usually so good about being in touch."

"I know. I just wish I could get her take on all of this."

Becca nodded her agreement. "Well, it seems like Jack was genuinely happy to see you. And, like, interested in you, which is crazy!"

Rachel had managed to convince herself that she was long over Jack, but any time she saw him over the years she was reminded that she had never fully let him go. Sure, Jack seemed to feel it, too, but he was an actor—who knew how real any of that was? She couldn't trust that any connection between them last night was genuine. And what did it matter anyway? She was married, and he was a movie star. She had to push it away.

"I shouldn't be focusing on Jack." As much as that was all she wanted to think about. She knew the far more pressing question was whether her marriage was salvageable. "Dan was so pissed at me this morning when he saw the *Page Six* thing. I wanted to shake him—he did this to us!"

"Dan knows how much he messed up."

"I think so." Then she said the words she'd been thinking all week, and hadn't been ready to admit aloud. "I don't know if I can forgive him, though. Is that awful? I just keep wondering what kind of person does this to their wife?" She stopped walking and started to cry again in earnest.

Becca put her arm around her friend, acutely feeling her pain. "I promise we're going to figure it out."

Rachel leaned into her. At least she wasn't totally alone.

17

THAT NIGHT, AS SHE WAS PUTTING MAX TO BED, HE FINALLY brought it up. "Mom, Jonah and some of the other guys said that the guy from *Last Licks* is your boyfriend. I told them they were wrong."

Rachel had debated all week whether she should say something to her son and immediately regretted her decision not to get ahead of it. "Oh, sweetie, he's definitely not my boyfriend. Jack Bellow, the man from that movie, is an old friend of mine. We had dinner last night and pictures were taken, but it was all a big misunderstanding."

"So you aren't leaving us to move to California?"

"What? Of course not!" Rachel knew it was only a matter of time before Max sensed the tension between his parents, but she was caught off guard by the question. "Max, honey, I would never leave you and your sister."

"But you keep sleeping in the guest room, and why isn't Dad home tonight?"

Rachel felt awful that they hadn't done as good a job of pretending as she thought. Max was so into his friends and video games, she forgot how intuitive he could be when he was paying attention. But she wasn't ready to have this conversation with her son, not until she knew where she and Dan stood.

"Sweets, Daddy met Uncle Josh for dinner. He'll be home soon and then we'll all be at your game tomorrow, okay?"

"You promise?"

"I promise that you'll see Dad in the morning. And I'll tell him to come in and give you a kiss when he gets home tonight."

"Okay," Max said, seeming to accept his mom's response.

"Hey, have you come up with an idea for the science fair yet? I was thinking maybe we could work on it together? Wouldn't that be fun?"

Max became animated telling her about wanting to build a rocket using a soda bottle. "And it really flies, Mom. Can we do that one?"

Rachel agreed and promised to take him to buy the supplies after his game the next day. She kissed him good-night and headed downstairs.

Rachel grabbed a bag of chocolate chips from the pantry and then plopped on the couch in the family room, turning on *Real Housewives*. She scrolled through Instagram as she half watched and saw a photo of an old friend from her sorority's anniversary, a woman she hadn't spoken to in probably ten years. Look at her, celebrating in Hawaii. She cared zero percent, but hearted it anyway. Ugh. Was Rachel going to start posting family pictures without her husband in it, hoping people would read between the lines? She certainly wasn't going to make some kind of bold statement that her marriage was over, like Becca's high school friend had earlier that year. God, that was embarrassing. Wait, why was she even thinking like this? She had to find a way to get over it.

It was strange having Dan mad at her now. She hadn't heard from him all day. Not that he was big on checking in, but the last week he had at least been trying. She was the one who was supposed to be angry. Rachel tried to clear her mind and focus on the show. One of the housewives was lecturing another for talking too much. She clicked it off and headed upstairs.

She wanted to forgive Dan. She really did. They used to be so happy. Dan was the first boy that she was truly giddy about since Jack. She had plenty of crushes, and more meaningless hookups and dates than she cared to remember. But Dan was different. He balanced her out; he was always so social and upbeat. Rachel knew she took everything so seriously. When they were third-years, Dan would make her race him around the law library every two hours when they were deep into studying for finals. He insisted her brain would rot if she didn't take a break. And she would do it, for him. As much as she never wanted to put down the outline she'd been dutifully copying over and over to memorize. Their friends would loudly whisper "go!" and she would take off, squeezing past him, and sometimes she'd beat him, but mostly he would grab her back, lifting her easily and placing her behind him to slow her down. He made it all so much fun. He made her fun, she thought wistfully.

And, she reminded herself, they had serious chemistry. Even their first time, before he knew exactly what she liked, exceeded all prior sexual experiences. He had taken her ice-skating in Rockefeller Center on their fourth date and insisted on teaching her, even though she was awful and unbalanced.

"Just lean into me," Dan said, skating backward, a remnant from his ice hockey days. "You're doing great. Now stand up straighter. Look at you. You're doing it."

"Do not let go of me," she remembered shrieking, clutching his forearms.

"You got this," he'd said encouragingly. "And you look so cute." He touched her face with his big gloved hands and leaned in to kiss her, and she immediately lost her balance and pulled him down with her. They couldn't stop laughing and stayed down on the ice until people started checking on them. Rachel always said she fell in love with him in that moment. She brought him home with her that night and was surprised by how much heat he brought into the bedroom. There was something about how oversized he was that she'd expected it to be clunky. But Dan took his time and was so focused on pleasing her. It was electric between them. Mostly, without fail, everyone that knew her well commented that Dan brought out the best in Rachel, a lightness that was otherwise hidden.

They got married a couple of years after law school and were both working at Silver and Frank. It was a giant law firm, and they were never assigned to the same matters, but comparisons between the young spouses were to be expected. Rachel was a worker bee. She had started bringing in her own clients, mostly small litigation matters, but it got her some attention. She was also named a Rising Star in the *New York Law Journal*, which impressed no one in the know but thrilled her parents. Dan was never as dedicated, or valued. They both knew it. If it wasn't for his connection to Jerry Rich, he would never have been hired there in the first place. After about eight years at the firm, around the time both were being evaluated for partnership, Dan was asked to provide comments on a purchase agreement for a client who was competing for a deal. He didn't turn the document around on time, and the client lost out on the bid. Rachel lobbied for him to be given another chance, pretending she had a "medical issue" to excuse his malfeasance, putting herself on the line in the process.

When Rachel got word that she was making partner, and Dan decidedly was not, they knew Dan would probably get pushed out of the firm within a year or two. She started putting feelers out for him, and eventually heard through a friend about an opportunity at Parker Daly Schmidt.

"It's a chance for you to stand on your own, and maybe even bring in some of your own business," Rachel assured him at the time.

"Maybe I should be thinking about other options, outside of the law." ˙

Rachel brushed him off. What else was he going to do?

His new job was fine for a while. He didn't love his colleagues, and he earned less money, but the work was interesting enough and his hours were more flexible. But as time went on, he complained more and more that he was bored there, and they both noticed he was being passed over for promotions.

"Maybe you should look at other firms, or go in-house? Remember Mark from law school, he works at Related now, and I think one of the other guys from our section is at CBRE. I can ask Gabe to put you in touch," she said to him one night after they had put the kids to bed.

"Do you ever feel like we have the same conversation over and over? It's fine. I'm not going to find something better." He was clearly sick of discussing this with her.

She realized now that Dan had been telling her he was unhappy at work for years. Why didn't she encourage him to explore other opportunities outside of the law? She always tried to see things from other people's perspective; her mom had drilled empathy into her from birth. But she hadn't done that with her own husband. Was she maybe a little bit at fault, at least for the way things had been between them lately? Rachel was suddenly ashamed by how dismissive she'd been.

She attempted to go to sleep, with her anger and now guilt banging around her brain. She heard Dan come in the house and the door to the guest room opened shortly thereafter.

"You up?" Dan whispered.

Rachel debated whether to pretend to be asleep but instead asked him how his brother was.

"Fine. He's worried about me." He paused. "I'm sorry about this morning."

She sat up in bed and turned on the lamp. She felt an urgency to be nicer to him. "No, it's fine. I know how it looked. Why is Josh worried?"

Dan sat down on the edge of the bed.

"Everything." He sighed. "Mostly me being an idiot."

"How worried about you do I need to be?"

Dan looked at her. "If you're asking about the poker, I'm done with it. I got in over my head, that's all. My brother doesn't like seeing me upset."

"Whose fault is that?" she asked, forgetting the remorse she had felt just moments before Dan got home.

"I can't have you so mad at me."

"It's not like I want to be mad at you, Dan. I'm trying to figure it out." She paused, weighing her words. "Maybe we should get into therapy again?"

"I know I messed up. I don't need some shrink trying to figure out what happened in my childhood."

"You clearly need help. We need help." Rachel felt her eyes welling up. "And Max asked about it tonight, so it's not like the kids haven't noticed that something is going on."

"Did you tell him Daddy is a fuckup?"

"Are you drunk?" She was bewildered.

"I'm going to bed. This is bullshit."

Rachel watched her husband stalk off to their bedroom. She didn't even know him anymore.

18

2016

Just before the birth of their second child, Rachel and Dan left Manhattan and moved to the town of Ridgevale in Westchester County, a half hour north of New York City. Rachel had made partner at Silver and Frank that year, and Dan had moved to a boutique real estate firm where they expected he would also make partner. They found a home they absolutely loved in the same town in which their best friends, Becca and Matt Darner, lived. It was a few hundred thousand dollars out of their budget, so they ended up taking money for the down payment from her parents.

To their surprise, they both loved living in the suburbs. Besides spending many evenings with the Darners, they met several other young married couples, most of whom also had children around Max's age. Everyone they met was a recent city transplant, and eager to make friends. Rachel and Dan soon found themselves hosting potluck dinners, going bowling, and for Dan, attending men's poker nights. Rachel and Becca had even done one of those paint and sip classes with some of the other moms in their boys' nursery school class, which involved them attempting to paint a sunset while completely loaded on white wine.

Emma Rose Miller was born just after midnight on a Sunday in June. Her birth was far less complicated than her brother's, and they were booted out of the hospital thirty-six hours later. As a gift to their daughter, Elaine and Mitch hired a night nurse to take care of the baby so Rachel and Dan could sleep.

Emma was a perfect infant. She slept and ate well, and she and Rachel spent their days enjoying the summer weather walking around their new neighborhood with Becca and her own newborn daughter, Julia. The best friends pretended to anyone that asked, even their husbands, that it was a coincidence that they had babies three weeks apart, but in truth they had secretly started trying at the same time. A summertime baby was perfect, both mothers had agreed. What better time to enjoy your newborn and for Rachel, to take a break from work.

When her four-month maternity leave ended, Rachel returned to her law firm in Manhattan. Though she felt guilty leaving her baby, she was eager to pick back up where she'd left off; it was not in her nature to stay at home to take care of her kids. Rachel had been fighting one particular case for quite some time, and before her leave, had written a compelling motion for summary judgment that was years in the making. Her return to the office coincided with oral argument for the motion, and she spent much of her first two weeks back preparing.

Dan, who generally avoided overworking himself, thought Rachel was taking on too much too soon after Emma was born. He worried she might burn out if she didn't ease back into things and pointed out, repeatedly, that Rachel's colleagues had been handling her files ably in her absence. Rachel was exhausted, but passionate about this particular case, which involved a new mother who claimed that the folate she took during pregnancy wasn't strong enough to prevent her child's spina bifida. Despite the sympathy she had, Rachel had developed extensive evidence supporting the vitamin company she represented. She also felt strongly, as she explained frequently to Dan, that as a brand-new mother herself, only she could argue this motion.

She was also concerned about Jerry and felt she needed to show him she had her head in the game. Her second day back at work she handed him a draft of some discovery responses for him to sign off on, and he was displeased with her effort. He told her that she had to get out of "mommy zone" and back into lawyer mode. Rachel needed to show him that she could handle herself.

So Rachel resumed her eleven-hour workdays, stopping to pump twice a day and racing home each evening to get dinner on the table. She tried to spend at least an hour a day playing Legos or dinosaurs with Max so he didn't feel neglected, and it was worth it to have that time with him, even though she had to sign back online each night before bed.

Two days before she was scheduled to argue her motion, Dan had already left for work and Rachel waited at home for their nanny, Justine, to arrive to watch Emma before dropping Max at his nursery school.

"I didn't get that much milk out last night," she told Justine. "So you can use formula for her second feed, I guess."

"I got it. Don't worry! Say bye to Mommy, Emma," Justine said, taking Emma's little baby hand and waving goodbye.

Rachel gave her another little kiss and then got Max into the car. Then she realized she had left her breast pump in the baby's room. She left Max in the car seat as she ran back into the house to grab the pump. He was extra clingy that day at drop-off, and his teacher eventually had to pull him away from her. Rachel felt terrible leaving him upset, but she needed to make the 9:32 train.

Her calendar pinged at eleven, and she got up from her desk and taped a DO NOT ENTER sign to her door. She unbuttoned her blouse and zipped herself into the special breast pump bra she used with the nipples cut out, attaching the pumps and maneuvering the cones through the holes. She got desperately thirsty when she pumped, and realized she'd forgotten to get water, so she debated getting dressed again. She'd survive. She had way too much to do and needed to quickly pump and move on with the morning. Once the milk got going, she resumed her focus on drafting the outline for her oral argument. After a few minutes of typing, she felt her left hand seize up. She tried to stretch it out, but it was stuck sort of in a claw shape. She tried to keep working through it, but soon after felt her right hand tightening up as well. Her throat started feeling weird, too. Something was wrong with her.

"Beth, can you come in here?" Rachel croaked anxiously to her assistant.

Beth walked into her office and looked over at Rachel, sitting there with her breast pump going. She closed the door behind her. "Do you need something?"

Rachel held up her hands to show her. "I think something's wrong with me. I don't know. I'm feeling sort of panicked, I think. Can you call Dan? Please?" Beth reassured her but pulled out her phone and Rachel gave her Dan's number.

"Hi, Dan, it's Beth O'Malley," she said. They knew each other from when he too worked at Silver and Frank. "Rachel's not feeling well, do you think you can come get her from the office?"

Rachel couldn't hear Dan, but she could imagine he was confused.

"Honestly, I'm not sure. She's sitting here in front of her computer and her hands are kind of clenched up," Beth explained. She listened and looked at Rachel. "Okay. He's on his way."

Beth hung up the phone. She offered to help Rachel detach her breast pump and get her dressed, and although Rachel was embarrassed, she really had no choice. After getting her into her clothes and storing the breast milk for her in her cooler bag, Beth sat there with her until Dan arrived.

Dan burst into her office twenty minutes later. "Sweetie, are you okay?"

"Dan, you're here!" Rachel said, immediately feeling better being near her husband. "It's my hands. I don't know what's wrong with me. I'm freaking out. Do you think I'm having a stroke?"

"I don't, Rach. I'm sure this is all stress related, but why don't we go see a doctor?"

Beth helped him gather her stuff and handed him Rachel's bag. Dan thanked her, and Rachel begged Beth not to tell a soul about this. "Hey, Beth," Dan said. "Maybe you can have someone try to get that motion adjourned for a few weeks?"

Dan led Rachel out of the building and though he told her he was confident there was nothing other than anxiety at play, he took her to the emergency room. As they sat there waiting for several hours to be seen, Rachel's hands remained stuck in a weird claw shape. She was worried that something was truly wrong with her. She wanted to google her symptoms, but she couldn't use her phone and Dan would never do that for her. She tried to distract herself by periodically making Dan check her iPhone for messages from work. Dan bounced between their two inboxes, responding to e-mails that Rachel dictated and then responding to his own.

They finally made it through triage and Rachel was brought to a small room to be seen by an emergency room doctor. The doctor went through her vitals and asked her a series of questions about her health. He wasn't sure what was wrong and sent her for a CT scan of her brain and a neuro consult, who conducted a whole other series of tests on her. Despite assurances from the neurologist, who seemed generally unconcerned by her condition, Rachel convinced herself that she had an aneurysm or was having a stroke, or maybe it was brain cancer.

Another hour later, Rachel and Dan were visited by a different doctor, who announced that Rachel's scans, blood work, and neurological tests were all clear. The consensus was that her so-called frozen hands were purely psychosomatic and that she was suffering from an anxiety disorder, likely due to her postpartum condition. This doctor believed that the stress of returning to work, along with her other responsibilities, triggered the episode. It would resolve with rest, anti-anxiety medication, and more importantly, therapy. Rachel was sent home with a prescription for Lexapro and a doctor's note supporting his recommendation that she take a few more weeks of medical leave off work.

Rachel was relieved that she wasn't dying, but she couldn't understand how her nonworking hands, which were still clenched up, was a psychological problem. She had never been a particularly anxious person. She was fine. She just had a lot on her plate. When they called Rachel's psychologist mother, Elaine, from the cab on the way home from the hospital, she agreed with the diagnosis.

"You're so high strung, Rachel. A second baby, a job, all those cases. And that mean boss of yours. This was bound to happen." She told them she would call a therapist friend who she knew would get them in for an emergency appointment.

Rachel took her first dose of Lexapro that night. Dan, instead of Rachel, did the night feed for the first time since the baby nurse had left. And though she was feeling a bit better the following day, Rachel agreed to see the therapist her mom recommended, Mindy Black.

Mindy had an office in a ritzy residential building on Seventy-Ninth and Park Avenue, and Rachel felt awkward greeting the doorman and then entering the doctor's office off the lobby while he watched her go in. Despite having a psychologist for a mother, Rachel herself had never been to therapy.

Mindy's office was calming, with a box of tissues on her coffee table, and uncomplicated artwork on the walls. She was only a little older than Rachel and had a cheery disposition. Rachel liked her immediately, and willingly filled Mindy in on her life. She told her about the new baby and her older son, being an only child, and always pressuring herself to succeed. She mentioned that she needed things to be orderly and hated surprises.

As Mindy listened to Rachel, she told her that she thought her diagnosis made sense, and what she was experiencing wasn't as unusual as one would think. Rachel was a new mother of two with a stressful career and post-pregnancy hormones coursing through her body.

"So tell me about your husband."

"Dan? Dan's the best," Rachel responded.

"I've been listening to you talk about your children and your many responsibilities, and you haven't once mentioned your husband. I'm curious, what does he do to make your life easier?"

Rachel thought about what the therapist was saying. She barely knew her, and yet . . .

"Well, I guess I do most things around the house, everything our nanny can't get to, anyway. Laundry, meals, cleaning up. That kind of stuff."

Mindy asked her what else she did for their family.

"I guess I make most of the playdates for Max. I handle doctors' appointments, things like that."

"But you're an attorney, and you just had a baby. Do you think perhaps your husband could share some of those responsibilities to ease your load?"

Rachel did not, in fact, think her husband could share those responsibilities. She explained that Dan was not organized, or good at cleaning up, and this was just the way they managed things. "He would forget to pick up Max or feed him dinner if I didn't tell him to, you know? Like a few weeks ago, I asked him to mail in Max's preschool deposit and he forgot to do it. Thankfully, I know someone on the board and she gave me a heads-up. Max would have lost his spot!" Rachel shook her head, remembering how irritated she had been. "We actually used to work together, but he left the firm. He wasn't cut out for big law, if you know what I mean."

Mindy looked at her, urging her to continue.

"It's not a huge deal. He was only really hired there because his dad knew a senior partner. And one time he missed a deadline and I had to figure it out for him. It's kind of the same at home."

"I see. How's your relationship otherwise?" Mindy asked her.

Rachel said things were good. "Everyone loves Dan. He's one of those guys with a million friends."

Mindy waited for Rachel to say more.

"He's a good husband. He calms me down, keeps things more upbeat, you know? I can be a little serious, clearly."

"So that's what you need, someone who keeps things light?"

"I think so. I don't know."

"Does he give you emotional support?"

Rachel looked at Mindy. "He's not really a talker, if that's what you mean. I have great friends I can talk to about my feelings. And my mom, too. I guess I wouldn't mind if he told me that he loves me more, or, like, how good a mom I am." She paused, thinking. "Or that he appreciates me. That's not really who he is, though. He says it's obvious that he feels all those things, why does he need to tell me all the time?" Rachel was surprised to find herself tearing up.

Mindy asked her if she talked to her husband about how she felt, and Rachel admitted she hadn't.

Mindy said that it sounded like Rachel felt she needed to be in control all the time. That she saw herself as the only one capable of handling things. But pairing that with a new baby and a very stressful job was not sustainable, and she needed to learn to lean on her husband. Even if the way he did things wasn't good enough in her eyes. And there was nothing wrong with asking him for more verbal assurances, either, she added. Many people like to hear they are loved and appreciated. Rachel promised to try.

After a few days, Rachel's hands completely returned to normal. With the extra time off work and the Lexapro, she felt mostly like herself. Weekly sessions with Mindy also helped, and after a month of seeing her, Mindy suggested that Rachel bring Dan in for a session or two so she could help facilitate a discussion about some of their challenges.

Dan was resistant at first. But Rachel pushed, and eventually he said yes.

So a few weeks later, she and Dan sat together on her therapist's gray sofa.

"Dan, it's so nice to meet you," Mindy said.

Dan looked so uncomfortable. He had never been to therapy before, either, and while he was entirely sympathetic to the stress his wife was under, he didn't know what it had to do with him.

"Well, I just want to help Rachel," he said.

Mindy explained to Dan that this was a space for them both to talk about their feelings, without judgment. She asked Rachel to start off by filling in Dan about some of the things the two of them had been talking about in therapy.

"I love you, obviously," Rachel started, tearing up a little. "But I think with the new baby and now being back at work, I need a little more help around the house. It just seems that everything falls on me."

Dan looked at his wife. "Sometimes I think that maybe you say you want me to do more around the house, but when I try to help, you criticize me or redo whatever I've done. I guess it seems easier sometimes to let you handle it," Dan responded.

Mindy nodded, encouraging him to continue.

"Also, it's not like I don't play with Max," Dan continued. "I spend all weekend with him, taking him to the park and birthday parties while you're with the baby. I wish I could help more with Emma, but I can't exactly breastfeed."

Mindy asked Rachel what she thought about that.

"He's not wrong, I guess. I do think sometimes it's easier for me to manage it all on my own. But I don't think he does anything to try."

Dan disagreed. "You're always angry at me, though. Even when I do try to help. Nothing feels fun anymore."

Mindy asked them to explore that.

"He's like a big kid. He doesn't take on any adult responsibilities, he watches football all weekend and always wants to go out with friends."

"I work hard during the week. I want to be able to enjoy my weekends. But it's not like I'm dumping you with the kids," Dan said.

But Rachel often felt like she was being dumped with the kids. "That's not exactly true. It's like I just exist to take care of your children. I think if you told me you appreciated me once in a while, I'd feel better about things."

"We're adults, Rach. You don't get a trophy for taking care of your family. This is her problem. She works so hard. Too hard. Plus, she's spent her entire life being told how great she is by her parents. I can't compete with that."

Rachel was crying in earnest now. "That's really mean."

"You know I love you," Dan said, trying to soften his comment. "And I think you're a great mother. It just seems sometimes that your expectations of me are out of whack with reality."

Mindy took the couple in. "I think over the next few weeks, Rachel, you should try to let Dan help more around the house. If he does things a little bit less well than you, you have to find a way to let go."

Rachel nodded her agreement.

"Dan, you seem to want to help. Pick a couple of things each day that you know Rachel manages, like making lunch for Max, or throwing in a load of laundry. Don't worry about her being unhappy with how you do it, because she just promised both of us she won't complain."

Dan smiled tightly at Mindy and agreed.

"Dan, it also might go a long way to give Rachel the verbal reassurances she's looking for. This doesn't come easy to everyone, and it won't change overnight. But at least make an effort. And, Rachel, you have to be patient with Dan."

And they really did try. Within a few more weeks, Rachel felt much more relaxed. She was back at the office, but working from home on Fridays, and pushing assignments down to junior associates when she could. Dan came back again with her to see Mindy one more time, and Mindy commented that she was pleased to see that the couple was more physically engaged with each other. Dan still didn't text or call Rachel often during the day, but he was making a much greater effort to thank her and recognize her efforts when he remembered to. Rachel wasn't able to relinquish the majority of household tasks, but she came up with little chores for Dan to do and was always grateful to him when he complied.

They seemed back on track, and by Emma's first birthday, Rachel was generally happy with the way her life was going.

19

Present Day

THE NEXT MORNING, RACHEL SLEPT IN, ALLOWING THE KIDS unfettered use of their iPads, then rushed the family through breakfast to make it to Max's soccer game. Dan seemed hungover from his night out with Josh, and Rachel absentmindedly placed a cup of coffee in front of him. He smiled at her gratefully and she looked away, remembering what an asshole he had been to her when he'd gotten home the night before.

"Daddy, where were you last night? I made a butterfly in school yesterday and I wrote my name really big, and then Julia wrote her name on it too because it's our best friend butterfly!"

"That's so great, sweetie, I can't wait to see it!" he replied, grabbing her to him for a giant kiss.

"Mom, don't forget, after the game you promised we could get the stuff for the science project and then we're going to work on it, right? Will you help, too, Daddy?"

Rachel took note of his use of the word *Daddy*, which he'd given up using at seven. Prematurely, they had thought.

"Sure, bud," Dan said, "but first let's go win our game!"

When they got to the field, Coach and son walked off to greet the other players who had arrived early, and Dan started a practice drill to warm up the boys. Rachel and Emma walked to the other side of the field to set up. Rachel opened her chair and laid out an old picnic blanket for Emma, on which Emma immediately plopped. Rachel tossed a bag of LOL dolls, coloring books, and markers onto the blanket. Then she settled into her chair and was immediately overcome with anxiety about seeing some of the other moms. She took a sip of water and tried to steady herself. Just act like nothing's wrong, she said to herself repeatedly.

Rachel was happily distracted when Becca's daughter, Julia, bounded over to join Emma on her blanket and Becca placed her ten-month-old son, Asher, next to them. As was typical for the Millers and Darners, Matt and Dan were coaching their sons together.

"I swear, I feel like I've already had an entire day and it's only ten," Becca said, as she collapsed into the beach chair she lugged around to watch her kids' games.

"I told you not to go for the third!" Rachel said with a laugh.

Becca pretended to give her a dirty look.

"Hey, girls, be careful with the small toys around the baby."

"We will, Aunt Becca." Emma loved babies, often begging for her own little sister or brother, and was happy to play babysitter for a bit. She distracted the baby by making silly faces.

"Okay, we have maybe three minutes before everyone else gets here. How are you feeling today?" Becca asked.

"I don't know." Rachel threw her hands in the air. She legitimately didn't know what to feel anymore.

"I'm so sorry, Rach."

Rachel smiled at her gratefully, but clammed up as soon as she noticed Amy and her sidekick, Heather, walk over to set up their chairs a few feet away. Seeing Amy more than once in a week was more than Rachel could handle.

Fortunately, the women were far enough away and appeared to be deep in conversation about the school's upcoming spring carnival. Rachel tried to focus on the field as the game began.

The boys leapt into action. For fifth-grade soccer, Rachel was always amazed at how fast-moving it could be. She leaned forward in her seat as Becca's son, Jordan, dribbled the ball up the field, holding her breath as he passed it to Max. Max put the pressure on the defenders from the other team and moved closer to the goal. He passed to another boy on the team, who made a giant kick. The ball was knocked out of play by the opposing team and Rachel exhaled, disappointed as she clapped for the play.

"Becca," Amy called, "can you come chat with us? We really need your opinion."

Becca looked at Rachel and raised her eyebrows. True, Becca was far more involved in the PTA, but this felt like a very pointed exclusion. Rachel shrugged. She couldn't muster up the energy to care about the carnival, anyway. She had signed up to man a session of Emma's class's booth, a donut-eating thing, and felt satisfied with her contribution to the event. Becca got up and grabbed the baby, then walked over to the other women.

Rachel heard them ask her if she liked the idea of getting a couple of food trucks for the carnival and then tuned them out. The boys had moved the ball down the field toward their own goal, and she noticed Dan shouting at one of the players to knock it out. She couldn't imagine being the goalie's mom, too much pressure. Rachel checked her phone and saw she had a text from Jack.

> JACK: Hey, there. So much for a quiet dinner between old friends.

> RACHEL: Lol

> JACK: Sorry about that. Hope it's not too bad for you.

> RACHEL: I'm currently dealing with the PTA brigade, but I'll be fine.

JACK: Offer them a signed topless photo of me.
Use that clout, girl.

RACHEL: I'm definitely not mentioning you being
topless to these vultures.

JACK: Is it bad to say that I'd love to see you again?

RACHEL: Only if you tell me to wear my *Varsity
Blues* costume. Gotta go watch my son's soccer
game. XO.

Where did the "XO" come from? she thought. Ugh. Rachel
flung her phone into her bag, forcing her attention back to
the game.

A few minutes later, Becca's son had the ball again and was
charging up the field. Max ran alongside Jordan. Fully immersed
now, Rachel jumped out of her chair as the boys bypassed the
other team, inching closer to the goal. Jordan darted around the
last defender and passed the ball to Max. With one giant kick,
Max scored. Rachel shrieked excitedly and jumped up and down.

"Wow, what a play!" Becca said, walking back and settling into
her seat. "Did you see Dan and Matt jumping on each other? This
is like their childhood fantasy come true."

"I know, I'm a little worried about them coaching the girls'
T-ball. They're going to scare all of the other second graders." She
looked over at Becca and said quietly, "So what did the Queen Bee
and her little lackey have to say?"

"What do you think? They're obsessed with you and Jack,"
Becca said, rolling her eyes and bouncing Asher on her lap. "They
want to know everything. Who sold the pictures, if you and Jack
hooked up the other night, how big his dick is."

"They didn't ask you that!"

"No. But they're wondering," Becca said with a chuckle.

"So what did you tell them?" Rachel asked.

"About Jack's dick?" Becca said.

"Mommy, I'm hungry," Emma said, quietly coming up behind her and poking Rachel's shoulder. Becca covered her mouth in mock horror. Rachel opened up her bag and handed her daughter a pack of goldfish and then grabbed a second one for Julia, tossing it to her. Emma returned to the blanket with her back to the game and chatted away with Julia as they snacked.

"Sorry about that. I wanted to tell them to fuck off, but that didn't feel productive. I said I wasn't going to talk about it, and that they could ask you themselves."

"I seriously couldn't function without you."

"I know you'd do the same for me." She reached over and grabbed Rachel's hand and gave it a quick squeeze.

Rachel sat there, looking over at the women, who were pretending to be looking at the field but she knew they didn't care at all about the soccer game.

"People's lives are so boring they can't help themselves. And they're all just jealous. I'm jealous and I knew Jack before he had a sick body," Becca said, trying to lighten the moment.

Rachel laughed. "He was already hot when we were eighteen, don't take that away from me."

"F them, Rach. This will go away soon. Focus on your family," Becca said.

Rachel nodded her agreement. People were going to talk about her regardless and she would just have to accept it. It was only meaningless gossip, and it would die down. It had to. For the rest of the game, Rachel and Becca and their daughters made up a mini cheering squad, and they all jumped up and down together as they watched Max score his second goal to end the game three to one.

Leaving the field, Emma ran ahead and jumped into Dan's arms. Rachel found Max and grabbed him for a hug. "Amazing playing, buddy. That second goal was incredible!"

Rachel and Max walked over to join the rest of their family, and Rachel could feel people's eyes on her as she congratulated her husband and Matt. They all migrated out to the parking lot as a group, to make way for the next set of players. She smiled at Dan, attempting normalcy, knowing she was being observed.

"Wow!" Rachel said. "They killed it."

"I can't believe he scored twice!" Dan's face was lit up with pride.

Rachel couldn't help but share his enthusiasm. "I know," she said, her voice filled with excitement. "It was insane. So I'm thinking we grab lunch and then stop at the hardware store for the science project. Sound okay?"

Dan seemed relieved that his wife was acting normally, and he threw his arm around her as they walked. Rachel restrained herself from wriggling out from under him. She was not going to give these women any more ammunition.

20

THERE WAS A NEWS VAN PARKED IN FRONT OF THEIR HOUSE when they got home. Rachel's heart immediately started racing and she told the kids to go right into the house. As she made her way toward her front door, she heard her name being called.

"Ms. Miller, just a few questions," a reporter shouted out at her, followed by a cameraman.

"You need to leave," Rachel said emphatically.

"Are you and Jack getting back together?" the reporter asked from the base of the driveway as Rachel stood outside her door. Dan stepped in front of her, protectively. "My wife is not answering questions. Our children are here," he said angrily. "Come inside, Rach," he said, shutting the door behind him.

"Dan, this is ridiculous. It's all such a mess." Rachel started to cry once they were inside. Of course the press was interested in her and Jack. Why was she such an idiot for going to see him? she silently berated herself. Dan told her to go up to their room to relax, and he would deal with the kids.

Rachel walked into their bedroom and lay across the bed. She felt so cloudy. About Dan. About Jack. Dan hadn't always delivered on all her needs, but he had never before breached her trust. She knew she should be focusing on him, and his possible gambling problem that someone—her?—needed to fix. But she didn't want to fix him anymore. And if he didn't have a real problem, as she suspected, but was just so dissatisfied with his life that he needed to distract himself by playing excessive online poker, well, what did that say about them?

Her dinner with Jack was the first time she'd felt seen in years. The way he hung on her every word, wanting to know about her career, her life, and reminisce about their shared history. Even the way he texted her earlier during the game, just to check in. Every time she closed her eyes she found herself picturing his face. What was she doing?

Rachel eventually passed out from the emotional exhaustion. After two hours, she got up to take a shower and clear her mind. Dan came into the room as she was drying off, and Rachel sat down next to him on the bed in her robe. "We got a ton of the science project done. Kids are watching TV."

"The science project! I promised Max I'd help him."

"Hey, don't worry. I got it covered. Is pizza good for tonight?"

"Whatever you guys want."

"I'm so sorry, Rachel. I know this has gotten out of control."

Rachel started crying again and Dan began rubbing her back. She forgot herself and leaned into him. Rachel realized how much tension she had been holding in since this whole thing began and let it all fall out. She cried until she hiccupped, and he sat beside her, continuing to rub her back and occasionally wiping her face with his white T-shirt. As her breath returned to normal, Dan kissed her temple.

"Sorry," she said to him, finally feeling calm again. "I guess I needed that."

"Oh, Rach, how can I make this up to you?"

"I don't know," she whispered. "I don't know if I can move past it." It was the first time she had acknowledged that out loud to him.

"I know I messed up." His voice broke.

"I know this is hard on you, too. I just need time to figure everything out."

"I'm so incredibly sorry. I need you to believe me."

"I know. I really do, and I appreciate that. I just wish I didn't feel so betrayed." She was overwhelmed by the attention and confused by her renewed connection with Jack, but Dan's actions had left her bereft.

"I'm not excusing what I did, but I feel like I've never been able to meet your expectations."

"What?" Her emotions quickly ping-ponged from loss to anger. She was perfectionist Rachel again in his eyes, putting too much pressure on her husband.

"Not making partner, not doing enough for the kids, not worshiping the ground you walk on. I clearly can't compete with your movie star ex-boyfriend. Or, honestly, your parents."

"Why do you always come back to this? I have never once said you aren't enough for me."

"How do you think I feel that everyone's asking if my wife is running off with a movie star?"

He couldn't be serious. She stood up and looked down at him, feeling some of the power that height gives. "You tell them that you sent me running into his arms. How about that? Everyone thinks I was the one who sold the Jack stuff. Do you know how embarrassing that is for me?"

"Rach, I'm sorry. Forget I brought it up. Just sit with me," Dan said. "We need to figure this out."

"Things with us have been incredibly shitty lately, and you basically made it a hundred times worse." There was no use pretending—she didn't know if she would forgive him, but she knew she wasn't happy.

"What are you talking about?"

"Seriously? I thought you were bingeing bad television at night, not gambling our savings away. And the way you always look at me, like I'm your annoying mommy trying to get you to be an adult."

He sat there, unable to speak.

"Forget it," she said. "Let's just order dinner. I'll be okay." What could they possibly accomplish with the kids downstairs?

He shook his head at her sadly and walked out of their bedroom. She heard him call down to the kids, asking them what they wanted from Sal's Pizza. Rachel stood in front of her bathroom mirror and stared at herself for a moment. How did we get here? she wondered to herself. She put on an old pair of Cornell sweatpants and a T-shirt, not bothering to put on a bra, and threw her hair into a messy high bun.

She waited until she heard the pizza delivery man ring the doorbell to go downstairs and was surprised to see that Dan had set the table and opened a bottle of wine for them. She poured herself a large glass, then poured one for Dan, too.

"Hey, Max, how's the science project going?"

Max launched into his plans. "It's going to be so cool!"

Rachel smiled at him. "That does sound cool, bud. I'm sorry I couldn't help, but glad you and Dad made some headway."

"Mommy, I opened up a hair salon while you were resting. Wait until you see my Barbies!" Emma said eagerly.

Rachel laughed at her adorable little doppelganger. "I hope I'm not going to find a mess in the basement, my love."

"Daddy helped me clean it up already. Don't worry."

Rachel looked at Dan again. "That's great, sweetie. You can show me your Barbies after we eat."

"We need to do roses and thorns!" Emma exclaimed. They had a tradition every weekend of saying all of the good things that happened to them that week, and all of the bad. Rachel squirmed.

Emma went first, as usual, and told them how her teacher made her the line leader and also that Grammy promised her a new LOL doll the next time she went over to her house. Her thorn was that her brother pinched her earlier. Dan gave Max a stern look and told him it was his turn. Max said he was excited about winning the soccer game.

"I guess my thorn is that some of the guys were kind of mean to me this week."

"What do you mean, Max?" Rachel asked him, concerned.

"It's what I told you about, Mom, like you and that movie star? They just keep bringing it up to me and asking me if I'm getting a new dad." He started to sniffle, and Rachel could see his eyes tearing up. Her heart broke. After meeting Jack in public, she was nearly as responsible.

Emma looked up at her parents quizzically. "We're getting a new daddy?"

Dan laughed. "Guys, no. Don't worry, Em. Max, you can tell those boys they need to get their facts straight."

"But what about those reporters coming over here?" Max asked.

"Hey, sweetie, this is all a mistake. I told you, Jack is an old friend, and I think people just like gossiping, especially about celebrities," Rachel said, trying to reassure him, wondering how much he was picking up on the iciness between his parents.

Max still looked concerned but seemed to accept their answer for the time being. Emma resumed pulling the cheese off her pizza. Rachel would have to do a better job of pretending, she knew.

Fortunately, neither kid remembered that their parents hadn't done their roses and thorns.

As they finished up dinner, Dan grabbed the plates from the table before Rachel could get up and he asked if anyone wanted ice cream.

The kids jumped up to go pick out their selection from the freezer, as Rachel sipped her wine, watching them. She noticed Dan put his hand on Max's shoulder, pulling him in for a quick squeeze. He was a good father. As Rachel observed her family, she wondered how different her life might have turned out if she'd ended up with Jack.

21

2013

RACHEL WAS BACK AT WORK AFTER HER MATERNITY LEAVE ENDED and was desperate for a girls' night out. She asked Alex and her girlfriend, Tara, to meet her for dinner. She happily passed the childcare duties off to her husband. When she walked into the restaurant, she made a beeline for her friends and threw her bag down on the table, collapsing into the seat across from Alex.

"Oh my god, guys, I'm completely exhausted. Max has been waking up almost every night this week," Rachel complained about her six-month-old.

"I thought you did that whole cry-it-out thing," Alex said, turning to Tara, who like her had no experience taking care of a newborn. "Apparently, you leave your baby in a room to cry and then they eventually never cry again."

"That's not exactly it, Al." She paused. "Well, yeah," she admitted sheepishly, "we sort of did that. But the pediatrician told me to! Anyway, I think he's having a regression."

"That sounds awful," Tara said, perhaps less sympathetic than she was grateful that she enjoyed uninterrupted sleep. Alex had met Tara at Henrietta Hudson one night through mutual friends. She was skinny and flat chested, with a Joan Jett haircut, and clearly way too cool for a baby.

"We are going to get you so plastered tonight that Max won't be able to wake you even if he tried." Alex was compassionate as always.

The women quickly ordered cocktails and once Rachel had her first sip of vodka she felt more relaxed. "Sorry, I'm just having a tough week. Being at work is just a whole other level with a baby. But I'm fine. Ignore me. Tell me about you guys!"

"Did Alex tell you her news yet?" Tara asked, happy to change the subject.

"No! She's too nice to me and lets me drone on and on about my baby," Rachel said.

"Obviously that is not true, Rach," Alex said, grabbing her friend's hand. "I happen to be madly in love with that baby. And I know how hard it can be, working and taking care of him. It's a lot!"

Alex was so good to her. Rachel deflected and apologized again for being so self-involved.

"Please. I'm used to it," Alex said, teasing her old friend, who had steadfastly seen Alex through her own strife over the years. "I do have some news. I got a job as a staff writer on a television show!"

"Oh my god, Alex! That's incredible!" Alex had been trying to meaningfully break into the entertainment business since they'd graduated college ten years ago, and Rachel had been nearly as eager for her to land something.

"But it's for *Plus Size*."

Just hearing the name of Jack's show made Rachel's stomach flutter.

"I know it's a little strange that I'll be working with Jack. Are you horrified?"

"What, no! This is huge. I just didn't realize you guys were still in touch."

"We aren't. I don't think I'd spoken to him since around the time you got married. But I had this idea for the show, so I reached out."

Tara chimed in. "She's been writing for a while, and you guys were all so close, why wouldn't he want to help her out?"

"In other words, Tara made me call him," Alex said, smiling. "He was so nice about it, he invited me right away to meet him at the set." Alex filled Rachel in, trying to get her excited about it. "I have to say, he's way better looking than when we were kids. Like, ridiculously gorgeous," Alex added.

"Wait, do you think he had work done?" Rachel asked.

"No way," Tara interjected. "Men always look better as they age. It must be so weird for you that Jack is huge now."

"Honestly, my life is too crazy to think about anything, although yes, it is sometimes bizarre that I can't go to the grocery store without staring at his face when I'm checking out," Rachel replied. He was everywhere these days. *Plus Size* had taken off a few years ago and now everyone wanted to know who he was dating and what he ate for lunch. She felt herself picturing him; there was that photo last week of him walking in SoHo holding a Starbucks cup. He looked so good.

"Can you let me tell my story, people?" Alex exclaimed. Tara pretended to zip her lips. "After he toured me around the set, we were talking in his trailer, just catching up, and he asked me what I wanted for lunch. Literally within seven minutes this huge thing of sushi shows up for us. Like ten people could have eaten with us."

Rachel looked at her friend, desperate to hear the details of the glamorous lifestyle her ex-boyfriend lived.

"So, I told Jack that I had made the shift to writing full-time and asked if he would be willing to look at a spec script I had prepared for the show."

"And he loved it!" Tara said proudly.

"Hello, my news," Alex said with a chuckle. "But yup, he was really into it. Oh, and he told me some amazing Ben stories I need to tell you!"

"So, what happened?" Rachel asked her.

"I left my script with him, honestly not really knowing what he would do with it. I thought maybe he would get me an introduction to someone on his writing staff or an agent or something, which is really all I was hoping for. But he called me that night and said he loved what I wrote and asked me to come back the following week to meet with the executive producers."

"That's crazy!"

"Right?" Alex responded. "Anyway, I went back for the meeting with one of the producers and the head writer, and they told me they loved my script and wanted to buy it. And then they said they had a staff writing position open and asked if I was interested!"

"Are you serious? That's incredible!" Rachel said excitedly.

"I know. It's insane. So, of course I took the job. I'm a full-blown television writer! Finally!"

Rachel was visibly happy—and relieved—for Alex. It had been hard watching her struggle all these years. It was sort of weird that Alex and Jack were going to be back in each other's orbits, but she tried to push that thought out of her head.

"I am so proud of you. This is amazing news."

Rachel was dying to ask Alex if she came up during their meeting but didn't want to make this moment about her.

"He obviously asked about you." Alex had a knack for reading Rachel's mind. "I told him how great you're doing with your successful career and amazing husband and gorgeous little boy."

"I'm sure he was so interested in my exciting life. So tell me about the script!" As Alex shared the details, Rachel wondered if maybe now she'd have a chance to see Jack again.

22

May 2014

ALEX'S FIRST EPISODE AIRED DURING MAY SWEEPS EIGHT MONTHS later. It coincided with her thirty-third birthday, and so she threw a party to celebrate both milestones at her favorite bar in the East Village. Rachel asked her parents to watch Max at her apartment, which they were thrilled to do. Then she booked a room at the downtown Ritz, eager for a night away with her husband.

Rachel and Dan walked into the bar, and Dan made a beeline for Alex, grabbing her in the air and twirling her around. Alex and Dan adored each other, sharing a mutual love of teasing Rachel, among other things. Rachel rolled her eyes at them as Tara walked over to say hi.

"What did you think of the episode?" Tara asked her. "So good, right?"

"She killed it," Rachel responded, proudly. "Alex, get your hands off my husband and come say hi to your actual best friend."

"I thought we were all best friends, no? Hello, my love," Alex said, grabbing Rachel in for a hug. "Tell me what you thought."

"I already told you what I thought for an hour on the phone yesterday. You're incredible. The show was fantastic. I'm so proud of you," Rachel responded, pulling Alex in for another hug.

"Okay, okay. Go get a drink, and then I want you guys to meet my friends," Alex said, pointing them to the bar.

Dan whispered into Rachel's ear. "Open bar. You better watch out tonight, baby."

She lightly pinched his butt in response.

They got their drinks and Tara introduced them to some of their friends. Rachel recognized several of them from other parties and got into a conversation with a woman she knew through a few litigation matters.

Alex mentioned that she had invited friends from the show, including the actors, but told Rachel she didn't think Jack would come. He was filming a movie during the show's upcoming hiatus and had been preparing during most of his free time.

"What are you wearing to this thing?" Becca had asked her earlier that day. "What if he does show?"

"Can you not make me more nervous? Dan finally stopped obnoxiously referring to him as my boyfriend when he comes on our television screen."

"I'm just saying, you want to be prepared." Becca was disappointed that she and Matt couldn't make it. She and Alex had gotten close from all of them living in the city after college, but they had just moved out to Westchester and had their own one-year-old with whom they had to contend.

Rachel wore a Becca-approved outfit: a cute pair of skinny jeans that she had finally gotten back into after Max, with a basic tee and a leather jacket. Her hair was longer than it had been in years, and she had thrown a few waves in with a curling iron after straightening it. She had to admit she looked good, and even Dan, who rarely noticed these things, made a comment.

About an hour into the party, after she had already consumed two vodka sodas, she saw them walk in. Jack and Ben. Rachel felt the air around her still. She watched Alex walk over and throw her arms around both of their shoulders, but she herself was unable to move. Dan looked at her, and seeing her freeze he turned around, laying his eyes on Jack for the first time.

She ran her fingers through her hair as he walked toward her.

"Jack, Ben, wow!" Rachel said, reaching up to hug each of them and masking her nerves. "It's crazy to see you."

Dan stood there awkwardly, looking at Rachel. "Oh, I'm sorry, this is my husband, Dan Miller. Dan, Jack Bellow and Ben Danforth."

Dan shook Ben's, and then Jack's, hand.

"So what's it been, fifteen years?" Ben asked Rachel, looking between her and Jack.

"Something like that. How're you doing, Ben?"

"You know me, living the dream." Rachel laughed. He hadn't changed.

"It's great to see you, Rach," Jack said.

"You, too. It's been so exciting watching you. Congratulations on the show and everything." She felt like she was seeing a ghost. Was she acting normally? Her heart was beating erratically.

"Yeah, man. Alex's episode was great," Dan threw in. Complimenting Jack on his own success was a step too far for him.

Rachel was in a haze and had forgotten her husband was next to her. She glanced at him, and gave him a look he interpreted to mean that he didn't quite belong at this reunion. He went to grab another drink for himself, and Rachel barely acknowledged him as he walked away.

"Rachel Stone. I wasn't sure I'd see you here. You look exactly the same." Jack had to lean in close to make himself heard over the loud din of the music.

"Please," she shouted back at him. "You look great. I guess that's part of your job description. It's surreal to be standing here with you." She inwardly groaned at how pathetic she sounded.

Jack laughed, making her feel better. "I get that a lot, actually."

Rachel smiled back at him. She heard Tara and Alex pointing out their single straight friends to Ben, and was glad she could focus on Jack.

He led her to a nearby table with two barstools, so they could hear each other better without shouting.

"How have you been?" she asked once they sat down, leaning close to him.

"I can't believe I'm in the same room as you."

"I'm the one staring at a movie star." She slapped his arm teasingly. How was he still so familiar to her?

"Tell me about the last, oh, decade of your life."

Rachel laughed. "Let's see. I'm a lawyer. I have a one-year-old son. We're considering moving to Westchester. Real exciting stuff."

"It is exciting. I'm not surprised that you became a lawyer. You were always so smart. Though I can't believe you have a kid."

"Really?" Almost all her friends had kids these days.

"Maybe it's because you're still, like, eighteen in my mind." Jack gave her a look, one for which he was becoming famous, and Rachel felt it run through her. She suddenly noticed how close they were sitting, her legs now wedged between his. Ben and Alex walked over with a glass of wine for her. Rachel accepted the glass and was both relieved and disappointed to no longer be alone with Jack.

"Just like old times, guys!" Alex said, clinking glasses with each of them.

"To Alex," they collectively toasted.

"Guess who I saw the other day," Ben said, after they each took a sip of their drinks. "Remember that kid, Noah, from drama? I was at a work conference last week and he came right up to me. He works at J.P. Morgan and apparently has a ridiculously hot girlfriend."

"Noah Rittenhouse? I always felt so bad for him. That skin. And he had the biggest crush on Rach," Alex said.

"He did not have a crush on me. What are you talking about?"

Jack started laughing. "You don't remember him following you around? He hated me with a passion because of you." Rachel had zero recollection of this.

"Wait, where's Dan?" Rachel asked Alex, suddenly realizing she hadn't seen him in at least fifteen minutes.

Alex glanced around the bar and shrugged. "I don't know."

"Be right back." Rachel pulled away from Jack and spun off the stool, heading toward the bar. She didn't see Dan anywhere. Maybe he went outside? She smiled at the bouncer and ducked out. There were a few people standing outside smoking, but no Dan. She looked down at her phone. Nothing. She called him.

"Where are you?" she said when he answered.

"On my way back to the hotel."

"What are you talking about?"

"You seemed to be quite cozy with your old friend, I didn't really think you needed me there."

"I'm sorry, you just left? Without saying anything?"

"Rachel, go have fun. Clearly you want to spend time with him. I'm not going to stand in your way."

"I literally don't know what to say to you right now."

"So don't say anything." He hung up the phone.

Is he serious? she wondered. Was there something wrong with catching up with an old friend? She wouldn't admit that Dan wasn't entirely off base.

She walked back into the bar and was stopped by Tara.

"Rach!" she exclaimed, drunkenly. "Come take a shot with us!" Tara had gathered Ben and Alex and a few of their friends up by the bar. Rachel noticed Jack didn't join.

Dan ditching her left her feeling reckless. She knocked back a lemon drop shot and Tara handed her another vodka soda. Then she walked back to Jack.

"I'm here," she said, a little woozy, as she climbed onto the stool and let her legs graze his. "Remember when we went to the Hamptons before senior year?" She kept her eyes on him, wanting to see his reaction. "My mom found the letter you wrote me after that weekend. Remember? She gave me this whole sex talk. It was horrible." She paused. "I knew you'd be mortified back then if I'd told you. I don't know why I'm telling you now."

Jack fortunately wasn't as embarrassed hearing this now as he might have been at seventeen, and thought it was hysterical. "I can just imagine her psychoanalyzing the whole thing. *All those feelings you must be having, Rachel*," he said in a fairly decent approximation of her mother. She was surprised he still remembered Elaine so well.

They continued to reminisce about high school. Rachel felt herself leaning close to him, unable to stop herself from the magnet that was Jack. They stayed like that, talking and drinking for hours, and Rachel momentarily forgot her real life.

"I know I'm, like, twelve years too late, but I owe you an apology," he said sincerely. "I didn't mean to disappear on you."

Rachel cut him off. She was no longer harboring any anger. She moved a smidge closer; she had an overwhelming urge to kiss him. "Let's talk about the good stuff."

Eventually Alex intervened, telling them it was time to end the party. Jack led her outside and helped her get a cab. She grabbed on to him, reaching up to kiss his cheek and getting the corner of his mouth. Or maybe she was aiming for his mouth, and he turned to give her his cheek. She couldn't think straight.

"Don't be such a stranger," she garbled, getting into the open taxi.

She dozed on the ride back to the hotel and finally stumbled inside, not realizing until she was outside the room that she didn't have a key.

"Dan," she sang out, banging on the door. "Wake up, Dan."

Her husband opened the door in his underwear, hair mussed from sleep.

"Hi, baby," she trilled.

"Oh my god, Rachel. Get inside."

"Why are you so mad at me? We have big plans tonight, remember?" She reached for the elastic on his underwear and gave it a tug.

"Jesus," Dan said. "I'm going back to bed."

Rachel stared at him, confused, and wanting sex. "I don't understand, don't you want me?"

"You're drunk," he said, walking toward the bed. She followed after him.

"Come on, don't be a baby. Oh wait, we can make a baby!"

"I don't know what kind of messed-up foreplay for you seeing Jack Bellow was, but I'm zero percent interested."

"Fine! I don't care!" She kicked off her heels and stalked away, unsteadily, toward the bathroom.

Dan huffed at her and got back into bed.

Rachel noisily opened the door to the giant bathroom and stripped off her clothes. She stood in her underwear, washing her face angrily. Her thoughts were jumbled. Dan was being such an asshole. What did she even do to him? She grabbed her phone to text Alex to complain, but instead decided to text Jack.

Jack would have happily taken her home with him. She typed "I missed you" without thinking. She put down the phone and started brushing her teeth.

The phone remained silent in response. She stared at it, willing it to ping. Why wasn't he responding? She turned off the light to the bathroom and slid next to Dan in bed. She wished she had somewhere else to go, away from him. She listened to Dan, deeply breathing, not giving a shit about her.

Rachel tried closing her eyes. The room spun around her. She was never going to sleep. She would probably throw up. Finally, she heard the sound of a text come in and grabbed her phone to see what he said.

JACK: Me too. G'night, Rach.

She slammed the phone back down, mortified. Jack didn't give a shit about her, either.

23

Present Day

WHEN RACHEL GOT INTO THE OFFICE ON MONDAY MORNING, SHE had an e-mail from Jerry waiting for her, asking her to stop by his office that morning to discuss the "current situation." She checked her calendar and sent his assistant, Joan, a quick note asking if Jerry was free at ten. May as well get this over with, she thought.

Rachel walked down the hall to Jerry's office. There was Joan, sitting in her cubicle right outside his door. "Hi, sweetie. Jerry is expecting you. Go on in."

Joan was the nicest administrative assistant they had, and certainly the only one that could put up with the mercurial Jerry Rich. He was often found yelling at her about one thing or another, but she always laughed it off. The truth was, despite his unpredictable nature, Jerry adored her.

Rachel knocked on the half-open office door and walked in. Jerry told her to take a seat.

"Rachel, thanks for coming in. How are you doing?"

"I'm fine, Jerry."

"Good, good. As you know, I've always found you to be an excellent attorney. I'm also impressed with the way you've worked on your business development. Many women have difficulty balancing their work and other firm responsibilities, but you've really proven yourself. Especially lately, with the Carraway business."

Rachel let the misogynistic tone slide and thanked him.

"But"—and of course there was a *but*, Rachel thought—"I do have some concerns about your focus, with the recent publicity you've gotten," Jerry continued. "A couple of our clients were curious about it."

"Jerry, thanks for checking in, but I'm very focused on my work. This has nothing to do with the firm and it certainly isn't impacting my commitment to our clients."

"Well, that's good to hear. Even so, I'm going to be running point on the Carraway matters now."

"What?" she exclaimed. "Why? Carraway is my client. I brought them here. It's my relationship."

"Well, not exactly, Rachel. You were given a small local matter through your friend, but they never would have given us their national counsel work without my expertise. I spoke with Fred, and he agreed that it would be better for me to manage the relationship," Jerry said, referencing the CEO.

"What are you saying here, Jerry?"

"Well, you can still work on the file of course, and I'm allocating 10 percent of the origination to you, which is extremely generous. But I'll oversee all matters and manage the staffing."

Rachel was shocked. Carraway was supposed to be her ticket. "Jerry, I had hoped I would be up for equity partner this year, and I was banking on Carraway to get me there."

Jerry laughed. "Rachel, you're still quite young. We can revisit that next year."

"Jerry, with all due respect, I feel like I'm being punished for something I had nothing to do with. And I find it hard to believe that Carraway even cares about this. Gabe hasn't said anything to me."

"Rachel, this is done. Gabe isn't the one who decides, and neither are you. I'll be managing Carraway and I'll let you know what work is required."

Rachel stood up and walked out. She knew there was no further discussion to be had with Jerry. She thought back to their meeting with Carraway a couple of weeks earlier, when they persuaded the company to move its litigation work over to their firm. As the meeting had wrapped, she heard Jerry tell Fred that he had friends who belonged to his golf club. This really should not have surprised her. Yet she had done everything right.

Rachel went back to her office and stared blankly at her computer. A half hour later, Kaitlyn showed up at Rachel's office, breaking Rachel from her trance.

"How's it going?"

Rachel waved her into the office and Kaitlyn closed the door behind her. "Jerry just pulled my client from me."

"You're kidding, that big medical device company?"

"Yup." Saying it aloud made it even more real.

"You worked so hard on getting that business! That's total bullshit."

Rachel put her head in her hands. She felt like her entire life was falling to pieces. "Yeah, well. It's over."

"Listen, screw Jerry. You'll get this client back, or land a better one." Kaitlyn paused, weighing her next words. "I do think we need to get some control over this situation. Those pictures the other day weren't a great look."

Rachel groaned. "I know."

"Yesterday's news. But I talked to a couple of PR friends and I think you need to make some decisions here."

"Can't we just focus on making this go away?" Rachel asked her.

"Have you spoken to him again?"

"Jack? Just over text. He felt bad about meeting in public, I guess he thought no one would spot us," she answered.

"Right, because celebrities don't control everything that ends up in the paper."

Rachel looked at her quizzically.

"Never mind." Kaitlyn got up from her chair and pulled it around the desk so she could sit next to Rachel, setting her laptop between them.

"I pulled some stuff together over the weekend." Kaitlyn flashed through a couple of headlines, starting with the original article and then other pieces picked up by the media. Rachel looked at everything closely. There were several posts that she hadn't seen before, on websites she'd never even heard of. The crux of each story, Kaitlyn noted, was that Jack was madly in love with his high school sweetheart and that he was unable to commit to other women as a result.

"That's all sort of nice, no?"

"Yeah, for sure, but the last few days there has been an obvious shift. Safe to assume you haven't looked on Reddit?"

Rachel barely knew what Reddit was.

"Forget it. Did you see the article on PopSugar from this morning?"

Rachel said she'd gotten an alert but didn't have the stomach to look as Kaitlyn pulled it up on the screen.

Why Jack Bellow Is Giving His
High School Girlfriend Another Look

Here's What We Know:

Jack and Rachel dated when they both attended high school on Long Island. They met performing in the classic musical, *Grease*, playing, what else, but a Pink Lady and a T-Bird. They attended prom together, of course, and were even voted

"Cutest Couple" in their high school yearbook. Jack writes of his love for his teenage girlfriend in letters published exclusively by the *Daily Mail*. Even the couple losing their virginity to each other is documented in painstaking detail.

The sweethearts had every intention of being together forever, but according to sources, poor Rachel had her heart broken by Jack unexpectedly when they attended separate colleges. Fortunately, Rachel moved on, finding love again with her law school classmate, Dan Miller. The couple have two young children. Rachel is now a partner at the reputable law firm Silver and Frank.

Jack's romantic trajectory is slightly less traditional. After a speedy marriage to a former co-star, Fiona Drake, which ended disastrously, he's been linked to several models and actresses. We all thought his playboy ways had come to an end last year, when he made his first red carpet appearance with the stunning Cassandra Willis. Wedding bells and babies seemed to be in their future, but that's all been called into question by Jack's reunion with his high school sweetheart.

Here's What We Don't Know:

How is Cassandra Willis taking this resurfaced relationship, and how did she feel seeing those pictures of the former couple together outside famed New York City restaurant Carbone? Cassandra is currently on location filming the movie *Live and Let Live*, with none other than Jack and Rachel's old high school friend, up-and-coming director Alexandra Hirschfeld.

Is Rachel going to jump ship on her career and follow Jack to Hollywood? Did Rachel herself sell those old letters and photos to make a buck? Or was she looking to get Jack's attention? What does their old mutual friend Alexandra think of this? And will Cassandra show up to Jack's film premiere next week?

What's Next:
The rumor mill is in overdrive as we wait and see whether the old flames resume where they left off. We suppose only time will tell. But for now, we'll be on the lookout for more Jack and Rachel sightings.

"Obviously, it's more of the same," Kaitlyn said, as they finished reading. "But I've been thinking, if we do want to respond, it will help us tell a good story if we could explain how it got out there."

"No way. I'd rather people just speculate it's me."

"I totally get it. But maybe if you tell me how it got out I can help spin it?"

"Not happening." Rachel was too embarrassed to admit to anyone else that her own husband had sold her out.

"Here's the thing. I know you're a successful lawyer and mother, with no interest in blackmailing your ex-boyfriend or trying to steal him away from his actress girlfriend. The rest of the country doesn't. We need to find a way to tell your story."

"I'm honestly not sure I care about telling my story. I just want to be left alone," she said.

"Fine." Kaitlyn brought up a document on her laptop.

"You made a PowerPoint for me?" Rachel said, touched.

Kaitlyn smiled at her. The first slide had three separate columns under the title "Next Steps." Column three was, in fact, do nothing. "The way I figure it, you can let people think what they want, and hope that in a week or two this all goes away. Which it probably will, assuming it's not a terribly slow news cycle. I'm sure someone will get divorced in Hollywood this week."

"Well, I'm definitely not looking to capitalize on this, which I can see is column two."

"I just want you to know your options. If you want to, you can probably get a book deal out of this."

Rachel looked at her friend pointedly and Kaitlyn let it go. "Fine, the news cycle is fast and you'll eventually be forgotten. And it's not a scandal; right now all they have is that Jack once loved you and you had dinner recently and maybe you slept together. Whatever. But no one has any proof of that and if you are never seen together again, this will absolutely go away."

"Great. So we're done here," Rachel said.

"I'm just trying to prepare you for the shitstorm of publicity that will come your way if you're seen with him again."

"I know, I'm sorry." Rachel looked gratefully at Kaitlyn and squeezed her hand. "Thank you for helping me through all of this, seriously."

"I don't think you realize how famous this guy actually is."

Rachel knew exactly how famous Jack was, and for the last few years, she couldn't stand who he had become. But he seemed so different now.

"So say I do want to see him again," she finally relented. "What the hell am I supposed to do?"

24

Thanksgiving 2018

RACHEL USHERED MAX OUT OF THE CAB. THEY ENTERED THE lobby and were greeted by an austere man with an earpiece and a clipboard.

"Who are you here for?" he barked at her.

"Um, Jack Bellow?" She briefly wondered whether she was supposed to use a code name.

"And you are?"

"Rachel Miller." Would he have put down her married name? "Or Stone, maybe? Rachel Stone."

He gave her an annoyed look. "ID?"

She pulled out her wallet and handed him her license. He studied it and then handed it back to her after he found her name on his list. "Penthouse."

Rachel grabbed Max's hand and they walked toward the elevator. There was an older man in a maroon uniform inside and once they got in, he cranked the rotary. What would happen if he forgot to put in the floor? Would the elevator go up and up and up? She noticed Max staring at the man, and he tipped his hat at him. She squeezed her five-year-old's hand; this was as foreign to her as it was to him. The elevator opened and they stepped into a palatial hallway that led to one single apartment.

Rachel felt her heart beating rapidly as she pushed open the door, pulling her son along with her. A young woman greeted them, offering to take their coats. Rachel smiled tentatively, as she shrugged out of her puffy jacket and then helped her son do the same. The woman pointed them onward.

Rachel took in the high ceilings and artwork on the walls high-lighted by library-style lighting. She was surprised to see that Jack was a collector. All the paintings seemed to have a moody vibe, nothing like the bright, fun art and photograph prints that Rachel had chosen for her home. There were several clusters of people, and she didn't recognize anyone she knew among the guests.

She saw a woman holding a tray of mimosas and quickly grabbed one.

"You made it!"

All of a sudden, he was standing in front of her.

Jack leaned in to kiss her cheek, and Rachel felt herself grow flushed.

"I'm so glad you're here! You look great, Rach."

She felt a laugh escape her. This was far from true, particu-larly since she was still holding on to her Emma baby weight. She decided to ignore the platitude.

"Thank you so much for inviting us. This is my son, Max. Max, say hello to my friend Jack."

Jack glanced down at him and back at Rachel, shaking his head.

"What?" she asked.

"I still can't believe you have a kid. Aren't we kids?"

"I have two now, actually. I left my little one at home."

Rachel's mom had offered to babysit so Dan could come with her, but he wouldn't consider it. "Um, can we discuss this ridicu-lous apartment? I cannot believe you live here."

"I know." He perked up. "I had nothing to do with it. I have this incredible decorator who handles everything."

"I'd ask for her number, but I'm sure we couldn't afford her. Plus, we're still in the phase where nice things get markers and Play-Doh on them."

Jack laughed, as she chided herself for reminding him that she was a boring old mother. "You should see my house in LA, at least I spend time there."

"Look at you, two fancy houses, fancy decorator," she joked.

"I've come a long way from the wrong side of the tracks. My friends all wondered why I didn't get an apartment in Tribeca, but I love having a place overlooking the park. And my nieces insist I throw a big party for the Thanksgiving Day parade." He gestured around them, as if to emphasize the grandeur, and Rachel was a bit taken aback.

"Well, they must love it." Rachel couldn't think of what else to say to him. They lived in entirely different universes. She noticed the children lining up along the glass pane windows, waiting for the parade to start and see the giant balloons float by. She crouched down and pointed. "Hey, Max, want to go take a look?"

He shook his head and tugged on her hand.

"I guess that means I'm joining him." She was grateful that her son wouldn't go off on his own; she didn't want to attempt more small talk with Jack.

"Yeah, of course. There's lots of food, the bar is in the dining room. Find me later, I'll give you a tour or something."

He turned to greet someone passing by and Rachel was left off-kilter. Alex was insistent that she come today, that Jack wanted her to bring her family. That he mentioned it to her repeatedly the last time they had dinner and followed up with a text message. Alex had even screenshotted it, as proof for Rachel. "Great time, as usual. Bring Rachel and her kids to the parade. Love to Tara."

For three weeks, Rachel debated it. Alex didn't see why it was a big deal; they'd spend the morning in the city at Jack's, and then drive to Long Island together for their respective Thanksgiving dinners back home. Alex was eager to see Max and Emma. "This isn't a big deal. It's a ton of kids, Max will love it!"

"I know. It's just, last time I saw Jack, things got weird, remember? I don't entirely understand why he'd want me in his apartment."

"That was, what, four or five years ago? Why are you being like this? You're an old friend!" Alex hated when Rachel over-thought things.

Rachel turned to Becca for the reality check.

"Rach, I really think this is fine," she reassured her. "This is a get-together for kids. No one's getting sloppy."

So she agreed, but then Alex was called away for a reshoot on the film she had written, and Rachel still went, figuring it would be a once-in-a-lifetime experience for Max to see the floats up close. She left Dan at home with Emma. She wasn't bringing him to Jack's without her best friend there as a buffer. He didn't even seem to care that she was going. Finally, she thought with relief, he was over it.

Until last night. Friendsgiving. As they'd been doing for nearly a decade, Becca and Matt hosted a bunch of the guys' old friends for a potluck. Unfortunately, Greg was there because Matt always insisted on including him.

"Rachel," Greg called across the table as they were finishing up dinner, his arm thrown over the chair of his current twenty-four-year-old girlfriend. "Settle a bet. Brie here thinks Hollywood actors are all gay. But I told her that you know firsthand that isn't true. Can you please enlighten her?"

Rachel and Becca eyed each other. "Our friend Alex works in the business," Becca seamlessly responded. "She's given us lots of celebrity intel and I can assure you that isn't true."

"Ooh, like what?" Brie leaned toward her.

"Come on, Rach, just give her a little something," Greg goaded her.

"Dude. She doesn't need to talk about it," Dan said. Rachel was grateful, and a little bit surprised that he'd stand up to his friend. He never liked rocking the boat, even with an ass like Greg.

"Why do you care so much? She dated Jack Bellow in high school. She also fucked me in college."

"Jesus, Greg!" Dan stood up and Rachel jumped up, too, to make sure he didn't do anything stupid.

"I'm kidding, man, relax. Since when is this a big deal?"

"It's fine, babe," Rachel said, trying to break the tension.

Dan stood there for another beat, eyeing Greg, then her, icily. He wasn't really mad at Greg, Rachel suddenly realized. Her hooking up with Greg in college was something he teased her about; he wasn't jealous. This was about Jack. It always was with them. He couldn't stand the idea of her seeing him again, but was pretending he didn't care. She was so sick of it.

"Okay, then, ladies, want to help me clear?" Becca, ever the host, defused the tension. "Matt, why don't you all head into the living room? The kids' movie should be over in about a half hour."

The evening ended shortly after, and Dan barely spoke to her as they left their friends' house.

"Are you mad at me for some reason?" Rachel asked Dan on the car ride home, knowing full well the reason for his aloofness but forcing him to admit it.

"I just think it's crazy that you're going to his apartment." There. She knew it.

"I'm sorry, you knew about this for weeks and didn't say a thing."

"It was one thing if Alex was there." His voice softened slightly. "You know how I feel about this."

"I know you harbor some ridiculous resentment toward a guy I haven't been with since high school. Jack was just being nice by including us. Max will love it."

He was silent for a moment as he drove. She watched his face. She knew he was weighing whether he wanted to keep the disagreement going. His eyes were squinting a bit in the dark. She needed to book him an eye exam. She pulled out her phone to set a reminder.

"I seriously don't know what's wrong with Greg," he finally said, apparently ready to move on. "That's the last time we're hanging out with him."

"Hello! I've been saying that for years." Rachel was happy to shift the conversation. "And that girl? He gets older and keeps picking younger. What does anyone see in him?"

"He must have a huge cock. Oh, wait, does he?" He laughed to let her know he was kidding.

"Gross!" She grabbed his hand across the console. "Hey, if you really don't want us to go tomorrow, we don't have to. It's not that important." Dan shook his head no, and she was glad, because despite her jitters at seeing Jack again, she had been really looking forward to it.

"Mommy, look!" Max's voice exclaimed, bringing Rachel back to earth. She watched as Woody from *Toy Story* floated by Jack's apartment. She walked with her son closer to the windows and he inserted himself among the other children, all entranced by the passing balloons. They stood there for a while, admiring all the passing floats and balloons. Then she took him into the dining room to make him a plate of food.

"Rachel Stone?" Rachel looked up at the sound of her old name as she was scooping berries onto her son's plate.

"Megan!" Rachel set down Max's plate and gave Jack's sister a hug. "God, it's been forever!" She helped Max get settled at the table.

"I was so happy when Jack said you were coming today."

"Which ones are yours?" Rachel asked.

Meg proudly pointed out her young daughters and commented on how adorable Max was.

The two women caught up. "How ridiculous is my brother's life?" Megan said.

"Oh my god, I wasn't going to say anything. He told me he has two houses!"

"Three actually, he has a condo in Park City. Apparently, he skis now." She laughed, but her admiration was apparent.

"He's definitely come a long way."

Megan shook her head. "For sure, although I'm ready for him to settle down a bit. The kids want cousins. Too bad you're not available!"

Before she could joke that she was the last person Jack would be interested in these days, Max interrupted them. "Mommy, I have to go to the bathroom."

Megan smiled at Rachel knowingly and waved her on.

Rachel found a bathroom and sent Max in by himself, keeping with her current push toward independence. She leaned back against the wall and checked her phone.

"I'm glad you're here, man. I know hanging out with a bunch of children isn't exactly your thing." Rachel cringed as she heard Jack's voice.

"You're my best client. You invite me, I come," another man said.

"I appreciate it, man."

"Hey, who was that woman you were talking to? The one with the frizzy hair and big tits?" Rachel's heart stopped. Was he talking about her? She patted down her hair. She'd been rushing and hadn't had a chance to flat-iron it that morning.

Jack laughed. "That, my friend, is the woman I had once assumed I'd marry. We dated in high school."

"Whoa. That's random, no?"

"Nah. Our other friend was supposed to be here, too, but she bailed."

"She's pretty hot for her late thirties. Think she's down for a little reunion?"

"Well, she's married with two kids. I'm pretty sure that ship has sailed."

"You never know," the other man chuckled.

"You watch a woman wipe up her kid's snot and she sort of loses her appeal, no?"

Rachel couldn't make out what the other man said in response, but the next thing Jack said came through loud and clear. "I mean, I guess I'd still bang her."

The other man laughed loudly, and Rachel was mortified. Coming here was obviously a terrible idea. Max exited the bathroom and Rachel didn't even bother asking him if he'd washed his hands. She steered him toward the front of the apartment.

"Mommy? Aren't we going to see more balloons?"

"Oh, sweetie, we saw the good stuff, we have to get back to Emma and Daddy."

Rachel pulled their coats off the hanging rack, not waiting for the girl to help them. She felt such an urgency to escape and didn't care if she seemed frantic. Clearly her world was completely different from Jack's, and that was just fine with her.

25

Present Day

RACHEL WAS SITTING ON THE 8:40 TRAIN HEADING TO WORK when she felt a woman's eyes on her. She looked up, and the woman quickly looked away, but she saw her whispering to her seatmate moments later. Rachel resumed looking at her phone, but had a sensation of being stared at for the rest of the ride.

"Excuse me." The woman approached her as they stood to exit into Grand Central Station. "Are you that woman, the one who used to go out with Jack Bellow?"

Rachel was ill-prepared to be recognized by a stranger; managing the attention from friends was bad enough. She smiled weakly and shrugged, and made a beeline for the exit.

She decided to walk the fifteen blocks to her office, rather than take the subway. The weather was starting to turn for the better, and she needed air.

She got to work and grabbed coffee. Then she set about drafting an outline for a deposition she had the following week. She was finally able to focus again at work, and felt like she was playing catch-up from the haze of the past couple of weeks.

She perked up a few hours into her day when Jack texted her, as was becoming more and more common for him.

JACK: Hey, lady

RACHEL: Do you remember when Brenda hit on you?

She had been reminiscing about their senior year the night before as she'd tried to fall asleep.

JACK: Our acting teacher, Brenda?

RACHEL: Yes! She told you that you were a perfect Shoeless Joe, and kept stroking your arm?

JACK: Rachel, that never happened.

RACHEL: It certainly did happen. Alex and I kept trying to catch her in the act so we could report her.

She was chuckling to herself.

JACK: You're making this up. How's work?

RACHEL: Well, since I'm texting you and not working, it's great.

Since they'd started texting more regularly after they'd met up, she found herself telling him about the struggles she'd been having at work and the invasive dynamics of suburban living. It was funny, since she couldn't talk to Dan, and Alex was apparently unavailable; she was grateful to have an old friend to talk to. Even though he was at the center of her current problems.

She was still texting back and forth with Jack when the school called.

"Mrs. Miller, this is Dean Whittley from Max's school. I'm sorry to call you like this but your son was in a fight today. I need you to come get him."

Rachel was stunned. "A fight? With who?"

"We would prefer to discuss this when you come to get him."

"Well, is he okay? My husband and I both work in the city. I can have my nanny come get him right now and then Dan and I can set up a conference call with you?"

"He's not hurt, but I do think it's best that a parent come to retrieve him. He can wait in my office in the meantime."

Rachel agreed to pick her son up at school and dialed Dan's number.

"What's up? I'm about to head into a meeting."

"It's our son. Apparently he was in a fight at school. I have no details, but the dean wanted me to come get him," Rachel reported.

"Is Max okay? We can't just get on a conference call with the guy?"

"That's exactly what I asked. I think he would have told me if Max was hurt, but he refused to discuss the details. I guess I'll grab an Uber and head home now. I can move some stuff around. Do you want me to pick you up?"

Dan agreed and Rachel picked him up ten minutes later. They sat silently in the back seat as they both stared at their phones.

They finally pulled into their town's train station to get Dan's car. "I can't believe Max got into a fight. It's so unlike him."

"I know," Rachel said, worried. "I told you how upset he was the other night. He seemed to be doing better, but those boys must have kept teasing him about it."

"I can't believe he would get into a fight about it!" Dan sounded irate, and Rachel wasn't sure who he was angry at. She felt terrible for Max.

Dan pulled up to the elementary school and they exited the car and walked up several steps to the main entrance. The security guard buzzed them in and collected their licenses. They were pointed in the direction of the administrators' office, and, after telling the secretary who they were, they sat down and waited.

"I feel like I'm back in junior high," Dan said quietly to Rachel.

"This is legitimately the first time I've ever sat in a principal's office!" she replied with a short laugh. "I'm starting to get nervous. They would have said if something was wrong, don't you think?"

Just then, Dean Whittley came out and waved them into his office. Max was sitting in a chair across from his desk, and it was obvious he had been crying. His face looked red and blotchy but there were no discernible injuries on his body.

"Max, baby," Rachel said, running over to hug him and stroking his hair.

"What happened, Max?" Dan asked, hanging back.

"Mr. and Mrs. Miller," said the dean, "thank you for coming in. I know it was difficult to get here from work, but we take violence very seriously and Max is in quite a bit of trouble."

Dean Whittley explained that Max was on the lunch line with several of his friends when he grabbed his tray and smashed one of his friends, Jonah, over the head. "Of course, I contacted Jonah's parents and they already took him to the doctor to get checked out."

"Oh my goodness, Max! Is Jonah okay?" Rachel asked.

"I think he'll be fine," Dean Whittley said. "He just seemed a little dazed."

"Max, what happened?" Rachel asked.

"I'm sorry," Max started, beginning to whimper and trying to catch his breath. "Jonah has been talking about you and a lot of the other guys said stuff, too, and I just got so mad. I think I snapped."

"We talked about this, Max. You aren't supposed to let the rumors bother you," Dan said.

"Dan, let's discuss that later." She turned to her son. "Baby, sometimes kids can be mean. We know that. But we need to stick with our words, right? Violence is never the answer. Dean Whittley, what's the protocol here? Max was clearly provoked."

The dean explained that any physicality among students resulted in an immediate three-day suspension. They also expected letters of apology. "If it happens again, the suspension is much longer, and after that we are talking about expulsion. Max, you're a good kid. I've never seen you in my office before and I don't expect to see you back after today. I agree with your mom that even when our friends really upset us, we should never resort to hitting. Can you promise me that this will never be an issue again?"

"I promise. I'm sorry, Dean Whittley. I'm sorry, Mom and Dad."

Dan and Rachel shook the dean's hand and agreed to discuss this further with Max at home. They left the building and got into Dan's car. Dan immediately turned back to Max. "What were those boys saying?"

"Basically, the same stuff, but it just got me so angry. They said Mom is dumping you for a movie star and moving to California. And Jonah said that you're a pussy because you couldn't keep her happy."

"What?" Dan exclaimed. "Jonah's dad ran off with the au pair!"

"Dan, Jesus! Max. Ignore what your father just said. And watch your language, please," Rachel said.

"Mom, there are, like, a million articles about you."

Dan and Rachel looked at each other. Clearly their son was more aware than they had given him credit for. "And you guys have been so weird lately and you don't tell me anything, so is it true? Are you leaving Dad?"

Rachel turned around to look at her son in the back seat. He wasn't a baby anymore. He was nearly as tall as her and was approaching puberty. He also had almost unfettered access to the internet, and Rachel underestimated how much he'd noticed the distance between her and Dan.

"Max, your dad and I both love you so much and we love our family. You're right that we're having a bit of a difficult time, but all relationships have ups and downs. As for the things you've read, well, this is all stuff that happened years and years ago, before I even knew your dad. But when someone is really famous, like Jack, they get a lot of attention. You really shouldn't be reading celebrity gossip, honey."

"But, Mom, there was a picture of you and him together from, like, the other day. I know it was now because you looked a lot younger back then."

Dan looked at his wife again. "Max, Mom went to have dinner with an old friend. They were just catching up. Things you read online aren't always true. In fact, they are usually not true when it comes to celebrities."

Rachel nodded, gratefully.

Dan pulled up to their house and into the driveway and put his car in park. "Max, the bigger issue here is that you lost your cool and instead of telling Jonah to stop, you physically hurt him. That's not acceptable. No iPad and no plans with friends for a week."

"But I have Sam's birthday party on Saturday!"

"Not happening, kiddo," Dan said.

Dan opened the door to the house and Max ran in, eager to escape his parents. "You better be working on that apology note, Max," Rachel called up the stairs after him.

Dan and Rachel walked into the kitchen. Dan sat in one of the stools, looking at his wife in disbelief. "Suspended, Rach? I can't believe he did this. And to Jonah!"

"I know. I better call Sarah," Rachel said, grabbing her phone from her bag.

"Wait. Don't you think we need to talk to each other first? I know I totally fucked things up. But clearly it's impacting the kids, and I think we need to start figuring out how to move past this. Don't you?"

Rachel stared at her husband, assessing him. "You know, I've been thinking about it a lot, and I can see how people get sucked into gambling. I'm not excusing it, I just want you to know I do kind of understand."

Dan looked up at her. This was the first time she was focusing on the problem, and not on the aftermath.

"I know you've been unhappy at work, and maybe if I'd encouraged you to find your passion . . . I don't know. You wouldn't have done this?" Dan wasn't wrong about her expectations. She was so used to everything coming so easily, and their success was supposed to be a foregone conclusion. She always brushed him off whenever he said he wanted to consider other careers. When was the last time she'd really listened to him?

"Rach, this is obviously on me. I'll go to therapy. I want to work on it."

"And you should. Absolutely."

"But what about us?"

"I don't know. This feels different than us just having trouble communicating." She felt her pulse speed up, trying to find the words to tell him what she was really thinking.

Dan looked at her, waiting, willing her to forgive him.

"I just don't see a way to move on from this," she admitted, as much to her husband as to herself. She felt an immediate sense of relief finally saying it out loud.

"Rachel, this is insane. You have to forgive me. How can you not even want to try to figure this out? Unless this is about Jack and the articles are true."

"Oh, come on," she said, angrily. "The moment you sold that stuff was the moment you decided you didn't care about us anymore. You know if you had come to me and said you messed up and lost this money, we could have figured it out. Together. But you didn't. You took me completely out of the equation. I just can't get past that."

"So what are you saying?" Dan asked. "You want to end our marriage because of one stupid thing I did?"

Rachel had spent the last few days wondering what she wanted. Did she want to end her marriage? Was it just three weeks ago that she'd been living her normal life?

"It's not just one stupid thing, Dan. It's a major thing, and we were already struggling. I'm trying to be honest with you." She paused, considering her next statement. "Maybe you can go stay with Josh for a bit."

"I don't want that, Rachel."

"I know, but I think I do," she said to him, sadly.

Dan put his head in his hands, taking in his wife's words. Letting himself absorb it. She wanted him to leave.

"What do we do about Max? He's going to think this is his fault," Dan said dejectedly.

"I think we should be honest with him. We're having a hard time; it has nothing to do with the ridiculous gossip he read. But that it's not acceptable for him to act out and he has to bear with us as we figure this out. And Emma will be fine. As long as she sees you, I think we can keep it very simple."

Dan pushed his seat back from the kitchen island and stood up. "Fine, if this is what you want, let's go talk to him." He was challenging her to stand by her words, but she wasn't backing down.

She headed upstairs with Dan right behind her. Rachel paused outside Max's door, building up her nerve, then knocked once and pushed open the door to his bedroom. They found him facedown on his bed. Max sat up when he heard them come in.

"You're getting a divorce, aren't you?"

Rachel sat down next to him and put her hand on his back. "Sweetie, things have been really tough for Dad and me lately. We just need to take a little time apart."

Max started to cry, and Rachel's eyes filled, too. She looked at Dan, hoping he would say something, but he was staring there, immobile, unable to speak.

"This is just so we can figure things out, okay? You'll still see Dad. He'll just stay at Uncle Josh's for a little bit. And he's going to come coach your game every weekend, just like normal."

Dan finally chimed in. "I'll come take you and Emma for dinner during the week, too. You'll get to see me a lot, buddy."

"Just go then. I don't want to talk anymore." Max turned away from them and refused to acknowledge his dad as he went to hug him. Rachel looked at Dan sadly and followed him out of the room.

Dan went to their room to pack a bag and Rachel gave him space. She tried to do some work, but she couldn't focus. She knew this was the right thing for them, but it all felt so strange and sudden.

She could hear him go into Max's room again and hoped Max was speaking to him about his feelings. He came down a little while later with his things and stood there, seemingly not sure how to address her.

"This is difficult for me, too," she said.

"Are you going to see him now? Is that what this is?" Dan's anger showed through; it was as if in the short while it had taken him to pack up he'd forgotten why this was happening.

"This is about you and me. You know that."

Dan looked at her sadly and then walked out the door. She watched him pull out of their driveway and shook her head in disbelief. There was nothing she could do right then, but she needed to figure out what she wanted.

Max came out of his room after a few hours and was acting normally, almost as if nothing had happened. Rachel knew she would have to talk to him about it, but was trying to give him time to digest. While Emma was curious where her dad was at dinner, she took the news that he was spending some time with their uncle in stride. After a quick ice cream dessert, and two Pinkalicious books, Rachel put Emma to bed. It was just her and Max.

"Do you want to call Dad to say good-night, sweetie?" she asked him.

He shook his head no. "It's okay, Mom. I'm really sorry about the thing with Jonah. Maybe I can text him?"

Rachel suggested she try Sarah first, who she had forgotten to call. After smoothing things over with her friend, who was particularly sympathetic having gone through her own scandal when her husband left her, they put their boys on the phone. Rachel heard Max apologize, but she also heard him accept his friend's apology, too. They decided to hang out the following weekend, when both were no longer grounded.

Rachel walked Max up to bed and asked if she could sit with him for a while. Tonight, Rachel needed her son about as much as he needed her.

"I'm sorry about all this, sweets. I know how confusing it is. I just want you to remember that none of this is your fault. Your dad and I have been unhappy for a little while, and we both have done some stuff lately that made each other angry. I think taking time apart is going to be a really good thing for us," she explained.

"But when Dad was leaving earlier, he promised me you aren't getting divorced, right?" he asked, earnest and hopeful.

Of course, Dan promised their ten-year-old something he had no right to promise. "Honey, I can't say for sure whether Dad and I are going to fix things. All I know is that right now, being apart is what's best for us, but we both love you and Emma more than anything in the world. And even if he and I can't work things out, we will do everything in our power to be there for you no matter what, any hour of the day. None of that changes."

"Don't you love Dad?" he asked her.

"Oh, Max, of course I do. He helped me make my two beautiful kiddos. But even though I love him doesn't mean we are meant to be married anymore. That's what we're trying to figure out."

"Okay. I think I get it. Do you mind lying here with me while I read?"

Rachel snuggled up close to her son as he read *Diary of a Wimpy Kid*. She was so exhausted that she drifted off and didn't notice as her son turned off the light. Max gave his mom a kiss and fell asleep beside her.

26

AFTER DAN LEFT TO STAY IN THE CITY, RACHEL FELT LIKE SHE could think about their marriage more freely. She was also happy to be back sleeping in her own bed. The kids were adjusting to the change. They had been FaceTiming with Dan each night after dinner. For the time being, he planned to come up one night a week to take them to dinner, and to be with them on the weekends.

Her first Sunday night apart from Dan, Rachel had her parents over for dinner. As her dad played Connect Four with Emma in the family room, she and her mom cleaned up and she filled her in.

"It just seems like he completely failed to consider the impact of what he did," Rachel lamented. "Maybe he didn't expect this to become as big of a story as it is, which is partially my fault for having dinner with Jack in public, I know that. But Dan is supposed to be the person I trust more than anyone else, and I feel like he stole from me." She looked at her mother, wishing she could fix this all for her.

"Honey, I think Dan got caught up in something and made a lot of bad choices."

"So I'm supposed to just move on?" Rachel asked, surprised her mother wasn't angrier.

"Let's talk with your father. I know he wants to be part of this discussion."

Rachel and her mom finished in the kitchen and then grabbed Mitch and went into the living room, so they could have space from the kids. Rachel's parents settled into her couch and she sat down across from them in a bright oversized floral chair she had taken from their house when they'd moved from Long Island a few years before.

"Okay, what do you guys want to say to me?" Rachel asked, bracing herself and knowing her parents would not hold back.

"You can't leave Dan," Rachel's seventy-three-year-old father burst out, tears immediately welling in his eyes.

"Oh, Dad."

She watched her father sniffling.

"I know you're aware of what he did to me, correct?" Rachel questioned him calmly.

Mitch looked at Elaine for encouragement. "We are, and we are very angry at him. We can't understand how he got himself into this mess. But, Rachel, he's your children's father."

Rachel's parents had done nothing but support and love her, albeit sometimes in a smothering and overwhelming way. She needed them to understand her now.

"Dan broke us. He spent the last year apparently resenting me for having a better job than him. Then he gambled away our hard-earned money. And instead of trying to come up with a solution together, he sold me out to the highest bidder," she said, tears beginning to fill her eyes also. "I know you love him, and I know you think our family needs to stay in one piece, but he did this to us, not me."

"Baby, we love you so much, and we know you will do what's best for your family. But we're worried that if you keep going in this direction there will be no coming back," Elaine said. "We don't want you to get so caught up in this fantasy of reuniting with Jack that you forget what you have right here."

Rachel stared at her parents dumbfounded. "I told you, Mom, I had one dinner with Jack. Are you so obsessed with gossip magazines that you believe what you read over your own daughter?"

"You don't need to have an attitude," her dad reprimanded her, jumping to her mother's defense and speaking to her as if she was a child. "You told Mom you've been talking to him. Jack is not a real option for you. What are you planning to do? Move to California? Ship the kids back and forth? Shouldn't you at least try and work on your marriage?"

"Mitch, she's an adult. I'm sure she's thinking about the impact of this on the kids," Rachel's mother said, clearly not believing that her daughter was considering her children at all.

"This conversation is not particularly helpful for me," Rachel finally interjected. "I appreciate your opinion of my marriage and my kids' mental health. But what's happening between me and Dan has nothing to do with Jack. And it has nothing to do with the two of you, either."

Rachel took a breath and looked at her parents, willing them to understand what she was going through. "Dan completely betrayed me. I can never trust him. Would you be saying this if he had cheated on me? How is this different?"

Rachel's parents were silent for a moment too long. Mitch looked over at Elaine, who nodded. "What?" Rachel asked.

"Honey, I am so embarrassed to admit this, but a long time ago, I had an affair. I will always regret it, and I'm so grateful that your mother forgave me. It took her a long time to get back to trusting me," Mitch offered.

Rachel was stunned. Her dad, her sweet and unassuming father, who never missed a performance or a tennis match, the nerdy accountant?

"Don't look so shocked, Rachel. People cheat all the time. I forgave your father. I had you to consider. I have always been so glad that I kept our family together," Elaine said.

"I'm not sure what to say. I'm sorry that happened, Mom, and, Dad, wow. I can't believe you did that to Mom," Rachel said. "God, when was this?"

"You were in middle school, it was a woman from work, and it was the biggest mistake of your dad's life. We just wanted you to know so you could see that we know what you're going through. And as painful a time as that was for me, it made our relationship even stronger. We think you need to give Dan an opportunity to fix this."

Rachel considered her parents. She was somewhat nauseated by their disclosure, as it evoked unpleasant images of her father.

"Mom, I get why you forgave Dad and I'm so grateful. But I don't feel like I need to get over this. And the kids are resilient. Whether I move to California with my movie star ex-boyfriend, or I make Dan officially move out of our house, the kids will be fine. Half their friends have parents who have split up." She finished her monologue, realizing as she said it that it was all true. She didn't need a man, and she certainly didn't need Dan after what he'd done to her.

Rachel's parents were clearly surprised by how adamant she was. "We know we can't tell you how to live your life. But we feel strongly that this is a mistake. Dan is a good man, and he loves you. The kids need him as their dad," Mitch said.

"The kids will always have him as their dad, guys."

"We just don't want you to do anything rash. You have too much at stake," Elaine chimed in, trying to soften her husband's words. "But of course we know you can take care of yourself. We're so proud of you for that."

"I love you guys. I understand how you feel. I am not going to do anything stupid. I just have a lot to think about. On my own."

"Just promise us you and Dan will go see a therapist. You need to at least talk through this. And maybe he needs some help of his own?"

"Yeah, I hear you." She stood up. "It's getting kind of late." Rachel was done analyzing this with her parents.

She really hoped they would give her space to figure things out. She called in Max and Emma to say goodbye to their grandparents and sent them upstairs to get ready for bed.

Rachel ushered Elaine and Mitch out of the house and caught a glimpse of herself in the mirror near her front door. She felt for the first time in a while that she looked old. The concern about her leaving her husband for a gorgeous movie star was crazy. Forget how she felt, the likelihood that Jack would actually be interested in dating her was ridiculous.

Before bed, she tried Alex again. "I know you're busy, and I probably don't even understand the extent of it, but I need you to call me. Dan and I are splitting up. He completely betrayed me and I am a total mess. I wish I could talk to you about all this. I just really need you. Can you please please call me?"

27

2009

RACHEL COULDN'T DECIDE BETWEEN BECCA AND ALEX, SO SHE appointed them as her co–maids of honor. Two months before her wedding, Rachel, Becca, Alex, Nicole, and a few of Rachel and Becca's college sorority sisters went to Miami for Rachel's bachelorette party. Rachel wanted an easy and relaxing weekend on the beach, which her friends accommodated, though Becca insisted they hit up at least one club while away.

The same weekend of the bachelorette party, Dan and his friends went to Vegas. Unlike the women, who were focused on spa treatments and relaxing by the pool, the men had plans to party.

The girls arrived Thursday evening and laid low. They spent Friday by the pool and went to one of the local hot spots, Prime 112, for dinner, followed by drinks at the hotel bar. Becca insisted that Saturday night be their big night out, so the girls made a big thing of it, dressing Rachel up in a veil, drinking out of penis straws, and pre-gaming in Rachel and Becca's hotel suite beforehand. Alex surprised Rachel with a montage of her life, with interviews of friends, photos, and old home movies. She included pictures of Rachel as a baby growing up, recorded her parents talking about how amazing their daughter was, and showed the cutest pictures of her and Rachel from childhood. Alex hesitated but ultimately added some pictures and video from high school. There was a whole section of the group of them, including a short clip of a movie they'd made in Ben's basement. Rachel was pretending to be choking, and Jack was behind her giving her a very sexualized Heimlich maneuver.

"You guys did some weird shit in high school," Rachel's friend Ivy, from Cornell, said as she watched. Alex, Rachel, and Nicole were hysterically laughing, all of them remembering how the guys were obsessed with making fake how-to videos, usually about something catastrophic.

The video moved on to the Cornell days, and the rest of the girls were now shrieking with laughter. They looked so ridiculous in their tube tops and black pants. There were a ton of photos of Rachel and Becca, from their dorm room to the sorority house to their apartment on College Avenue. They moved on to life in the city, in law school and current day, and Alex transitioned to an interview with Dan. She had asked him some risqué questions, and Dan had a lot of fun with it. He was such a good sport. He had no hesitation answering questions like where was the craziest place they had ever had sex, what Rachel's nickname for his penis was, and if they could have a threesome with anyone who would it be. Dan joked that it was Alex, which everyone loved.

At the end, everyone clapped and toasted Alex for making the video.

Then Alex raised her glass. "To my best and oldest friend, I remember when we were five years old playing with our Barbies and you always wanted to act out a Ken and Barbie wedding— I was more interested in Barbie and Barbie, but that's not important." Everyone chuckled at that. "I'm so glad you found your real-life Ken. You deserve everything you ever dreamed of, and I know Dan is the one for you. May you live happily ever after."

Rachel grabbed Alex into a giant hug and their friends *aww*ed.

"My turn," Becca exclaimed, jumping up from the couch. "Co–maid of honor here!"

"Pretty sure you're a matron," Alex teased.

"Is matron worse than maid? Like, why does your title change just because you're married, it's the dumbest thing," Becca said.

"Okay, feminist, time to focus," Rachel said. "You're about to tell me how amazing I am!"

Their friends all laughed, drunkenly.

"Yes, sorry." Becca steadied herself. "I always wished for a sister and got stuck with two brothers instead. But when I finally met you, I felt like I found my person. Thank you for always being my biggest cheerleader. You are so smart and you always keep me in check when I come up with crazy ideas. And thank you for stopping me from stalking all of the boys in college I was convinced I was in love with."

"You did end up marrying one of those guys, but I'll take it!" Rachel chimed in.

"True. Well, then thank you for accidentally reuniting me with my husband, then finally agreeing to marry his best friend. I truly love doing life with you. I know you and Dan are going to be so happy."

Rachel grabbed Becca in for a hug and then looked at each of her friends and said how happy she was to be celebrating with them.

"You are the world's best bridesmaids, I can't believe how lucky I am. Alex and Becca, you really are my sisters. Thank you for planning this for me and for putting up with me as I neurotically plan my wedding."

"Doesn't every bride carry around a color-coded binder wherever they go?" Alex teased her.

"Hey! I can't help myself if I want to stay organized."

After one more shot each, Becca rallied up the girls and insisted they leave the hotel.

The music pumped through the club, which was filled with skimpy-clothed twenty-somethings jumping around and gyrating against each other. Rachel's friends loved it, drunk enough to let loose and dance. Rachel kept on her veil, and her friends circled around her, bringing in various men to dance with them.

About an hour later, Rachel gestured to Alex that she wanted a drink, and the two of them headed toward the bar.

"I keep thinking about the video," Rachel shouted over the music.

"It was so much fun to put together."

"No, I mean, I'm freaking out about it!"

"What are you talking about?" Alex asked, pulling her outside so she could hear her better. "We're having so much fun."

"You're going to think I'm crazy. It's just that seeing us all back in high school, I can't stop thinking about Jack."

Alex looked at her quizzically, seemingly unsure of how to best respond to her friend.

"What if I'm supposed to be with him? You know he texted me a few times this year. And he's not with that girl from his show anymore. I didn't really engage because Dan and I are so happy, and it just seemed like a bad idea. But what if this is all a huge mistake?"

Alex grabbed Rachel by the shoulders. "Listen to what you just said. You and Dan are so happy. Dan loves you. How could you be making a mistake?"

"But does Dan love me the way Jack did? Remember how he would write me all those love notes? And he put me on such a pedestal. Dan hasn't texted me once this weekend. He never tells me I'm pretty anymore. I have to remind him to say *I love you!*"

"Rach, you're getting married. Dan adores you. It's obvious to anyone around you. He may not be the best communicator but that doesn't mean he isn't right for you. He can learn that stuff. He's a lawyer, he's smart, he's funny. He makes you less serious! Everyone knows you guys are perfect together."

"But do you think Jack still thinks about me?" She was not letting go of the thought.

Alex looked down at the ground, seemingly contemplating how to respond. "There is no doubt that what you and Jack had was special, but he's in an entirely different world right now. I'm sure Jack occasionally thinks about you, just like it's okay for you to occasionally think about him, or what might have happened between you. But Dan is your future. Dan is real."

She took in Alex's response. She was right. "I don't know what I'm thinking. I guess that video just threw me for a loop."

Alex was obviously right. Things between her and Jack had ended years ago. She hadn't seen him in forever anyway. Dan was kind and outgoing and perfect for her. This was crazy.

They went back to the group and found their friends still dancing where they left them.

"Are you okay?" Becca asked her, shouting to be heard over the music.

"Just needed some air," Rachel loudly responded. "I might be losing steam, though." She tapped at her wrist to signify the time to make sure Becca understood. "Will you let us go back to the hotel soon?"

Becca smiled at her, a little relieved. She flagged the other girls and they followed them outside.

"Oh, man," Ivy said, "anyone else feel like they're still inside? My ears!"

Rachel laughed. "Yes, mine are totally ringing."

"Okay, old ladies, back to the hotel." Alex flagged down a cab and they all piled in, loudly singing along with the radio and making their driver turn up the music.

When they got back, Becca and Rachel went to their room to get ready for bed after hugs with their friends, sad that they all had to head back home the following morning.

As she was brushing her teeth, Becca asked Rachel if she saw Bryn kissing that guy on the dance floor.

"What? No!" Rachel said. "Guess things aren't so great with her and Justin. It must have happened when I was outside."

"Was everything okay tonight? You looked kind of freaked out when you went off with Alex."

Rachel looked at Becca sitting on her bed and remembered how they used to stay up talking all night back in college. They were randomly thrown together as freshmen and chose to live together for three more years. Rachel trusted her with everything, but she'd just gotten married to Dan's best friend.

"Oh, nothing, Alex is just having girl trouble. You know how it is for her."

Becca shook her head. She did know. Alex had dated practically every single lesbian in her twenties in Manhattan. Both she and Rachel had been dragged to gay bars and themed brunches more times than they could count. "You would think meeting a girl would be so much easier than meeting a guy."

"I know. She just doesn't seem to pick very well." Rachel was happy Becca accepted her answer.

"Oh my god, Matt just sent me the funniest text!" Apparently Greg, who she and Rachel both couldn't stand, got thrown out of the strip club for getting too handsy. He wanted the guys to leave with him and go somewhere else, but they wouldn't because no one wanted to hang out with him.

"Well, that's amazing," Rachel said. "So the guys are at a strip club? Are we supposed to care about this?"

"Please. Look but don't touch is what I tell Matt. Our boys would never do anything."

Rachel had noticed Becca and Matt texting throughout the weekend and occasionally talking, too. She didn't mention that Dan hadn't texted her. She reached out to him to say good-night yesterday, and he sent her a quick text back. Becca would tell her that this was just how Dan was. When they were apart, she almost never heard from him. He didn't understand why that was an issue. For him, out of sight was out of mind, but not like permanently out of mind, he said. Rachel was trying to train herself to get over this minor flaw of her fiancé's.

"Can you believe the wedding is in two months?"

"It's going to be so amazing!" Becca exclaimed. "I still can't believe we're going to be married to best friends, Rach. How lucky are we?"

"I know. If we could go back and tell those naïve Cornell girls what was ahead for them, they wouldn't believe us!"

As Rachel tried to fall asleep that night, she typed Jack's name into the browser of her new iPhone. Several articles came up, and she clicked on one she had practically committed to memory.

Jack Bellow and co-star Amanda Coyne have split after less than one year together. The *Sanctions* actors were first linked when they were spotted strolling arm in arm in New York City's West Village last March. "Jack and Amanda hit it off immediately on set, but it wasn't until Amanda ended her longtime relationship with basketball star Shaun Michaels that they hooked up," a source exclusively revealed. Neither were looking to rush into a romance, Jack reportedly concerned about its impact on the show. There was no denying their chemistry, however, as shown on their recent trip to St. Barts and various spottings around Boston, where their show was filmed. With *Sanctions* currently airing its last episodes, it seems their relationship has simply run its course.

Rachel wondered what happened. She couldn't believe she was getting married. And that Jack was single. She turned off her phone and lay awake for another hour, thinking about her old boyfriend and willing herself to fall asleep.

28

Present Day

WITH DAN STAYING AT HIS BROTHER'S, RACHEL AND THE KIDS settled into a good routine. She still got calls from reporters, but at least they hadn't shown up at her house again. A few nights earlier there was another story about Jack on *Entertainment Tonight*. This one focused on him and Cassandra. Some anonymous source had reported that their relationship was over. Apparently, they hadn't been seen together in over a month, which Rachel thought was because of filming, but no one seemed to care too much about logistics. They also interviewed a woman who claimed to have hooked up with Jack earlier that year in Los Angeles. She was clearly seeking attention, Rachel thought, and had no proof of their meeting. Rachel felt sick that Jack was getting all this scrutiny. But one thing he had said to her at dinner was that it came with the territory, and he was too lucky in his career to begrudge the attention.

Rachel wished she had his attitude, but she saw no upside for herself as just a regular person. She knew the best thing she could do would be to put this whole situation behind her. Like Kaitlyn had said, eventually people would forget that she existed.

Even so, she and Jack continued texting. She started to get a sense of his schedule: gym in the morning, usually a breakfast or lunch meeting with one producer or another. He was shooting another car commercial later that week, so he had been prepping for that. Then he'd be back in New York in a few days, in time for his movie premiere and more meetings. She knew this was dangerous territory, when she caught herself staring at her phone one day waiting to hear from him, but talking to him was the only thing keeping her going.

She was texting him one night before bed when she told him that Dan was staying at his brother's in the city while they figured things out. Jack immediately called her.

"I'm so sorry," Jack said, assuming responsibility.

"Please, it's not your fault. There were other things going on."

"But Alex always said what a good relationship you guys have, and I feel like meeting up with me came between that?"

In the last couple of weeks, Rachel had forced herself to really evaluate her marriage. She was seeing things now that she had brushed under the rug for ages. How Dan would linger in the family room at night, claiming not to be tired, but really just avoiding spending time with her. How their conversations centered on the kids, and never about what either of them felt about anything real. How he never told her that he loved her anymore, or that he wanted her, or that he was grateful for any of the number of things she did for their family. How she ignored how unhappy he was, because yes, she saw that now. So they pretended things were good between them until one of them did something destructive, shattering the false veneer, and leaving them crumbled.

"I think this thing happening forced me to confront our relationship in a way I hadn't done before. I'm not sure I was as happy as I thought," she finally responded.

"I get it," he replied, not wanting to push her. "You know I was married once, right?"

Rachel laughed, shoving her thoughts about Dan back down. "Jack, everyone in America knows that." Jack's wedding and eventual divorce from Fiona Drake were something about which Rachel had read extensively.

"Right. I guess you would. I'll never get used to that. Once Fiona and I got married, it became clear that she went after me because she thought my career would help hers. It was all about how my success could serve her. Then she got a role in this big movie, and she sort of bailed."

"Jeez," Rachel said, sympathetically. That was not how the tabloids had spun it.

"I only figured this out when I started talking about us having kids one day, and it was clear that she had no interest in ever starting a family with me."

Rachel took this in. She remembered reading about Fiona getting a Marvel movie, and that Jack was reportedly pissed because he was also up for a role in the same film.

"I thought you didn't want kids."

"Why would you think that?" He sounded surprised.

Rachel remembered what she'd overheard him say about her and Max at his apartment. She hesitated whether to admit that she'd eavesdropped, but she'd always been completely honest with him. "When I came for the Thanksgiving parade? You seemed sort of horrified that I was a mother. And then I heard you making some comment to another guy. It sounded like you were happy not to be living my life." She felt her cheeks turn red as she admitted something that had mortified her so deeply at the time. She was glad he couldn't see her face.

Jack was silent.

"Hey, I get it," she backpedaled. "It was so long ago. I'm over it."

"Rachel, are you serious? That's why you rushed off like that?" He chuckled. "My sister figured I did something stupid. I should have listened to her and called you. I'm so sorry. If anything, I was jealous."

Rachel thought back to how turned off she had been by him then, how unlike himself he had seemed. She assumed celebrity had turned him from the sensitive, thoughtful boy she had known into a self-obsessed prick. "Water under the bridge. Seriously."

"Okay." He seemed unsure of whether she really meant it, but decided to move on. "Well, my point in bringing up Fiona is that sometimes we don't see people for who they really are until they hurt us."

"Well, that's depressing."

"I realized I was better off without her, even though it took her ending our relationship to get there." He paused. "Honestly, I compared her a lot to you, which was part of our problem. You knew me when I had no money and a shitty family situation and still thought I was amazing. I think I've always been looking for that unconditional love."

Rachel wanted to tell him she felt the same. It was essentially the same thing Dan had been accusing her of for years.

"It's not too late for you," she said instead.

"What do you mean?"

"You're a man, you can have a baby until you're, like, eighty. Haven't you and Cassandra thought about having kids?"

"Me and Cassandra? No. That's definitely not happening."

"Really? I heard on *Entertainment Tonight* that you're about to propose to her."

Jack seemed disappointed. "Do I seem like the kind of guy that would be texting another woman every night if I'm about to get engaged?" He didn't. At least not the Jack she knew.

Now Rachel felt like an asshole, since she actually *was* married and spending her days waiting for another man to text her. Somehow the fact that they'd once been together made it seem okay to her, more like it was just two friends staying in touch. Was this what people meant by emotional cheating?

"You shouldn't believe everything you see on celebrity news shows," he chided her.

"I know. Sorry." She needed to change the subject to safer territory. "Have you heard from Alex lately?"

Jack hesitated for a minute, then said he hadn't. He explained that the filming schedule could be so hectic, plus she was probably watching the dailies every night.

"I guess," Rachel said. "But I've tried calling her a bunch of times and it's sort of bizarre that she's barely been in touch. She must have at least five minutes to call her oldest friend!" The absence of Alex's support was heavily weighing on her. Alex could unemotionally dissect any situation and help lead her to the right answer.

"Yeah." Jack was quiet. "Maybe I'll give her a buzz."

They talked a bit longer and Jack asked her about her parents.

"Well, they confessed something super weird to me the other night. Apparently, my dad had an affair when I was in middle school."

"I'm sorry, what?" he exclaimed. "Your dad cheated? I'm shocked." He had spent so much time observing her parents and assumed they were completely in love.

"I know. I was, too," Rachel said. "I think they wanted me to see that nothing was so bad that you can't forgive your spouse."

"So they want you to stay with him," Jack said quietly.

"Yeah, of course. They love Dan," Rachel said, not considering how that might make Jack feel. "But my mom and I are in completely different situations."

"How do you mean?" he asked her.

"Things were so different when we were kids. I guess I have this career, and my own money." And, she thought, unlike her mom, she was distracted from her broken marriage by daily texts with a handsome movie star.

"Right, but your mom worked, too, and I'm sure it wasn't all about money for them. They're good people, you know?" Even all these years later, he thought they could do no wrong.

"I'm grateful, obviously. They are good people. And they're great parents. I was lucky, I know," Rachel said. "Anyway, I better go to sleep. I'm covering a deposition for someone tomorrow, since apparently I can't manage my own clients." Rachel had already filled Jack in on what her boss had done to her.

"Okay. Good luck. Night, babe."

Rachel stared at the phone as he clicked off. Did he mean to call her *babe*? Was that how he ended all of his calls, or was it by accident? She felt like a teenager again, as she did more and more lately, dissecting the way a guy she liked said goodbye.

She washed up and then walked down the hall to check in on the kids. She loved the way they looked when they slept. Emma slept like a little frog on her belly, her curls sprawled out around her. She kissed her and breathed in her sweet scent, as Emma stirred and rolled onto her side. Max was starting to look and smell more like a boy, the little-kid version of her son disappearing. She brushed his hair off his face and kissed him. He didn't move. He was always a deep sleeper.

When she got back into bed there was a text waiting for her.

JACK: Is it a terrible idea for us to see each other again?

Rachel knew in her head that it was totally crazy, and definitely unfair to Dan. But she desperately wanted to see him.

RACHEL: Probably.

JACK: I'll ask anyway. Are you free this weekend?

This weekend was perfect, since Dan was with the kids, but seeing Jack again was reckless. And yet . . .

RACHEL: What did you have in mind?

JACK: How about you come to my apartment for dinner Saturday? No chance of anyone seeing us together.

Rachel's mind swirled with thoughts of being near him again. Breathing him in, looking into his eyes. She was so overtaken by the possibility of being with him, she quieted the voice inside her that shouted her husband's name.

RACHEL: I can do Saturday.

29

Spring 2000

RACHEL PACED HER DORM ROOM WILLING HER LANDLINE TO RING.
She was bewildered by Jack's lack of responsiveness. Their first
semester had gone as they had planned: occasional weekend visits
between Albany and Cornell, meeting each other's new friends, jokingly scheduling conjugal visits so their respective roommates gave
them privacy. Then they had an uninterrupted month together over
Christmas break, and Jack practically lived at her house. Her parents
finally acknowledged that she was going to do what she wanted with
her boyfriend now that she was in college and let him stay in her
room. So long as he came home for Sunday-night dinner, Jack's own
parents didn't seem to care how he spent his time.

Returning to campus had been a whirlwind for Rachel. She
immediately launched into sorority rush. She went from house to
house, meeting girls, assessing their clothes and mannerisms and
the guys with whom they socialized. She heavily debated between
two sororities, leaning toward the one for "nicer girls," but ultimately
her roommate, Becca, insisted they both pick the one with a more
fun reputation.

She missed a few calls from Jack that first week. When her
schedule allowed, she tried calling him right before dinner, as had
been their guaranteed time to connect first semester. Sometimes the
phone would ring and ring.

One evening, Ted, Jack's roommate, answered. "Hi, Rachel, he's
not here. Not sure when he'll be back but I'll give him the message."
She sat at her small wood desk, staring at the cork board above it

with photos of her and Jack, and Alex and Nicole and the rest of their friends. "But he's okay, right, Ted?" she asked.

"Oh, yes, Jack is definitely fine."

Jack's instant messenger was never active, so she tried e-mailing him. "Hey, babe, been trying to reach you. Not sure if you check this very much but call me as soon as you can. Just feels weird not to talk. Love you."

Rachel tried to focus on her friends. But she was a distracted pledge, and her new "sisters" were noticing.

"Rachel, name the girls in this photo. Becca got it on her first try. We're not making you run around in a bikini, circling your fat"—which had been all the rage until the administration intervened—"the least you can do is memorize a composite."

Rachel couldn't focus. Not on school, not on her friends, and certainly not on a photograph from 1994 of girls she had never met. Jack had been her constant for over two years. Without him, even from a distance, she was unmoored. She was grateful when pledging finally ended, and they were officially part of the sorority so she could get back into a more normal routine. Unfortunately, the lack of contact from Jack made it nearly impossible.

"Hey, Al," she called her best friend one night when Becca was in the shower.

"Rach, what's wrong?" Alex exclaimed, knowing her old friend so well that it was clear from her voice that something was not quite right.

"I haven't heard from Jack in weeks," she said, her voice cracking and tears filling her eyes.

"Oh, Rach."

Hearing her friend's voice unleashed the sobs that Rachel had been holding in for weeks. She cried so hard she lost her breath.

She heard Alex's voice trying to soothe her, but she needed to let it out.

When Rachel finally stopped, with just the occasional lingering gulps for breath, she asked Alex what she thought had happened.

"I wish I knew. I really do. But maybe being apart and meeting new people is what you're supposed to do. Sitting home and waiting for your boyfriend to call you is not how you should be experiencing college, Rach."

"So you think he met a new girl?" Rachel asked.

"I definitely did not say that. But as your friend, I don't think it's such a bad thing for you to take a step back from Jack and get out there a little." Rachel knew that Alex had been having many new experiences in college, those she had been limited from having back home.

"I just think if you're going to be together forever, like you guys always said, you'd benefit from having some time without him. You know?"

While a part of her agreed with Alex, Rachel thought at the very least, she and Jack would have discussed taking time apart before he disappeared from her life. She could not figure out what had changed in the month since winter break.

"You're probably right. It just hurts so much." She began to cry again.

Alex continued to listen and comfort her until Rachel felt calm enough to get off the phone. Becca walked in wrapped in a towel to her very sad-looking roommate.

"Oh my god, Rach, what happened?" Becca exclaimed.

"It's Jack. I feel like we're basically over," she said, a new wave of tears overtaking her.

Becca sat down on Rachel's bed, still in her towel, and put an arm around her friend. "You and Jack seemed so perfect, there must be some reason you haven't spoken? Are you sure he knows you've been calling him?"

Rachel rehashed the number of times she had called and spoken with his roommate, Ted, who undoubtedly thought she was a stalker by now.

"Listen, it's Friday night. You're coming with me to the Pike mixer, and you are going to hook up with someone. Fuck Jack. If he doesn't want to act like an adult and hash out whatever is going on with you two, then you need to start to live your life here."

Rachel sniffled in response.

"I love you, but I am sick of you not coming out with me because of your boyfriend! We'll have so much fun!"

Becca was right. If Jack was going to push her away, she was not going to force him to be with her. She was going out that night.

After drinking an obscene amount of alcohol, Rachel made her way back to her dorm room and threw up twice in the middle of the night. She woke up the next morning feeling somewhat refreshed. She noticed that Becca wasn't in her bed, and then remembered that she had gone home with Steve, who lived on West Campus. She lay there thinking about the party and suddenly remembered that she had made out with someone. Her first college kiss. It was so strange to kiss someone other than Jack. She couldn't remember his name, just that he had a crooked nose. He had said something about breaking it playing soccer, hadn't he? She vaguely recalled his friends calling him Gonzo—maybe that was his last name? Or like the Muppet? She needed coffee.

Her hurt by Jack's unexplained disappearance came flooding back to her. Maybe she should write him a letter. If he didn't want to be with her, she could accept that, but ditching her like this was just cruel, and completely unlike him. She threw some clothes on and ran down to the dining hall to grab a muffin. She needed to write this before she lost her nerve. Or her mind.

Becca finally wandered in around eleven, just as Rachel finished her letter. It was long, too long, but she particularly liked her ending, which was a quote from the Exposé song "I'll Never Get Over You (Getting Over Me)."

"How was Steve?" Rachel asked.

"Honestly, I think I'm over it. He's so nerdy about school. He asked me to leave so he could, and I quote, 'hit the stacks.'"

"We go to Cornell. Everyone is basically a nerd, Bec."

"I know, I know. But there are much cuter boys in that house that are older, and I think I owe it to myself to meet them!" she replied with a giggle. "Speaking of hot Pike boys, did I dream that I saw you kissing Gonzo last night? Did you go home with him?"

"No! That was the first guy I've kissed other than Jack since I was sixteen. So, his name actually is Gonzo? I wasn't sure if I'd heard that correctly. Is it because of his nose?" Rachel said.

"Not just his nose! According to Ivy, the rumor is his dick is just as crooked!" Becca shrieked with laughter.

"Wait, so why did you let me hook up with him? I'm dying. Does everyone talk about this poor guy's penis?"

"Joke's on you. I told the girls you would get to the bottom of it!"

The girls could not stop laughing and Rachel felt immediately better. Becca had a way about her of making things so much more exciting. They rehashed all the other ridiculousness that had transpired the night before on their way to grab lunch, picking up other friends from their dorm as they went. Rachel grabbed the letter on the way out to mail to Jack at Albany. If he wasn't going to call her back to talk this through, she needed to at least say her piece.

The rest of the semester was a blur of classes, fraternity parties, and for Rachel, sex with three different guys. That included Gonzo, or Jeff Goodman, who did in fact have a very crooked, but nevertheless effective, penis. Lingering in the back of her mind, always, was Jack. She wondered what he was doing, who he was kissing. If he ever thought about her.

She finished school in May and decided to spend that summer at her old sleepaway camp as a counselor, dragging Becca with her, rather than rejoining her old crew at home and working at her dad's boring accounting office as she had planned. Anything to avoid Jack, who by then she hadn't heard from in five months.

When she got home from camp, her mom handed her a letter with Jack's name on the return address. She gave her a sympathetic look and said she could sit with her while she read it. Rachel shook her head no. She could face whatever half-baked apology Jack was offering by herself.

Dear Rachel,

I know I waited too long to respond to you. I had been planning to see you this summer and was hoping we could talk in person, but you left for camp before we had a chance. I'm going back to Albany early, heading there right after I finish this letter to you. The work-study job didn't really work out, but I got a job at a deli near school and the pay is decent.

I know I owe you an explanation. This kind of all happened because I failed my calculus class first semester. I didn't tell you over Christmas because I knew you'd be disappointed in me, plus I was going to retake it. When I got back to school after the break, I found out they were revoking my scholarship and the work-study job (please do not tell your parents). I was more scared to tell you about this than my parents. By some miracle, my dad found the money to help pay for tuition (finally the dude steps up, right?) and I applied for more financial aid. But I sort of fell into a hole anyway, because it freaking sucked.

I also kind of resented you. It's not your fault, but it's not like you need to worry about paying for college. Plus, you would do well in school even if you didn't try, and since you always work so damn hard, you make the rest of us look like idiots.

I don't know, maybe us being so young and completely involved with each other through half of high school made us both miss out on certain things. I'm sure you want to know why I didn't tell you this at the time. After those first couple of weeks last semester when you were so busy, it became easier to stop trying to talk to you. I started drinking more and to be truly 100 percent honest, I started hooking up with girls, too. I guess I didn't want to face you.

I am sure you hate me. I know I deserted you. I got your letter. I am so sorry. So so so sorry. I just hope you know how much I did love you and that I will always regret how we ended. You'll always be my first love and have a very special place in my heart.

Love,

Jack

How much he *did* love her. That line reverberated painfully in her head. Rachel had convinced herself that she was fine, but it felt like Jack had ripped her heart from her chest for the second time. How many times had she wondered why he left her, doubting everything that they had. She could have helped him figure this out. Did he really think she wouldn't understand? she wondered. She lay back in her bed, looking over at the pillow next to her, envisioning Jack beside her. She wanted him to comfort her, to hold her again. But he didn't even ask her to try to forgive him. She felt so alone, dismayed that the tears continued to come for the boy who had broken her heart.

She finally stopped crying. She allowed herself to read the letter once more, then put it back in the envelope and added it to the box of Jack keepsakes she kept under her bed. He had clearly moved on from her. It was time for her to do the same.

30

Present Day

RACHEL BOOKED HERSELF A ROOM IN THE CITY THE FOLLOWING weekend. She felt bad about missing Max's soccer game on Saturday, but she and Dan had agreed that soccer was going to be his thing. Max didn't seem to mind, as long as his dad was there to coach him. Becca would send videos of any impressive playing. She knew the women would talk, but Rachel no longer had the energy to care. She promised to be home Sunday for the school's spring carnival.

The first weekend Dan had the kids, Rachel realized there was something sort of delightful about being separated and having a break from your family. Eating and sleeping and showering and peeing without children clamoring all over her or waking her at 6:30 in the morning was a bit of a dream. She missed them of course, but being alone allowed her to feel more like her old self.

Friday night Rachel ordered room service and caught up on Netflix. She woke up late on Saturday and spent the day walking around SoHo. She loved wandering in and out of the stores, although she tried not to buy anything. She gave in at Bloomingdale's, picking out a flowy skirt and silk tank to wear that evening to Jack's. She also got her makeup done. She wasn't exactly competition for his supermodel girlfriend, but she might as well make a little extra effort.

Jack had told her to come to his place around seven, so she grabbed an Uber and headed uptown. As soon as she got in the car, her nerves started to set in. She knew it was futile but she tried Alex yet again. The phone rang twice and then went to voice mail. What was going on with her?

"Hey. I know you're busy, but I'm sort of freaking out here. I'm meeting up with Jack tonight. At his apartment. I can't even believe I'm saying that. You're the only person I want to talk about this with and for some reason you won't call me. I don't get it. I want to understand. I know making a movie is insane. But my life is so messed up right now and it's weird you aren't here. Okay, I'm rambling. I guess call me tomorrow if you can. I miss you."

She clicked end and stared at her phone, flipping back to her most recent message from Alex a few days before.

> ALEX: This is going to be fine! I'll be home in three
> weeks. We'll figure it out.

Alex had been the one to lift her out of her spiral when Jack broke her heart, and stood beside her under the chuppah when she married Dan. She told her that taking Lexapro after Emma was born was not a sign of failure. She'd held her hand in fourth grade when Rachel cut herself and needed stitches, and refused to go back to her own class while they waited for Rachel's mom to arrive. This was a crisis. So where the hell was she, if not picking up the pieces and telling her what to do?

The Uber pulled up in front of Jack's fancy prewar building on the Upper West Side. Rachel was doing this, with or without Alex's support. A man in a dark suit greeted her, obviously waiting for her, and led her up the stairs through the front door into the lobby. The elevator opened and Rachel was guided toward it by who she now assumed was Jack's security detail.

When they reached the top floor, Rachel and the man in the suit stepped out. Rachel turned to thank the elevator operator, who smiled and nodded at her, then closed the doors. The door to Jack's apartment opened and Rachel was greeted by a smiling older woman in black pants and a white button-down.

"Hello, Ms. Miller. I'm Marjorie. Mr. Bellow will be with you momentarily. Can I take your coat and get you anything to drink?"

Rachel stared at her for a moment and glanced at the man who had accompanied her. He nodded to both of them and turned around and left the apartment.

"Don't mind Randall. He's very stiff. Why don't you come into the study and I'll grab you some water for now," Marjorie said, kindly.

Rachel followed her through the apartment and into a room she hadn't noticed the last time she was there. The study was wood and homey, with panels on the wall and rows and rows of books. Rachel sat on the cozy leather love seat and Marjorie left her alone. She eyed the books, noting to herself that there was no way Jack had read any of them, when she spotted what looked like photo albums in the corner of the room. Rachel got up and pulled one out and flipped through it. It was their senior year. She couldn't believe that Jack displayed this stuff in his library, whereas she had all of her old memories crammed into boxes stacked in her basement boiler room.

She sat back down with the album on her lap, and flipped through the pages more slowly. There was their senior parade. Rachel was in several of the photos. Her hair was up in a high ponytail and she was wearing overalls and a tight ribbed tank, which Jack had loved. She remembered how he used to slip his hand under her overalls to touch her stomach. She flipped a few pages and found the group of them at Ben's house. They had been trying to be discrete about their drinking, but now that she was a parent, Rachel quickly noticed the wine coolers and beer behind their backs and realized they hadn't fooled anyone. She and Jack were always next to each other. His arm flung over her shoulder, or her on his lap. They couldn't keep their hands off each other.

"So you found my Rachel shrine?" Jack's voice interrupted her as she started looking at their senior year musical.

"Ha, hardly a shrine. But man, we were so into each other, weren't we?" Rachel replied, standing to give him a hug.

"I'm so glad you came," he said. "Okay, drinks. Want a Manhattan?"

"Sure. But you may need to carry me out of here."

"You got it." Jack walked to the bar in the corner of the room. As he measured the ingredients, he asked, "How was the ride in? Randall walked you upstairs?" He pulled out two glasses and dropped a fancy cherry in each, pouring the Manhattan over the cherries and giving a final stir.

"Yes, he's really chatty. I'm actually staying in the city this weekend. Dan has the kids." She shook her head, acknowledging the oddness of that statement.

She accepted the glass from Jack and they clinked. "To old friends," he said.

Jack sat in the leather chair across from her. "I wasn't sure if you'd want to see me again, after last time."

Rachel joked that as long as there was no paparazzi hiding in his apartment, she was glad to see him.

"I promise you this will blow over. It always does," Jack said.

"I'll be honest, I'm still not entirely sure that I should be here." Rachel stopped speaking, noticing that Jack was smiling at her as she rambled. "Why are you looking at me like that?"

"Take a drink. Relax. I promise you Marjorie is not taking pictures of us. And I'm looking at you because I really like looking at you."

Rachel blushed. She couldn't believe this man could still have the same effect on her that he did when she was a teenager. "Fine," she said, taking a sip and feeling the alcohol calm her nerves.

"Rach, I know you're going through a lot right now, but I've really missed you. I'm not mad that a twist of fate brought us back into each other's lives." Jack took a sip of his cocktail and looked at his ex-girlfriend.

"By twist of fate, you mean my husband." Just a few sips of the Manhattan had loosened her up.

"I know how confusing this all is." Jack looked at her and smiled, sympathetically. "I'm sure the current photos of us didn't help."

"It certainly did not help." She paused, hesitating before continuing. "I don't blame you or anything, but isn't that something you should have considered before asking me to meet you at a celebrity hot spot?"

Jack looked at her, abashed, and waited almost a minute before he responded. Rachel stared back, understanding that maybe he wasn't as blameless as she had thought.

"I'm so sorry. My publicist thought it would be a good idea. I said no, but she convinced me that it wasn't a huge deal after all of the other stuff."

"You lured me to dinner to get publicity?" she said, horrified.

"No, of course not. That's not what I mean. I have all these people running my life, and when I told my team I was taking you out, there was some thinking that it might be good press if we were seen together. Which is awful, I know. I'm just so used to it and I wasn't thinking about the impact on you. Which I regret."

Rachel could barely take in what he was saying. Here was another man she cared about, callously, carelessly betraying her. "This was obviously a bad idea. I'm gonna go." She stood up.

"Rach. Don't go. Please. We just thought, we were already getting the attention, and a couple more pictures wasn't going to do anything. I know it prolonged the story a bit, but we'd been looking for a way out of the whole Cassandra thing. I shouldn't have let it happen. I know that now. I've been feeling terrible about it."

"What Cassandra thing?" she asked, then changed her mind. "You know what?" she said, making her way out of his study. "I don't care, I'm leaving."

He walked toward her and put his hands on her shoulders. His hands on her body softened her. Jack sensed her hesitation.

"Rach, look at me. I didn't consider how this would make things worse for you. I made a mistake."

She couldn't do this. Her feelings were once again sacrificed for someone else's gain.

"So, you invited me to dinner to have someone take our picture?"

"No! Absolutely not. I wanted to see you. I've been desperate to see you for years."

Her face remained dubious.

"Please come sit down with me. Let me explain."

Rachel stood there, torn by how awful the last few weeks had been, and the recognition that Jack lived in a world so unlike her own. He looked at her, those blue eyes piercing through her, breaking her resolve. She followed him back to the couch. She couldn't turn away.

"Rach, a lot of what you see with famous people is contrived. It's not real."

He looked at her, and saw she was listening. "Like when Fiona and I got divorced, people needed a reason. I couldn't come out and say I wanted kids and she didn't, or that she decided I was a loser because she got a better part in a movie, and of course no one would accept that we'd simply grown apart, which is how our publicists tried to spin it. So instead, Fiona was vilified for cheating on me, even though we denied it and we were already over when she got together with Andrew."

"Okay . . . ," she trailed off, not understanding what this had to do with their situation.

"I guess you could say I'm publicly exiting from the relationship with Cassandra."

"You broke up?" She wanted to stay angry at him, but the first thought that ran through her mind was that Jack was single.

"Not officially, we're working our way through it. My publicist thought maybe a little extra harmless attention on me and my high school girlfriend could help. Honestly, she was right."

"Why can't you just say you aren't together?"

"It's all really complicated. But can you trust me on this? I am so sorry for adding to your problems. I had no intention of doing that."

Rachel was betrayed by her husband, her oldest friend was making almost zero effort to help her, and now this. She didn't have the energy to stay angry at Jack for something she clearly didn't understand.

"Okay," she finally relented. "I wish you had been upfront with me about it."

"I should have been. I know things are already messed up for you."

"My publicist friend from work promised me it would go away. As long as I'm never seen with you again."

"Is that what you want?" Jack asked her softly.

"I don't know." She couldn't think clearly anymore. "What do you want?"

"I know it seems like I have all this amazing shit going on, but the truth is I'm pretty lonely these days. There are, like, five people I can trust outside my family. And two of the people I do trust are Marjorie and freaking Randall." He paused, debating if he should continue but deciding to put it all out there. "Then you walk into my life again and you're you, this person who still seems to know me better than anyone, and I just liked the feeling. I want to feel that way again."

Rachel knew what he meant. Sitting across from him, talking to him, it was as if the years of distance melted away. She had never felt so completely adored as when she had been with Jack. She knew Dan loved her, but she kept waiting for him to show her the same level of affection and he just never could. But she was married and a mother. Her own parents had reminded her that Jack was a fantasy, and they weren't wrong.

Jack finished his drink and stood up. He walked back to the bar, poured whiskey into his glass, and added an oversized ice cube. He tilted his drink to Rachel to see if she wanted more but she shook her head; she still had half her Manhattan.

"Come sit with me outside," he said.

31

RACHEL STOOD UP, A BIT WOBBLY FROM THE ALCOHOL, AND followed Jack out of the study and into his bedroom. There was a set of sliding glass doors and a large balcony off the room. Jack had two lounge chairs set up and a small table off to the side. He sat down in one of the chairs and waved Rachel over to join him. Rachel lay back and looked out at Central Park.

"How's your family doing?" she asked.

"They're pretty great. Meg had a third kid a couple of years ago. My mom is way more enthralled with her grandkids than she is with me."

"I doubt that. She must love having a famous son."

"I really think she just wants me to get married. But I did buy her and Stan a new house, which was a pretty amazing feeling. It's near your parents' old place."

"That's incredible, Jack. I love reading about celebrities that do things like that for their families."

"Celebrity. It sounds so weird for you to put me in that category. But yeah, it's definitely a perk. When I was younger, all I wanted was what you and Alex and Ben had. You had this security that I craved. Although I recognize that this is over the top," he said, gesturing around him.

"Well, I see why you picked this apartment, looking at the stars and the park. It's just so beautiful," Rachel said, turning to him. "Do you get to stay here a lot?"

Jack was rarely in the city. "Ben stays here sometimes. Actually, if you ever need a place to crash while you figure things out,
you're welcome to come here."

Rachel laughed. "I'm not sure that's the solution Dan and I are
looking for, but thanks."

They sat there together, lost in their own thoughts, drinking
and taking in the night.

"You know, I think about our relationship a lot," Jack said eventually, breaking the silence. "We were so young, but it felt so adult,
right? Sometimes I think I found that big love too early in my life
and so nothing else could compare. Especially living in this bizarre
fantasy world of mine."

Rachel had spent years searching for that level of devotion,
but she knew better now. "Maybe what we had then was the fantasy, though. I'm in a very real adult relationship. I mean, besides
the current hiccup. So it's like you don't have crazy sex anymore,
but you have all these responsibilities that bind you together. It's
just different."

Jack nodded.

"When we were teenagers, we had no problems, so of course
everything was easy and fabulous. Plus, I had a pretty good body
then, and now I'm just a mom who needs a breast lift."

"You might be a mom, but I'd argue that you still look
incredible."

"You haven't seen me naked," she responded without
thinking.

"But I'd like to."

Rachel covered her face with her hands. Jack leaned over
toward her chair and tried pulling them down but Rachel resisted

him. He moved to the edge of her chair and leaned in closer. "Come on, Rach, let me see that face of yours."

She put her hands down and looked up at Jack, who was now sitting on the edge of his lounge chair. He put his hands on both of her cheeks and told her she still looked eighteen to him. "For the record, I personally like natural boobs. Yours might have been the last pair I came in contact with."

"Oh my god, Jack." She went to cover her face again but Jack grabbed her hands.

"Rach, look at me. You're beautiful. You're still so beautiful."

Rachel didn't know how to respond and didn't have the chance as Jack leaned down and gently kissed her. She felt a pull in her lower belly as Jack grabbed her even closer. He touched her face and her hair. The kiss went on and on, until Rachel came back into the moment and pulled back.

"I don't know what I'm doing, Jack," she whispered.

"Be with me tonight, Rachel."

Jack leaned in and kissed her again, pulling her up out of the chair. As she moved her body even closer to his, she felt him through his jeans. He stopped kissing her and led her back through the glass doors into his bedroom. Rachel's mind was racing. But it felt so good to kiss him she didn't want to stop.

He walked her to the edge of his bed and she sat there. She watched Jack as he turned on the electric fireplace under his seventy-five-inch television. He fidgeted with a remote and simultaneously the lights dimmed as light jazz began to play through hidden speakers. Rachel looked at him walking toward her and started laughing. She couldn't stop herself, and he looked at her quizzically.

"It feels like we're in a movie, Jack. The lights, the music, the freaking fireplace. Is this your move?" she said, still in hysterics. "I'm sorry, I know I'm totally ruining the mood."

Jack grabbed his iPhone and all of a sudden "Kiss Me" by Sixpence None the Richer started playing. "Shut up and dance with me like you used to, baby," Jack said, reaching his hand out to Rachel.

"God, I loved *She's All That*. And you suffered through it with me, what, probably fifty times?" Rachel murmured in Jack's ear as they swayed together to the old song.

"I actually know Freddie Prinze Jr. He's much smarter than people think."

"Of course you do." Jack started singing along and twirling her around. They danced, like they did when they were kids, both singing loudly.

The song stopped and Aerosmith came on. "Armageddon!" Jack grabbed her closer and they continued singing to each other. "Um, is this a Rachel and Jack 1998 mix?" she asked him.

"'Iris' is definitely not coming on next."

They swayed to the music, both remembering a time long ago when everything was far simpler.

"I'm picturing us fake-cleaning out the prop room. Are you?" she asked him.

"I'm thinking of us sitting in the back seat of my car senior year during last period."

She pulled him closer to her, smiling at the memory. "We did a lot of kissing if I remember. You were so sweet."

Jack kissed Rachel's neck by her ear and made his way down her collarbone. She pulled his face to hers and kissed him deeply. "Just tonight," she whispered.

"Just tonight," he responded, and pushed her down on the bed.

Jack pulled Rachel's silk top over her head, and she lay there in her skirt and bra. He took off his own shirt and Rachel couldn't help but marvel over his muscles. "You didn't have these when we were eighteen," she said, rubbing her hand up and down his bicep.

"You weren't wearing bras like this when we were eighteen." He leaned down and kissed each breast, feeling her nipples grow hard through the black lace. Jack made his way down her belly, gently kissing her until he got to the top of her skirt. He slipped it down her legs, so she was lying there in just her bra and panties.

Jack stood back and looked at her. He undid his jeans and stepped out of them, standing in his tight boxer briefs. He pulled Rachel up off the bed and brought her close to him. He could feel her heart beating against his ribcage. He bent down to kiss her and she reached up to him, standing on her toes.

His kiss started gentle but became more intense. He ran his hands down her back and unhooked her bra. He left it in place as they kissed, running his hands up and down her bare back. She touched his back in return, so hard and strong, and let her hands rub his ass over his underwear. It felt so firm, and she couldn't help but grab on to him as he let out a slight moan. He stepped back and pulled down her bra straps so he could see her breasts. They were still round and full, and he could make out the pale pink of her nipples in the dim light.

For a moment Rachel felt self-conscious, and covered herself, but Jack told her that she looked beautiful and brought down her arm. He kneeled in front of her and peeled down her underwear, kissing her lower belly and thighs. He teased her with his mouth, and her legs began to shake with longing. Jack pushed her back on the bed and continued kissing her all over, up to her collarbone and by her ear. He gently grazed her nipples with his teeth. She arched her back to meet his mouth and he sucked harder. He made his way down, and she let go of every fear and question she had been holding on to as he pleasured her in a way she hadn't experienced in years. Her breathing accelerated and she loudly moaned his name. Almost too quickly, she felt the waves of sweetness overtake her.

Rachel pulled him back up to her and let him kiss her with her still on him, like she used to. She touched him, feeling his hardness. Jack pushed down his underwear and stepped out of them. Rachel moved against his thigh as she stroked him gently. He reached over her and grabbed a condom from the nightstand. So unlike when they were teenagers, in one easy movement he ripped open the condom and slid it onto his hard shaft. He kept one hand on himself and guided himself inside Rachel, as she moaned.

He started slowly and eased in and out of her, as she lay on her back with her legs wrapped around him. He pulled out of her and sat up, grabbing Rachel and placing her on his lap. She moved up and down on him as he held on to her. They kissed and kissed as they moved together, and Jack's breath started to quicken as Rachel sped her pace. She was still feeling the remnants from earlier as Jack came hard inside of her. He stayed put as he kept his fingers on her, making her finish a second time.

They lay there afterward on the bed side by side, catching their breath. Jack turned his head toward her. "I missed you. For twenty years, I've missed you."

Rachel chuckled. "If you were giving me multiple orgasms in high school, I would have missed you more."

Jack took his pillow from under his head and tossed it at her. "I remember lots of orgasms."

Rachel climbed on top of him and stretched her body out over his, her toes lining up with his shins. She looked down at him and kissed him softly.

"I missed you, too. I let myself forget how good we were."

Jack pulled her close to him and breathed her in. "How is it possible that you still smell the same after all this time?" he asked her. She confessed that she occasionally still bought her old shampoo and had used it that night for him. "I've moved on to nicer products, but nothing really smells as good as this."

"I love it," he said. "Should we order dinner? Anything your heart desires?"

"I feel like I need to take advantage of being with Jack Bellow. Can we get Nobu? Should I be embarrassed for suggesting that?"

"Your wish is my command." Jack picked up his phone and shot out a quick text. "Want to take a quick shower while we wait?" She definitely did.

32

RACHEL FOLLOWED JACK OUT OF BED AND INTO HIS GIANT
bathroom. The shower was as large as her closet, with dual shower-
heads. He stepped inside and Rachel followed suit. Jack pulled her
under his own stream of water and used the shower gel next to
him to lather her up. Rachel allowed herself to be cleaned by him
and when he was done, she returned the favor.

"Did you have a C-section?" he asked her. Rachel reached
down and felt her scar, along with the immovable pouch of skin
above it. At this point in her life, she mostly ignored it. Of course,
until earlier that day, only her husband and children were seeing
her naked.

"Yes. With Max. It's not a great scar. I got an infection and it
was a whole mess. Luckily I had a VBAC with Emma," she explained.

"What's that?" Jack asked.

"Oh. It's just, like, delivering the regular way after you have a
cesarean. I forgot for a second you aren't a father," she explained.
"Wait, you aren't a father, right?"

"Ha, not that I know of. Anyway, the scar isn't bad. I just wondered. And for the record, your breasts are still pretty fantastic."
She wondered how he could look at her, with her softening stomach
and breasts that had carried and fed two children, and find her
attractive. Especially compared to his own body, so muscled, down
to the V-shaped cut of his abs. But he did. He finished rinsing off
and turned off the water, reaching out to grab them the towels.

"Do you want a robe?" he asked her.

"You have a woman's robe laying around your apartment?" she responded.

He opened the massive closet off his bathroom and pulled out two robes that matched his towels. "I have a few extra unisex robes," he said, emphasizing *unisex*. "I love them. Shut up and put it on."

They walked out of the bathroom and Jack checked his phone. "Food is here. Let's eat." He opened the bedroom door and headed toward the dining room. The table was laden with an array of food. Candles were lit and the jazz Jack had started off their evening with was softly playing in the background. "What can I get you to drink? Glass of wine?"

Rachel was blown away by the ease with which things happened for Jack. He texted someone that he wanted Nobu, and thirty minutes later Nobu showed up inside his apartment. She shook her head yes and took the seat next to him.

Jack poured her a glass of Sancerre and she dug into the Kobe beef and spicy tuna, realizing just how ravenous she was. Jack did the same and they were comfortably silent for a few minutes as they ate.

"I can't believe this life you have."

"What, people don't usually eat Nobu in bathrobes?"

Rachel remembered for a minute how Jack was so awkward anytime her parents brought him out to dinner when they were kids. He never knew what to order and felt badly that they were buying him things, even though they constantly assured him that it was their pleasure.

"I guess you've come a long way from high school."

Jack smiled at her, shyly. "For the first time in a really long time, I feel like I'm that kid again."

"Oh my god, that was so cheesy."

He laughed and threw an edamame at her.

After dinner, they got back into bed with a pint of ice cream and Jack turned on Netflix. They laughed when the movie that came up on the home screen was one he starred in. "I swear I didn't plan that."

"I cannot believe I'm in bed with a legit movie star."

"I can't believe I'm in bed with Rachel Stone!" He smiled at her. They started kissing again, and didn't stop. Soon their robes came off and Jack was attentively stroking her body again. A little while later, satiated and exhausted, Rachel fell asleep. Jack lay down beside her, contemplating the turn life had taken, until he, too, closed his eyes and slept better than he had in years.

Rachel woke up early the next morning with a start and checked her phone. She needed to get home soon for the school carnival. She looked over at Jack. He looked so young and relaxed while he slept. She was taken back in time as she studied his face. The lines etched into his forehead and around his eyes made him cuter, somehow. She hadn't slept with anyone other than Dan in nearly twenty years, she hadn't imagined being close to anyone like that other than him for the rest of her life. Yet, here was Jack and in that moment she couldn't imagine loving anyone but him.

He must have sensed her watching him, and moments later he opened his eyes.

"Hey, you," he said, pulling her to him.

Rachel settled against him, and rubbed her hand mindlessly up and down his arm as they lay there together.

"What would you say if I stayed in New York for a while?"

Rachel pulled away from him and turned over so she could see his face.

"I've been asked to do a Broadway show. If I do it, I'll be rehearsing for the next few months and could be in New York for at least another six months or so, depending on the length of the contract."

Jack had the New York premiere for *Seamless* the following week, but spent most of his time in LA. She knew that his team had scheduled a few meetings for him with East Coast–based directors that he had been wanting to work with, but this was the first time she was hearing that he was also considering a move to New York. She looked at him, waiting to see where he was going with this.

"Ever since you came back into my life, things have finally made sense again. I feel like I've avoided any real committment because I never stopped waiting for you. And I think you feel the same way about me. I want to try to be together again."

For an instant, Rachel was taken back to college when all she wanted was for him to show up at her dorm and beg her to be with him again. Over the years, she would think about the way they had been together. That feeling that there was no one else in the world but the two of them. She'd see him in magazines or on television, wondering how her life might have gone if he'd come back for her.

She wanted it, so badly. Being with him, even just talking to him again, was better than she'd even dreamed. As she sat there, though, her heart and her mind butted against each other. She was a mother, first and foremost. If she could love him quietly, maybe, but the practical side of her, the side that always won, knew that could never happen.

"I know I can make you happy," Jack pleaded. It hadn't occurred to him that this might not be an easy decision for her.

"Jack, last night, us talking these last few weeks, has been incredible. But we're not in Hollywood. I have a family. I don't exactly see you giving up your lifestyle to raise two elementary schoolers."

Jack was silent for a moment. "You're not giving me enough credit. Look how good we still are together. I never stopped loving you, Rachel."

"So what happens? I end my marriage, you and I date for a bit, the paparazzi run wild with it, and my life, my career is over?"

"It doesn't have to be like that. No one would have to even know. We can figure it out."

"We both know this could never work. Not in the real world." She stood up from the bed, wrapping herself in the robe Jack had given her the night before and started collecting her clothes from the floor.

"Wait. Rach. I know you don't believe me, but I've spent the last twenty years wishing I hadn't screwed things up with you."

"It's easy to say that now. But there were plenty of opportunities for you to try to fix it, to come back for me, and that didn't happen." It was suddenly clear to her that she had never truly recovered from the heartbreak of her first love. Dan's jealousy of Jack had always seemed so ridiculous, but maybe he knew something she didn't. It was too late now, though.

"I moved on, Jack. I made a life for myself." The memories, their conversations, the sex—she had fallen deeply into a fantasy, and just as quickly, as he finally offered her everything she'd ever wished for, she woke up from it.

He watched her getting dressed, helpless. The innocent, empathic, and beautiful girl he once loved had truly become an adult. Maybe he had some growing up to do, too.

"I'll have Randall give you a lift back to your hotel. I'd walk you down, but you know how it is."

He pulled her into a hug and Rachel leaned into his embrace. She turned her face up to kiss Jack a final time, pouring everything she felt for him into it. "I never stopped loving you, either," she whispered.

He shook his head sadly at her, and Rachel walked out of his apartment and back into her reality.

33

RACHEL CHECKED OUT OF THE HOTEL AND TOOK A CAR DIRECTLY to her kids' school. She ran over to Emma's class booth with seconds to spare for her volunteer shift. The other class parent greeted her warmly and explained how the donut-eating contest worked. It looked simple enough, albeit messy. Rachel was glad she was wearing an old sweatshirt.

The kids lined up and Rachel was totally focused on hanging fresh donuts on string and making sure the children followed the rules. She barely noticed when Amy showed up at her booth with her younger son.

"Rachel, I heard about you and Dan splitting up. I'm so sorry." The comment was clearly disingenuous.

"We didn't split up. We're just taking some time."

"Yeah, well, Dan is clearly heartbroken."

"Have you been talking to my husband or something?" Rachel asked, not hiding her annoyance at Amy's intrusiveness.

"It's pretty obvious. We heard you've been seeing Jack Bellow for years."

Rachel was shocked. "What? That's insane!" she said.

Amy looked up at her, hands in the air. "Hey, I'm not judging. I just feel bad for Dan."

Rachel was stunned by how brazen Amy could be. She'd finally had enough. "Amy, all you've done is judge me since this happened. You'd think you'd show a little compassion for someone going through a hard time. But sure, you go be a friend to Dan."

She turned away from Amy and noticed that there were other women nearby, listening to them. Rachel wondered how her life had become a soap opera. She looked at the other class volunteer, and asked if she'd mind finishing up their shift without her. Then she grabbed her things and walked out of the carnival, without even stopping to find her children or Dan. This was too much.

When Rachel arrived home there was a black town car sitting in front of her house. Her breath sped up. Were there really reporters here again? she wondered, nauseated. She walked briskly up the path toward her front door.

She heard a voice call out. "Rach?"

Rachel turned around and saw her. "Alex? What are you doing here?"

"Hey, you." Alex smiled at her sheepishly. She walked toward Rachel and grabbed her in for a hug.

Rachel pulled away after a moment and looked at her friend. Alex had dark circles under her eyes that weren't there before she'd left for London. Her dark hair, which Alex usually wore long and wavy, was in a frizzy bun on top of her head. "Come inside. Do you have bags?"

"Just this," she said, gesturing to her tote. "Kind of a last-minute trip." There was a nervous energy coming off of Alex that was so unlike her usual confidence. Rachel unlocked the door to her house and Alex followed her inside.

Rachel went to the kitchen to grab them each water as Alex headed to the family room and collapsed on the couch. Rachel called out from the kitchen. "How long are you in town?" she asked.

"Just the night, actually," Alex said, as Rachel walked into the family room and sat down next to her, handing her a glass.

"Seriously? From London? I honestly can't believe you're here."

"Me either. I've gotten, like, six hours of sleep in the last forty-eight hours. I'm a mess."

It was disorienting seeing her sitting there, after so many weeks of essentially silence.

"So, I guess you know everything that's been going on?" Rachel asked her friend. "And that it was Dan who did it?"

"I'm sorry, Rach. I know how hurt you must be." Alex reached out to touch her friend's hand, but Rachel pulled away.

"Why are you here? Did Jack tell you to come?" Rachel asked, with an edge to her voice.

Alex shook her head no and sighed audibly. "I spoke to him on the way from the airport, though."

"Okay."

"I've been avoiding you."

"I noticed."

"Yeah." She laughed lightly. "I'm so sorry."

Rachel was quiet, waiting for her old friend to continue.

"There's a lot to tell you, and I'm not even sure where to start." She took a breath. "I love you, obviously. You're my best friend, like my sister. But I've done a couple of things I'm not proud of, and it's been weighing on me for years. I guess I'm worried you won't forgive me."

"Just say what you need to say." She felt emotionally exhausted. It was better to believe Alex was too busy than to be confronted by her like this. She wanted to rip off the Band-Aid so she could crawl into bed and pretend the last few weeks never happened.

Alex stood up and walked over to Rachel's fireplace, which was lined with family photos. She stood there for a minute, looking at the one from Rachel and Dan's wedding with the entire bridal party. She turned to Rachel. "Remember at your bachelorette party when you had a freak-out about Dan? And you told me you were thinking about Jack?"

Rachel shook her head yes. Alex started pacing and seeing her so unsettled was making Rachel uncomfortable.

"Can you please just sit down and talk to me?"

Alex walked back over and collapsed onto the couch with a sigh.

"I knew you never got over him. I mean it was obvious to me, even as much as you loved Dan, if Jack came knocking on your door back then, you would have left Dan in a heartbeat. So anytime you'd mention him, I made it sound like Jack didn't think about you anymore and that you should move on."

Rachel wondered where this was going.

"Jack called me about a year after you met Dan. But I told him not to reach out, that you were so happy with Dan and he needed to get over it."

"Why would you do that?" Rachel was thinking back to how hurt she had been that Jack had never once tried to connect with her, even when they were both in New York.

"I kept thinking about how miserable you were when he deserted you. Your career was taking off, you and Dan were talking about moving in together. I just felt like it was better to let sleeping dogs lie."

"You know me well enough to know I would have liked to make that decision for myself."

"I know. I screwed up. But Jack seemed to move on after that and you were so happy. Then when I told him you got engaged a few years later he, like, lost his mind. He still loved you. He wanted to tell you and see if he had a chance. So I told him I'd talk to you about it first."

"You never told me that." Rachel's mind was spinning, thinking back to that period in her life.

"I know. I told him you weren't interested."

Rachel's mouth opened in shock.

"I convinced myself at the time that I was protecting you, but I was being totally selfish. Do you remember the script I was working on for years while I was a PA?"

Rachel could barely look at her friend as she plowed on with her confession.

"Jack had agreed to help get it made. He was just starting to make a name for himself then, and I needed a star attached. I was in a no-win situation. He had to stay focused on the movie."

Rachel looked up in disbelief.

"And you were so happy with Dan. He was so perfect for you. I thought I was doing you a favor by not confusing things."

"Seriously?" Rachel said, unable to keep the anger out of her voice.

"I'm not making excuses, but I was twenty-eight years old, watching all my friends marry off and have these big careers. I finally had this amazing opportunity and felt like I needed to take it."

Rachel couldn't believe that Alex would lie to her like that, would lie about her like that. But a part of her wondered if maybe Alex had made the right call. Would she have chosen to leave Dan back then for Jack if she had known he was an option? And then what? she thought. Maybe they dated for a minute and he was lured away by a co-star? She and Dan had such a good life together, and their kids. She couldn't bear thinking about them never existing.

"I was right, Rach!" Alex said, reading her mind. "You created this amazing life with Dan."

"And look at us now!" she said, snarkily. "Wait, you never made a movie with Jack."

"Yeah, that's the kicker." Alex gave her a guilty look. "He got the leading role on *Plus Size* and bailed on me. I was so angry at him and just wanted to put it all behind me."

"So it didn't even matter?" Rachel asked.

Alex grimaced, acknowledging the truth in her friend's words. "Well, I think he maybe got me the writing job on the show because he felt like he owed me a favor. Rach, I'm so sorry. Truly. And now it's a whole mess."

"That still doesn't explain why you wouldn't return my calls for the last month."

Alex took a deep breath as if to steel herself. "Did Jack tell you he and Cassandra aren't together?"

Rachel nodded.

"I know this is going to sound crazy"—she paused—"but Cassandra is my girlfriend, not Jack's."

Suddenly, it all made so much sense. Jack saying he was publicly exiting from the relationship, using the photos of him and Rachel to his advantage. Not wanting to talk about Cassandra at all. And Alex, who for months had sounded happier than she'd been in years, and Rachel hadn't even bothered to ask her why.

"We've been secretly together for a while and Jack's been pretending to date her. I know, it's so Hollywood."

"I don't get it. Why can't people know you're a couple?"

Alex explained that most of the gay actresses she read about were either established actors before they came out or were young millennials and had always been open about it. Cassandra was a former model looking to break into acting—also, she was in her late thirties; the bar was much higher. "Being attached to Jack has been a huge thing for her, it's opened a lot of doors. Plus, she's from a super-conservative family and she hasn't been ready to tell them that she's with a woman."

"That seems a little unfair to you."

"I know it sounds that way, but I'm honestly so happy, Rach. We're planning to go visit her parents once the movie wraps to tell them about us."

Alex filled her in on how they met and their relationship. They had the same manager, who was one of the few people that knew Cassandra was gay. When the paparazzi first spotted Jack and Cassandra together, it was Alex, and not Jack, introducing a new girlfriend to an old friend. The media ran with the idea that Jack and Cassandra were together. Jack said there were worse things than pretending to be dating a model and agreed to keep it going as long as she and Alex needed. He really just wanted Alex to be happy again.

Rachel sat there silently, digesting this information. "I honestly can't believe you didn't tell me any of this. I didn't even know you were dating someone!" She wondered why Alex wouldn't trust her with this, and felt like she was partially to blame for being so focused on her own life.

"It felt too complicated with Jack involved. And I don't know, I think I also wanted to protect it."

"From me?"

"You had this perfect relationship in high school. Then you found Dan. It was so easy for you. You've always been so good to me, but no matter what, I felt like I was on the outside. After Tara and I broke up, I guess I just thought I wasn't going to ever find what you had."

"All I've ever wanted was for you to be happy, Al."

"I know, and it all just got so complicated. Can you forgive me?"

Rachel stared at her friend, in shock over all of the information she had just been given. "I still don't understand how you could let me marry the wrong guy when you knew the love of my life wanted to be with me again."

"Oh, Rach. Who even knows what would have happened with Jack? Dan is the man you wanted to marry. He loves you, and I know things are confusing right now, but you love him. And you have two beautiful children together. You can't possibly regret how things worked out."

Rachel thought about what Alex was saying and was finding it difficult to hold on to her anger at her. "I know. I love our life together. But I don't think I can ever forgive him." She started to cry and Alex scooted closer to her on the couch.

"I just feel like everything is so messed up," she continued. "My marriage, us, the kids. Max got suspended from school the other day."

"My Max? What could that angel boy possibly have done?"

Rachel laughed through her tears. "I'm still mad at you, okay? You've kept way too many secrets from me. You're right, obviously I don't regret marrying Dan. But I'm pretty sure we're going to break up, and I don't think I can handle losing another person I love right now."

Alex wrapped her arms around her friend and let her cry. Things would be okay between the two of them.

An hour later, Dan showed up with the kids to drop them off. They were overjoyed to see their Aunt Alex when they got home. They said goodbye to their dad, and then Rachel took Emma upstairs to wash off her face paint from the carnival. Alex walked

Dan outside to catch up for a few minutes. When Rachel came back down, she saw that Alex was teary.

"What was that all about?" Rachel asked her.

"I just hate seeing you both so sad."

"I do, too."

"He wants me to convince you to forgive him, and it was hard to tell him I couldn't do that. I'm so mad at him for doing this, but I also love him, you know?"

Rachel pulled her friend in for a hug. She couldn't begrudge her for caring about Dan; they'd been in each other's lives for so many years.

"I think we're all going to be okay. Eventually," Rachel said, feeling a little calmer now that she had Alex with her.

Alex was exhausted after dinner and fell asleep at the same time Emma went to bed. She had to fly back the next day; taking Monday off had already cost the studio tens of thousands of dollars. She said it was worth it, just to see Rachel and fix things between them.

Before Rachel went to bed that night, she texted Jack.

> RACHEL: Alex told me everything. I'm sorry I can't be more for you. But you deserve real love, Jack, don't give up on it.

He didn't respond.

34

WEEKS WENT BY, AND RACHEL FELT THE GOSSIP AROUND HER slowly ease. Becca had made her join the fifth-grade graduation party planning committee, which Rachel strongly resisted, but she found herself enjoying it. One evening, Rachel hosted the committee moms at her house, and after a couple of glasses of wine, their divorced friend Sarah told them that she had started dating her trainer. A couple of the other women confessed to having secret crushes, and their friend Katie regaled them all with a story about her husband catching her with her vibrator, after she refused to have sex with him. Rachel's face hurt from the laughter. It felt good to be part of a group, and more so, not to be the focus.

Without the distractions of Jack texting her all day, she was also a lot more focused at the office. She brought in a small matter, a vitamin manufacturer being sued for mislabeling, and she had high hopes that it would lead to additional work. She also made every effort to avoid celebrity news. Kaitlyn happily screened it for her, occasionally reporting on anything newsworthy. Apparently, Cassandra didn't attend Jack's movie premiere, which led to much speculation about the status of their relationship. Their refusal to comment fueled the rumors. Kaitlyn also saw an interview where Jack was asked about Rachel, but he shut it down quickly, saying she was an old friend, and they simply had dinner to catch up.

Dan continued staying at his brother's apartment in the city, visiting at least weekly and moving back in every other weekend while Rachel stayed at her parents' place. They had barely spoken, letting their nanny act as the go-between with the kids. Rachel was grateful that Dan was giving her space to figure things out, but she knew it was time to face things.

"I need to talk to him, don't I?" Rachel asked Becca as she drove her home from one of the fifth-grade committee meetings.

"Well, you can't just pretend your husband no longer exists."

"Can you talk to him for me?"

Becca laughed. "I wish I could. So what are you thinking?"

"I'm worried that if I confess about Jack, everything shifts to being my fault."

Alex, who was now checking in with her daily from London, thought she should come clean. Becca disagreed.

"You know how I feel about that. I'm not sure telling Dan about a one-night stand when you and he were separated helps anyone, especially if you don't know if you want to be with him. The bigger question to me is if you want to fix your marriage."

Becca was right. It was time to figure out next steps. The next morning, Rachel texted Dan and asked him to come home that Saturday night to talk, and asked her parents to take the kids. She had four days to figure out what the hell she wanted, but she always worked best on a deadline.

Rachel was finishing up packing an overnight bag in Max's room when she heard her parents and Dan come into the house. She couldn't make out what they were saying, but she heard her father laughing. She was grateful that they were acting normally, and was comforted by knowing that her parents would always consider Dan family, no matter how things ended up between them.

She came downstairs and kissed her parents hello. Initially, Elaine and Mitch had kept their distance from her after telling her not to leave Dan. They correctly sensed that any additional feedback on her marriage would not be well received by Rachel. She didn't blame them; not wanting your kid to get divorced wasn't an unreasonable position. But she also knew they didn't want to see her in pain. Rachel confessed to her mom about Jack earlier that week and explained that it was more clarifying than anything. Elaine surprised her by simply understanding.

"Be good for Grammy and Poppy," she said to her children. "See you in the morning."

"Mommy, did you pack Patch?" She had forgotten to pack the pink lovey Emma had slept with since birth.

Rachel slapped her head in disbelief. "I forgot her!"

Emma and Rachel bounded up the stairs to retrieve the missing doll. "Patch!" Emma said, holding it close. "How could we forget you! Okay, bye, Mommy." She grabbed her mom around her waist and squeezed. "Grammy said she's going to make us milkshakes tonight!"

"Not coffee!" Rachel called after her, as her daughter ran down the steps to her grandparents. She shouted another *love you* down to the kids, then sat at the top of the stairs as she waited for them to shuffle out the door.

After seeing the kids out, Dan made his way upstairs and sat next to Rachel on the top step. "So, I guess it's just us," he said to her.

"Yup."

They sat there for a moment, both lost in their own thoughts.

"I miss you," he finally said.

Rachel evaluated her husband sitting next to her. She took his hand in hers. She loved how big it was, like a paw. His nails were always neat and clean. His blond hair had grayed and thinned as they'd aged, but he still looked so handsome. She knew how awful he felt. She put her head on his shoulder as they sat there, quietly. Each waiting for the other to speak.

"Can I please come back home?" he finally pleaded, his eyes filled with tears.

"Oh, Dan," she said, her eyes also filling. "I don't think so."

Dan sat there, the tears now streaming down his face, silently.

"How many times can I tell you that I'm sorry?" Frustration crept into his voice. "I know I messed up with the gambling and clearly I miscalculated your reaction. But for it to end our marriage? Can't you find a way to forgive me?"

"It's more than that, Dan." She paused and wondered again if she should tell him the truth. "Something happened between me and Jack."

"What do you mean?" He pulled back from her sharply.

"I didn't mean for it to. I had been talking with him a lot after we had dinner," she said. "I don't know what to say. I went to his apartment, and well, you know."

Dan stood up and started walking downstairs, his pain so quickly shifting to anger.

"Dan." She tried to stay calm. "Come back here. Let's talk."

"I don't believe you," he shouted. "I would never do that to you."

"I'm sorry. I know this isn't what you were expecting." She followed him downstairs and positioned herself in front of the door. "Please don't leave. We need to talk."

"So you think this guy is going to drop his Hollywood life and become what, a stepdad to our children?" He scoffed at her.

"I don't know what you want to hear. Seeing him again after all those years brought a lot of things back. It felt like he knew the

real me before I became this, like, mom who has to keep everything in order and manage her husband and the kids' schedule
and fucking argue motions and volunteer for the PTA."

"I can't believe you dragged me here to tell me this. So you're
blowing up everything we've built here for that asshole?"

"No, Dan. Listen to me. It was one night. It's not happening
again. I'm saying that it gave me clarity."

"Clarity?" He threw his hands in the air. "What the hell are
you talking about?"

"I realized I've been unhappy in this marriage for a while."

"How can you say that? We were fine. I made a mistake and
you just decide we're done?"

"I tried so hard not to be angry at you. But I don't know if you
fully understand how bad it got when this whole thing blew up. I
was barraged with calls from reporters. People went on entertainment shows and talked about me. Dissecting my looks, my relationship with Jack, our marriage. The women in town were all
gossiping about me. It even impacted my job."

"I know it's been hard for you. It's been hard for me, too. But
to go screw another guy?"

Rachel looked away from him, the guilt momentarily overtaking her.

"Rach," he said, softening his tone. "I forgive you. I want to
forgive you. But you need to forgive me, too."

"It's more than that."

"Rachel, this is total bullshit. If someone had asked you three
months ago if you were happy, you would have absolutely said yes."

"You're probably right. I would never have admitted to myself
or anyone else how unhappy I was. We barely talk anymore. You
hardly do anything around the house to help me, and I let it go

because that's just how it's always been between us. You complain about your job and do nothing about it, yet still resent me for doing well in my own career and earning more than you. Then you take our money and you freaking gamble it away. Our savings. And you do all this behind my back, and then decide to fix the problem by making it ten million times worse. So what do you want me to say, Dan, I forgive you? I don't forgive you."

Dan stood there, silently. Listening to his wife, wanting things to be different, but knowing she was right.

"So, what are we going to do?" he asked her.

"I think we should make the separation more permanent. Maybe we could find a place for us in the city to be near work and then keep switching off here with the kids."

"Are you sure this is what you want, Rachel?"

She nodded, and looked at him sadly.

"I love you. I don't want this."

She told him that she loved him, too. It wasn't even about love anymore. She was so happy once with Dan, just like she was so happy long before with Jack. But she needed to stand on her own for a while.

35

TWO MONTHS LATER, ON THE FIRST SATURDAY AFTER SCHOOL
ended, Dan rang the bell at nine on the dot, as promised. He had
agreed to take the kids out for breakfast so Rachel could prepare the house for Emma's birthday party. She ran to get the
door for him.

"Dan, you can use your key," she said, after kissing him hello on
the cheek.

"I know, I know. Just trying to respect your 'space.'" He was
obviously quoting her. Things had moved quickly after they
agreed to formally separate. Within a couple of weeks, Dan had
found them an apartment in the city near his brother's. He stayed
there most nights, but came up at least a couple of times a week
for dinner to see the kids, and Rachel and Dan swapped on alter-
nating weekends. Rachel felt like she was in her twenties on those
weekends alone, wandering the city streets and meeting friends
she had barely seen in years for brunch and late dinners.

She smiled at him. So much had shifted between them in the
last couple of months. He followed her into the kitchen and she set
coffee in front of him.

"So, how did the interview go?" she asked.

"I think pretty well. I'm going back in this week to meet with a
few more people."

"That's incredible!" She was glad that Dan was finally pushing
himself, even though she had been begging him for years to look

at other opportunities. He started filling her in on the interview process and the potential job at Sycamore Developers when Emma came downstairs.

"Daddy!" Emma jumped on him.

"My birthday girl. Wow, you look so much older today!" He lifted his daughter into the air.

"I know!" Emma happily replied. Although Emma appeared to have adjusted, she had taken to sleeping in Rachel's bed since Dan had moved out. Rachel knew it wasn't healthy, but she secretly enjoyed having her daughter sleeping beside her. She would deal with it at some point.

"Where's your brother?"

"He's playing a video game with Jordan."

"Max, get down here," Rachel called out, rolling her eyes at her soon-to-be ex-husband.

He shook his head at her in return. Some things never changed.

Max finally walked in and greeted his dad with a wave. Dan grabbed him in for a bear hug instead. "Excuse me, I haven't see you since your graduation!"

The family had been joined by both sets of grandparents at Max's fifth-grade moving-up ceremony, followed by a family dinner at an Italian restaurant in town. Rachel and Dan were keeping to their promise to continue to celebrate special occasions as a family, and for now, it was working well.

"That was, like, three days ago," Max said, extracting himself from his father's crushing embrace. "Hey, Ma, can Jordan come over later?"

"Not today. We have Emma's birthday party. And Grammy and Poppy are coming for dinner."

Max looked annoyed, but Rachel knew he'd get over it. He'd shown far more empathy these last few months than she had ever expected.

"All right, kiddos," Dan said. "Let's get a move on. Anyone want pancakes?"

"Me!" Emma shouted, and Rachel watched the three of them head toward the front door.

"Don't forget to pick up the cupcakes," she shouted after them. She'd text a reminder to Dan in an hour, just in case.

She grabbed the balloons and the birthday banner from the basement and hung them up in the backyard. She was heading back downstairs to get a folding table when her phone rang.

She answered it, annoyed. "Bec, unless you're offering to help me set up an LOL-themed hip-hop dance party for fifteen eight-year-olds, I don't have time to talk."

"Did you see *People* yet today?" Becca asked, plowing ahead.

Rachel's heart sank. Not again. "No. Please tell me it's not about me."

"Not this time. About our friend Alex. Go look."

"Rebecca! I don't have time for this."

"Fine. I'm reading it to you. One sec, let me pull it back up. Okay, here we go.

From Dating Sexiest Man Alive to Taking a Ride on the Sapphic Love Train?

Cassandra Willis, former model turned actress and girlfriend of superstar Jack Bellow, has fallen in love with the director of her current film. Her female director. Mr. Bellow had no comment, but his ex was willing to talk. "The news that I am in a relationship with Alexandra [Hirschfeld] is true. We fell in love making her beautiful film and are so excited to share this movie with the rest of the world."

Ms. Hirschfeld declined to comment, but her representative noted that the film, Hirschfeld's directorial debut, is slated for release next Memorial Day weekend.

We expect more details to emerge, but based on a source close to the couple, this is Ms. Willis's first relationship with a woman and came as a surprise to both of them. The source added that Mr. Bellow was very gracious about it. In an odd twist, Mr. Bellow and Ms. Hirschfeld are old friends from high school. They, along with Ms. Willis, have been spotted having dinner together several times in the last couple of years. In fact, it is said that Mr. Bellow's convincing is the reason Ms. Willis was given the lead role in this film.

Interestingly, Ms. Hirschfeld's other BFF is reportedly Rachel Miller, Mr. Bellow's former girlfriend. Who can forget the news that was made earlier this year when photographs and letters between the old high school lovers were released? What a love quadrangle!'"

"Whoa," Rachel said, when Becca finished reading.

"I told you!"

"Guess that's better than people realizing Jack and Cassandra were faking it the whole time."

"I'm sure that will be the next thing that comes out."

"If this comes back to me again, I'm going to flip."

"Don't worry, it won't. Although, you could go have dinner with Jack again. Give them something to talk about?" Becca said teasingly.

"I might kill you. Get your ass over here and help me set up for this birthday party." Rachel hung up, laughing to herself about how ridiculous the tabloids were. What she had taken as gospel for years were half truths and the spin of celebrity publicists. She was done with that world.

Later that night, Dan stayed to help for bedtime. "I think my favorite present was the kitty cat Squishmallow," Emma said, reflecting on the day. "Or maybe my golden name necklace from Grammy."

"You made out pretty well, sweetie. Pajamas and teeth now, let's go." Dan gently reprimanded his daughter.

"She's too much," Rachel said lovingly, as Emma ran into the bathroom. One thing she missed was marveling over her children with their father. "I think the party was a success."

"You did a great job, Rach. Thanks for handling everything."

Rachel eyed him.

"I probably didn't say that enough over the years."

"Well, I appreciate you saying it now. So thanks."

"Hey," Dan said, as Rachel straightened up the dolls on Emma's bed and flipped on her nightlight. "I think I'll take the kids to a Yankees game one night next week, maybe Thursday. Do you want to come?"

Rachel thought for a moment. That had always been their thing. She loved to see Max's face as he recited the stats of his favorite players. The way Emma tried to follow along, but really only lit up when they bought her ice cream served in a tiny base-ball cap. She remembered the night she and Dan first connected again, after nearly two years of her avoiding him. Their first kiss and a glimpse into the possibility that lay ahead of them.

"No," she said. "You go ahead."

EPILOGUE

Memorial Day Weekend

RACHEL LEANED BACK IN HER DESK CHAIR AND SURVEYED HER new office. It wasn't as big as her old one, but she had a large window overlooking the lawn. When Gabe was promoted to Deputy General Counsel of Carraway, he offered his old position as the head of litigation to her. Rachel loved her job at the firm, and it was difficult to leave, but all lawyers dream of an in-house position like this. There was something so exciting about working directly for the client, and she found that she was passionate about more than just winning lawsuits. Plus, Carraway was significantly closer to her house, and she was only required to work in the office three days a week. A major bonus for Rachel as she navigated solo parenting.

She and Dan had tried sharing an apartment in the city for a while, switching off which parent stayed in the house with the children. That became too strange for them both when Dan started dating Jill. Rachel had to admit that Jill, a divorced pediatrician with two young kids of her own, was perfect for Dan. As a bonus, Max had quickly befriended her son, who was the same age as he was. It made shifting between homes a lot easier for all of them. They let go of the city rental and Dan found his own place in town near the train station, with enough room for the kids to stay. Rachel suspected he'd soon be moving into Jill's house, and they would have to adjust again.

Rachel loved her life these days. She felt a certain freedom in having the kids every other weekend and only on three school nights. She was quickly indoctrinated into a community of other divorced women in town, and they would go out together most Thursday nights. Rachel went with a few of the women to the Greenwich steak house she loved, and one of them ended up going on several dates with that guy, Tim, whom she'd met the night she found out about Dan's betrayal.

Rachel was often asked out by men she met on those Thursday evenings. She always declined.

Her phone rang and she heard her new assistant, Anne, answer the phone.

"Ms. Stone," Anne called out to her. "It's Ms. Hirschfeld. Are you available?"

Rachel smiled and said she would take it. Alex was very much back in her life, thankfully. "What's up, Mama?" Rachel said when she answered the phone. Alex and Cassandra had gotten married in January, and although the public wasn't yet aware, Cassandra was pregnant with their child. Despite using an anonymous sperm donor, Rachel suspected there would be plenty of rumors that she was carrying Jack's baby.

"So what's your story this weekend?" Alex asked her.

"I don't have one. Dan has the kids."

"Well, that's good to hear, because I booked you a suite at the Bowery Hotel," Alex said. "Surprise!"

"What are you talking about?"

"You have a movie premiere to attend!" Besides requiring moral support as the first movie she wrote and directed was finally shown to the public, Alex was worried that the news of her recent marriage and her wife's pregnancy would overshadow the movie. "In other words, I need my best friend to hold my hand," Alex pleaded.

"Alex, I love you. But I have somehow managed to get the press to forget about me. If I show up at some big New York City movie premiere and pictures are taken, well, I just don't think I can handle that."

"I completely get it. I do. I promise to sneak you into the theater. No red carpet. And the after-party is at the hotel and completely paparazzi and cell phone free! It's all arranged, Rach. Please say you'll come. I really wouldn't ask if it didn't mean a lot to me." Alex was typically the one offering support, not asking for it, and Rachel knew there was no chance she could refuse her oldest friend.

"It better be a sick suite," she joked, relenting as Alex knew she would. "Okay, I need to get back to work. I'll call you later."

That Saturday, Rachel took the train to the city and checked into the hotel. Cassandra had texted that she would arrange for a few dress options to be delivered to her room to choose from, and Rachel was stunned when she saw the rack of clothes waiting for her. She immediately started trying things on, ultimately landing on a black low-back Prada. Thank god she had packed Spanx. She texted Cassandra to thank her, who responded that she had jewelry options in their suite and to come over when she was ready.

Rachel quickly put back on her joggers and T-shirt and practically ran to her friends' room. Alex opened the door and the women threw their arms around each other.

Cassandra came to the door and ushered them both in. Rachel stepped back to assess her. "Your belly got so big since last month! Look at you!"

"Isn't she glowing?" Alex said proudly. "My gorgeous bride."

"Please, I'm a cow," Cassandra said, knowing full well she looked stunning. "So let me guess, you picked the Prada?"

Rachel laughed. She loved how well her friend's wife knew her already, even though they had only had a few dinners together. She liked her so much. She was incredibly warm, even though she was an absurdly beautiful and famous woman.

"I couldn't even see past it. It's stunning. What are we doing about my hair?"

The women laughed at her and said they had a team coming to do all of their hair and makeup and they had time to hang out until then. Cassandra showed Rachel the emerald chandelier earrings she thought would look best with her dress.

"You guys almost make me want to be a movie star!"

Rachel relaxed into the star treatment her friends bestowed on her, and sipped champagne as her hair was blown out and styled into a sophisticated low pony. Her makeup was perfection; even the false lashes the women forced on her looked natural and pretty. When her dress was on and she slipped into the matching black satin Prada shoes, she felt very much like a princess. She rode over to the premiere in her friends' limousine, but as promised, their publicist had someone meet Rachel and walk her around the press directly into the theater.

Rachel could hear them shouting at Cassandra and Alex to turn around, and there was a distinct murmur in the crowd about the obviously pregnant star. Rachel was brought toward the front of the theater and sat down in her seat. She took a quick selfie and sent it to Becca. Then she opened the Kindle app on her phone and continued reading the novel she had started on the train. Totally absorbed in the book, she didn't notice him as he sat down next to her.

"You clean up well." His voice shook her to her core.

She took in his well-cut suit and the new closely cropped beard he was sporting. "Jack," she breathed. "You're here." He leaned in and kissed her cheek.

"I'm here. Our girl made a movie."

"Shouldn't you still be out there greeting your fans?"

"I'm taking a break from all of that. Snuck in through the side. How are you doing? How's the family?" he asked.

"The kids are great. They're staying with their father tonight. Although my daughter would have killed to be there for the makeover I had today."

"Well, you look gorgeous, Rach. It's so good to see you," he said sincerely.

Rachel noticed that his hair was longer than it was when she had last seen him about a year ago, and there was a touch of gray around his temples. It only made him better looking.

The crowd started to fill in and Jack stood up. "I better get to my seat. It was great to see you, Rachel."

"You too, Jack."

Alex and Cassandra came into the theater shortly after and the lights went down. Rachel squeezed her friend's hand and whispered that she knew it would all be amazing.

"Did you see Jack?" Alex whispered to her. "I didn't know if he would make it, so I didn't want to say anything."

Rachel smiled at her. "Is this a setup, Alex?"

"I have no idea what you're talking about." Alex smiled at her innocently and then put her head on Cassandra's shoulder. With a baby on the way and her new bride, Rachel couldn't remember ever seeing her friend that happy.

The movie was beautiful. Rachel was so blown away and had tears in her eyes when it ended. She told Alex how proud of her she was. She loved having a front-row seat to her oldest friend's success. Alex and Cassandra had to stay after the movie and do more press, so they sent her ahead to the hotel. An assistant to their publicist brought Rachel outside and walked her toward a limo. Rachel asked if this was the right car for her. She didn't mind just taking an Uber.

The assistant checked her phone. "Confirmed. This one's for you. Have a good night," she said, hurrying back inside to her boss.

Rachel opened the door and got in the limo.

Jack was sitting there, waiting for her.

"I think you're in my car," she said to him.

"Actually, you're in mine," he said, as he pulled Rachel toward him.

ACKNOWLEDGMENTS

This book would still be sitting on my hard drive were it not for the tenacity of my agent, Elizabeth Bewley. You have shown me incredible patience and kindness throughout this process, and I am so lucky to have you in my corner. I am grateful to you and the entire Sterling Lord Literistic team.

Thank you to my inimitable editor, Claire Wachtel, who took a chance on *Love, Me*, and made it infinitely better, and to executive editor Barbara Berger, for your commitment and support along the way. Many thanks as well to the rest of the team at Union Square & Co.: Christina Stambaugh, Jenny Lu, Daniel Denning, Chris Vaccari, Rich Hazelton, Jo Obarowski, and Alfha Gonzalez. I am also grateful to Diane João for her copyediting prowess, and Sara Wood for the showstopper of a cover.

I am fortunate to have incredible friends from all walks of my life, many of whom read early drafts of this novel. To that end, I'd like to thank CHORT, my besties since birth; the girls of the BDP, who lift each other up at every turn; and finally, the Glitter Cups, who keep me laughing through this crazy thing called parenthood. An extra heartfelt thank-you goes to Rachel Jacobson and Ronni Arnold (first readers and true-blue friends), Letal Ackerman, Noa Arias, Dara Astmann, Katie Kreisler Black, Dani Heifetz, Sara Kopple, Michelle Levy, Nicole Plasky, Lindsey Raivich, Caren Sallada, Amy Silberman, Allison Sundel (for the multiple reads and so much more), and Lindsay Brooke Weiss (the fabulous @cocoincashmere).

To my happy surprise, there really isn't a more welcoming or encouraging group of people than writers. For answering my endless questions and offering phenomenal advice, thank you to Leigh McMullan Abramson, Neely Tubati Alexander, Julie Buxbaum, Jacqueline Friedland, Jessa Maxwell, Annabel Monaghan, Amy Poeppel, Allison Winn Scotch, Leigh Stein, and Karen Winn. I am also indebted to Gotham Writers Workshop for getting me started.

I have in-laws who exceed all expectations of what in-laws should be. Thank you, Sondra and Roger Eichel, for everything you do for us and our girls. To my two incredible sisters-in-law, Kate Eichel and Nicole Miller, thank you for the honest feedback (not just book-related) and friendship. I adore you both. And to my bro (bruh!), Scott Eichel, for always being there for me. Love and appreciation to my extended Fuchs and Most families as well, and to my nieces and nephew.

My parents have always believed in me, and never made me feel like I couldn't achieve whatever goal I set for myself. Mom and Dad, without a lifetime of your encouragement I would not have attempted this endeavor. I love you both more than words. And to Stephie: my sister, my forever best friend, and my biggest champion. Thank you for always getting it.

To my two amazing daughters: Sylvie, my reading buddy, you are the definition of wise beyond your years. It is remarkable to have your encouragement and enthusiasm pushing me forward. Frankie, just being around you lifts me up in so many ways. The character of Emma basically wrote herself, thanks to you. I love you both far more than I could express in these pages.

And finally, to Jeremy. Although you are not this book's target audience, you've always willingly been mine. Thanks for keeping the ship running. I love you endlessly.